Oliver Messel.

Oliver Messel

AN EXHIBITION HELD AT THE THEATRE MUSEUM
VICTORIA AND ALBERT MUSEUM

22 JUNE – 30 OCTOBER 1983

WITH CONTRIBUTIONS BY

Cecil Beaton · Richard Buckle · Thorold Dickinson
Philip Dyer · Christopher Fry · Peter Glenville ·
Stanley Hall · Leela Meinertas · R. Myerscough-Walker
Roger Pinkham · Sybil Rosenfeld · Alexander Schouvaloff
Agi Sekers · Roy Strong · Carl Toms
Rosemary Vercoe · Sarah C. Woodcock

EDITED BY
Roger Pinkham

VICTORIA AND ALBERT MUSEUM

*The Theatre Museum is most grateful
for help in mounting this exhibition, to:*

Berman's & Nathans Ltd
Black and Edgington
The Dorchester Hotel, London
Rank Film Distributors Ltd
Sekers International

Published by the Victoria and Albert Museum, London
First published 1983
© Crown copyright – text
© Copyright of photographs as listed in acknowledgements

ISBN 0 905209 50 8

Designed by Patrick Yapp
Phototypeset by Southern Positives and Negatives (SPAN), Lingfield, Surrey
Printed in Great Britain by Robert Stockwell Limited

FRONT COVER: Costume design for a Sprite, *Zémire et Azor*, 1955
FRONTISPIECE: Fig. 1 Self-portrait by Oliver Messel at the age of 19(?). Oil

CONTENTS

	page	
Roy Strong	7	A Tribute
Alexander Schouvaloff	9	Foreword
Roger Pinkham	10	Acknowledgements
	12	List of Illustrations
	15	Biographical Outline
Cecil Beaton · Christopher Fry *Peter Glenville · Stanley Hall* *R. Myerscough-Walker · Roger Pinkham (editor)* *Sybil Rosenfeld · Carl Toms · Rosemary Vercoe*	17	Oliver Messel and the Theatre
	36	Notes
	38	Chronology of his Involvement in Stage Productions
Richard Buckle	41	Messel's *Sleeping Beauty*
Thorold Dickinson *Roger Pinkham (editor) · Agi Sekers*	46	Outside the Theatre
	55	Notes
		Chronological Lists of:
	56	– Films
	58	– Exhibitions
	60	– Decorative Arts Commissions
	62	– Temporary Decorations for Festive Occasions
	64	– Interior Decoration Commissions
	66	– Designs for Houses and other Buildings in the West Indies
	69	Note to the Catalogue
Philip Dyer · Leela Meinertas *Roger Pinkham · Sarah C. Woodcock*	70	Catalogue (No. 1–108)
	191	Notes
	192	Concise List of Works in Collections
	195	List of Lenders
	196	Bibliography
	198	Index

A TRIBUTE

The most moving tribute I ever heard paid to Oliver Messel was that made by Dame Ninette de Valois at his memorial service at St Martin-in-the-Fields. She began by recalling her earliest awareness of him when she had been a dancer in Diaghilev's company performing in a regional theatre in France. She, together with three other girls, had to take a few steps forward, bend down and pick up a mask. She did that and, overcome by its beauty, asked someone in the wings who had made it. A voice replied, 'A young Englishman called Oliver Messel.' No less poignant was her recollection of the performance of his *The Sleeping Beauty* in Leningrad and how, in the interval, an aged Russian had come up to her and said, 'Tchaikovsky and Petipa should have lived to have seen this!'

These are memories of one intimately concerned with some of his most magical contributions to our theatre by someone who had the privilege of both knowing and working with Messel. Mine are the more humble memories and debts of a stage-struck young grammar-school boy from the suburbs of North London whose greatest ambition was to design for the stage. My earliest glimpses of his gossamer touch were all from on high, whether it was *The Sleeping Beauty* at Covent Garden, or *Ring Round the Moon* at the Globe. I also saw *The Little Hut*, *Under the Sycamore Tree* and Fry's *The Dark is Light Enough*, twice in the case of the latter to savour fully his décor, Edith Evans as the Countess, and Fry's poetry. Over the years I must have seen *The Sleeping Beauty* up to a dozen times as prosperity gradually enabled me to view it from a lower and lower and closer and closer vantage point.

Why was his work so hypnotic? He was, of course, a romantic of the Rex Whistler generation and after the starvation of the war years he swept his audiences away with his painterly stage visions, which belonged so closely to the English watercolour tradition. His effects always reminded me of Prospero's famous words: 'like an insubstantial pageant faded', because Messel's work always had that slightly unreal, transparent, bleached-out effect, as though we were being presented with an hallucination from an earlier century.

When he died in 1978 his work had been absent from the stage for more than a decade. A revolution in theatrical technique had rendered his approach virtually obsolete. Few arts are more transitory than theatre and this is borne out by the fact that my wife, when visiting the workshops of the Royal Opera House, was asked, 'Who was this Oliver Messel that your husband wrote about in the *Sunday Times*?' And this in a theatre that had housed his masterpiece. I hope therefore that this permanent loan of his work together with the exhibition will do something to answer that question for a generation that never experienced his spell as well as recalling it vividly to those who remember. Messel's place is not without significance. In that appreciation I wrote that he had 'lifted the professional status of the designer in the theatre. Those of today, even of the barbed wire and concrete schools, owe him therefore a remarkable debt. All of us owe him an even greater one for sharing with us a vision which was uniquely his.'

Roy Strong
DIRECTOR
VICTORIA AND ALBERT MUSEUM

FOREWORD

Oliver Messel was to be the title of the first exhibition at the new Theatre Museum. Lady Rosse invited Sir Roy Strong and me to her magically preserved Victorian house in Stafford Terrace to talk about it and make enthusiastic plans. We met Berkeley Sutcliffe, a designer and an old friend of Oliver Messel. Next day he took me to the disused chapel at Kensington Palace, where Princess Margaret had very generously allowed Oliver Messel's work to be stored. There were all the designs in piles of green portfolios labelled with names which conjured up for me so many evenings I had spent entranced in the theatre during my youth: *The Sleeping Beauty, Ring Round the Moon, Under the Sycamore Tree, The Little Hut* ... and there were the perfect evocations in miniature, the models in their decorated boxes, of other great productions: *The Magic Flute, The Barber of Seville, The Lady's not for Burning* ... That was in 1975.

The building of the Theatre Museum was then postponed, and postponed. Plans for the opening exhibition had to be laid aside. It was a bitter blow when Oliver Messel died in 1978 and I realized he would never see his exhibition.

Suddenly, in 1981, a mysterious telephone call from Lord Snowdon: would I be available to talk to him about something in a couple of months' time? Yes, of course. I began to have an inkling of what it might be about. Two months later, sitting in his car, Lord Snowdon told me what he proposed. He intended to make an indefinite loan to the Theatre Museum of the collection of Oliver Messel's work which he had now inherited. Did I agree? I was thrilled and delighted by his generous proposal. Details were arranged. Eventually two vans were sent to collect the portfolios and the models from Kensington Palace. By this time the future of the Theatre Museum in Covent Garden was still uncertain, but some galleries then became unexpectedly available at the V&A. We decided to delay no longer. We would present the *Oliver Messel* exhibition as soon as possible. Janet Steen, a Research Assistant at the Theatre Museum, made the inventory of the many hundreds of designs and drawings, the models, masks, costumes, photographs, from which Roger Pinkham has made the selection for this exhibition. We have been given enthusiastic and invaluable help by many people, but from the beginning the inspiration and constant support has always been that of Oliver Messel's sister, Lady Rosse. We have also received continuous advice and guidance from Lord Snowdon during the preparation of this exhibition. But a very special 'thank you' must go to Princess Margaret, who takes a personal interest in the collection and who, by preserving it for several years in her care, made this exhibition possible.

Alexander Schouvaloff
THEATRE MUSEUM

ACKNOWLEDGEMENTS

The Theatre Museum would like to thank HRH Princess Margaret for graciously attending, on 20th June, 1983, this exhibition of Oliver Messel's work. The difficulties of mounting this exhibition have been cleared away in many instances by the generosity and diverse assistance of Lord Snowdon. Anne, Countess of Rosse has been of invaluable help in lending from her private collection of Messeliana and in providing details of his career, which to some extent she shared at its beginning. To Mr and Mrs Thomas Messel we extend our thanks for the loan of material and for their warm welcome in Gloucestershire.

Without Mr Carl Toms' help we should not have had the charming mock-up of Oliver Messel's studio in Pelham Place nor the splendour of the tent room for, in a busy life, he put time aside to design both features. We have been exceptionally fortunate in that the Dorchester Hotel has sponsored the setting-up of the tented room by Black and Edgington; and in this connexion we should like to thank Miss Marjorie Lee of the Hotel who has been a great smoother away of difficulties as well as being a mine of information about Oliver Messel's work at the Hotel. To Monty Berman and Maya Koumani of the firm of Berman's & Nathans, the costumier, we are particularly thankful for delightfully recreating the costume for *Zémire*, and for understanding so readily our problems of display. Oliver Messel's long connexion with the firm of Sekers International was a fruitful one in many ways and we are touched and grateful that Sekers has not forgotten him. They have decorated the exhibition galleries in the sorts of materials we hope he might have liked. Mr Harry Barber and Mrs Mary Bacon freely offered their long experience and advice towards this aim. Rank Film Distributors Ltd have generously waived their royalty for the *Caesar and Cleopatra* film excerpts.

This catalogue would not have been so informative without the written contributions of Richard Buckle, Thorold Dickinson, Christopher Fry, Peter Glenville, Stanley Hall, Sybil Rosenfeld, Lady Sekers, Carl Toms and Rosemary Vercoe. All of them are heartily thanked here; and so are Philip Dyer and Sarah C. Woodcock, who have written the detailed and informative ballet, costume and head-dress entries. Mr Dyer has also delightfully arranged the cases of head-dresses, and the costumes. To Leela Meinertas has fallen the considerable task of implementing the photography for the exhibition and writing the entries on the Cochran Revues. To both she has brought knowledge, flexibility and skill. The rest of the catalogue I must take the blame for.

Lord Snowdon apart, the lenders are not numerous but their contributions are all of consequence, and we should like to thank Lady Diana Cooper, Ms Marianne Ford, Miss Kay Staniland and the Museum of London for generously answering our requests for loans. Mark Bowis has patiently cleaned the model sets, and Graham Brandon has photographed these and every object represented in the catalogue. His modest and very skilled work should not go disregarded; nor should that of Frank C. Scott-Stapleton, who had the complicated job of restoring the electrics in the model sets so they could be seen at their best. We also very much appreciate Judith Doré's work on the costumes, bringing them to life again, and Mike Ford for the audio/visual presentation. We should like to thank Janet Steen, Exhibitions Officer of the Theatre Museum, for the solution of many hair-raising problems, with calmness and efficiency. Thanks are proffered gratefully to the following for a whole variety of differing yet essential elements of help: June Averill (BBC TV Librarian), John Barber (*The Sunday Telegraph*), Mrs Betty Carillo, Barbados Public Library, Charles Castle, John Claridge, David Devenish, Dudley Dodd and Anthony Mitchell, both of The National Trust, Vivian Ellis, Francesca Franchi of the Royal Opera House Archives, Sharon Gater of the Wedgwood Museum, Mrs Lillian Gethic, Robin Gooden, Christopher Gowing of the Buckinghamshire County Museum, Lisbet Grandjean of the Danish Theatre Museum, Marion Hanscom of the State University of New York at Binghamton, Mark Haworth-Booth, Spencer Herapath, Sam Hunt, Bath Museums Service, M. Heymann of the Edward James Foundation, Chichester, Frank Holland of the British Piano Museum Charitable Trust, Dick Kasher, University College, London, Christine Kirby and Michelle Snapes of the British Film Institute, Gerald Lacoste, Bill Lorraine, Fiona MacCarthy, Lord Norwich, Norman Parkinson, the Rosehill Arts Trust, Lesley Smirthwaite of the National Army Museum, Jennifer Stewart of the Lefèvre Gallery, Christopher Warburton of *Architectural Digest*, Laurence Whistler, and Doris Zinkeisen.

For permission to quote from literary sources we should like to thank: Dorothy Dickson for the Cochran extract, Patrick Foster, the interviewer for and publisher of HERS *Magazine, Interview Magazine*, New York, for the McKendry interview extracts, Pitman Books Ltd., for the piece from Myerscough-Walker, Studio International (The Studio), and Weidenfeld and Nicolson, Ltd., for the Cecil Beaton extract. We would like to thank the following for permission to reproduce photographs and illustrations: The Arts Theatre, Batsford Publishers, BBC Hulton Picture Library, Columbia Pictures Industries Inc., Country Life, The Dorchester Hotel, Keystone Press, Louis Klementaski, Alec Murray, National Film Archives (Stills Library), The National Trust, the still from the film *Caesar and Cleopatra* by courtesy of the Rank Organisation plc, the Rosehill Arts Trust Ltd., Roy Round, Sotheby's, Syndication International, Thorn EMI, UPI.

We have tried without success to contact the copyright-holders of the *Illustrated and Dramatic News*, *The Sketch* and have been unable to trace John Seymour Erwin and Peter Waugh whose photographs are reproduced on pages 127 and 65; and we apologise to those parties should they feel injured.

For copyright permission to show the extracts from films we should like to thank Rank Film Distributors Ltd. *(Caesar and Cleopatra)*, Thorn EMI *(The Queen of Spades)*, Columbia EMI Warner *(Suddenly Last Summer)* and the National Film Archive for supplying copies from stock.

Lastly, without the prompt and efficient help of Mrs Barbara Riley and Miss Diana Hunter, who typed this book, it could not have been produced so quickly.

Roger Pinkham
THEATRE MUSEUM

LIST OF ILLUSTRATIONS

Fig.
1. Frontispiece; self-portrait by Oliver Messel; colour 2
2. Drawing, probably of *aucubana japonica* (spotted laurel) 16
3. Mask of a Faun, papier mâché, painted; colour 19
4. Tilly Losch as the Fu Manchu Marchioness in *Wake Up and Dream* 20
5. Oliver Messel by Cecil Beaton 21
6. Set design for the film *Romeo and Juliet*; colour 22
7. Costume design for Alizon in *The Lady's Not For Burning*; colour 25
8. The set for Act 3 of *Ring Round the Moon* 26
9. Set model for Act 1 of *Le Comte Ory*; colour 28–9
10. Costume design for Lady Teazle in *The School for Scandal* 31
11. Model of the final scene in *Helen*; colour 35
12. Design for a pouch for the musical *Twang!!* 37
13. Oliver Messel and his sister Anne, by Cecil Beaton 39
14. Costume design for the Cavalier to the Fairy of the Enchanted Garden in *The Sleeping Beauty*; colour 42
15. Cut-out design for Act 1 in *The Sleeping Beauty*; colour 43
16. Oliver Messel painting a mural at Flaxley Abbey, Gloucestershire 47
17. The interior of the theatre at Rosehill, Whitehaven; colour 49
18. View of the Penthouse dining-room, Dorchester Hotel, London 50
19. The screen in the bow drawing-room at Flaxley Abbey, Gloucestershire 51
20. View of the Ballroom of the Bath Assembly Rooms; colour 53
21. Elizabeth Taylor in *Suddenly Last Summer* 57
22. Oliver Messel working on his mask of Queen Elizabeth I 59
23. Oliver Messel, Graham Sutherland and Cecil Beaton at the Sekers Exhibition 61
24. View of the Crush Bar at the Royal Opera House 63
25. View of the façade of H. and M. Rayne shoe-shop 65
26. Tamar Gevergeva in *Zéphyre et Flore* 71
27. Masks worn in *The Great God Brown* 73
28. Stage view of *The Masks* 74
29. Lauri Devine and the masked chorus in *Dance Little Lady* 75
30. Lauri Devine and William Cavanagh in *Lorelei* 76
31. Tilly Losch as the Bluebird in *Wake Up and Dream* 77
32. Lifar and Nikitina in *Piccadilly 1830*, and the *Heaven* scene 78
33. Glen Byam Shaw as The Cripple being made whole in *The Miracle* 81
34. Diana Gould as a wood nymph in *The Miracle* 82
35. Tilly Losch as the Bride in *The Miracle* 83

LIST OF ILLUSTRATIONS

36 Costume designs for some characters in *Helen*; colour   85
37 Helen expresses her boredom with Menelaus in *Helen*, Act 1   86
38 The white bedroom in *Helen*   87
39 Orestes' girl friends, Parthenis and Leaena, in *Helen*   89
40 The set of *Mother of Pearl*   90
41 The Ballroom in *Glamorous Night*   91
42 Horner and Mrs Pinchwife in *The Country Wife*   92
43 Lady Fidget and Mrs Pinchwife in *The Country Wife*   93
44 Paolo and Francesca with the angelic apparition in *Francesca da Rimini*   95
45 Lubov Tchernicheva as Francesca in *Francesca da Rimini*   97
46 Set design for scene 2 and costume designs for Malatesta and Francesca in *Francesca da Rimini*; colour   96
47 Oberon and Titania in *A Midsummer Night's Dream*   98
48 A group of Titania's fairies dancing in *A Midsummer Night's Dream*   99
49 Prospero and Miranda in *The Tempest*   101
50 Advertisement for *The Infernal Machine*   103
51 Margot Fonteyn and Robert Helpmann in *Comus*   104
52 Comus attended by his rout in *Comus*   105
53 Julia brooding on her love for Faulkland in *The Rivals*   107
54 Princess Aurora and Prince Florimund, *The Sleeping Beauty*   108
55 Costume design for the Queen, *The Sleeping Beauty*   110
56 Design for the gauze before Acts 1 and 2, *The Magic Flute*; colour   115
57 Model set for *Die Entführung aus dem Serail*; colour   118
58 Oliver Messel on the set of *Ring Round the Moon*   120
59 Claire Bloom as Isabelle in *Ring Round the Moon*   121
60 Design for a sweet-dish, *Ariadne auf Naxos*   123
61 Costume design for Zerbinetta, *Ariadne auf Naxos*; colour   124
62 Costume design for a harlequin, *Ariadne auf Naxos*   125
63 View of the model for Act 2, scene 2, *Romeo and Juliet*; colour   128–9
64 Lady Capulet grieving over Tybalt, *Romeo and Juliet*   127
65 Design for props, *Under the Sycamore Tree*; colour   131
66 Design for Don Ramiro's palace, *La Cenerentola*; colour   133
67 Costume design for Cinderella, *La Cenerentola*   134
68 Costume design for Tisbe, *La Cenerentola*; colour   135
69 Costume design for Delia, *Letter From Paris*   136
70 Design for a hat for Delia, *Letter From Paris*   137
71 The Queen of the Waters, and Consort, *Homage to the Queen*   138
72 Costume design for The Queen of the Air, *Homage to the Queen*; colour   140
73 Costume design for Bella, *The Dark Is Light Enough*   142
74 Head of Gelda, *The Dark Is Light Enough*   143
75 Sheet of colours chosen by Messel for *Il Barbiere di Siviglia*; colour   145
76 Costume design for Dr Bartolo, *Il Barbiere di Siviglia*   146
77 Costume design for Countess Adèle, *Le Comte Ory*; colour   148
78 Costume design for a carnival dancer, *House of Flowers*   150

79 Costume design for Chief of Police, *House of Flowers*   151
80 Two designs for costumes, *Arms and the Man*   154
81 Scaled drawing, the garden, *Le Nozze di Figaro*   156
82 Portrait of Oliver Messel, *c.*1956   157
83 Costume design for Snake, *The School for Scandal*   158
84 Costume design, a reveller, *Samson*; colour   160
85 Costume design for a negro slave, *Samson*   161
86 Costume design for Dagon, *Samson*   162
87 Costume design for Sophie, *Der Rosenkavalier*   164
88 Costume design for Octavian, *Der Rosenkavalier*; colour   165
89 Costume designs for the ruffians, *Der Rosenkavalier*   166
90 Design for a hare, *Traveller Without Luggage*   168
91 Design for a Great Indian Hornbill, *Traveller Without Luggage*   169
92 Costume design for Gigi in the classroom; *Gigi*; colour   170
93 Design for a head-dress for Gigi; *Gigi*   172
94 Costume design for Gigi in the last scene; *Gigi*   173
95 View of the Morning Room at Flaxley Abbey   175
96 Design for the north elevation of The Gingerbread House   177
97 Designs for rattan furniture   178
98 Drawings for a knife and fork; prior to 1964   179
99 Mannequin wearing a Hardy Amies dress of 'Jungle' taffeta   180
100 The Royal Box, Covent Garden, 8th June, 1953   182–3
101 View of the Penthouse dining-room patio decorated for a marriage reception   181
102 Film still: Vivien Leigh as Cleopatra in *Caesar and Cleopatra*   186
103 Costume design for the old Countess, *The Queen of Spades*; colour   188
104 Film still: Herman and the dead Countess, *The Queen of Spades*   190

BIOGRAPHICAL OUTLINE

1904 Jan. 13 born the second son of Lt.-Col. Leonard Messel, OBE, TD., Eton.

1922 Jan. Enters the Slade School at the suggestion of W. A. Propert, owner of the Claridge Gallery, and writer on ballet. OM lives at Lancaster Gate.

1924 June Leaves the Slade.

1925 Apprenticed to John Wells, portrait artist and landscapist.

1925 Shows masks in the Claridge Gall. exh. *Character Masks*; brings him to the notice of Diaghilev and Cochran.

1925 Diaghilev's ballet *Zéphyre et Flore* performed in London, with masks and symbols by Messel, his first involvement in the theatre.

1926 – 1932 The main period of his work for C. B. Cochran in revues *Helen* and *The Miracle* (see cat. for details).

1932 – 1939 Work for films; with Tyrone Guthrie at the Old Vic, and for the ballet; books; is much written about and praised. Yeoman's Row studio.

1940 – 1944 Joins the Royal Engineers and works in camouflage – 2nd Lieutenant to Captain. This year begins work on *Caesar and Cleopatra*, film.

1946 – 1954 The year of *The Sleeping Beauty*, ballet; designs for Tennent productions directed by Peter Brook and Peter Glenville, plays by Anouilh, Fry. First Glyndebourne productions. Moves to Pelham Place, SW7, and meets Vagn Riis-Hansen who becomes his manager and friend. Carl Toms becomes Messel's assistant, 1952, until 1958.

1955 – 1956 Wins the Antoinette Perry 'Tony' Award for *House of Flowers*, (1954), (NY). Fellowship of Univer. Coll., London. Visits Buganda, Oct. The Glyndebourne period, particularly 1956 (Mozart bi-centenary), when 4 Messel productions, new or revived to be seen. Makes first visit to Barbados (1958).

1958 Awarded CBE.

1959 'Tony' Award (NY) for *Rashomon* (NY), tying with Oliver Smith's *Destry Rides Again*.

1960 Made Hon. Assoc. of the Regional College of Art (Manchester).

1966 Number of productions slows down. Arthritic hip operation this year. Moves to Barbados, and continues with house-designing which, in this region, he had begun in 1961.

1976 Almost no theatre work until *The Sleeping Beauty* (for American Ballet Theatre). Production based on that of 1946.

1977 Vagn Riis-Hansen dies.

1978 July 13 Messel dies of a heart attack.

OLIVER MESSEL AND THE THEATRE

It is almost twenty years since the last new production[1] designed by Oliver Messel, who died in 1978, was staged in this country; but though his name does not mean much now to the general public it is gleaming brighter in theatre history. Studying the chronology of his productions one can see that the apex of his career was reached by the mid 1950s. Thereafter the shows thin out and are interspersed by commissions in the decorative arts or ones for large scale interior decoration. In fact the last thirteen years of Messel's life were spent (except for time on two productions[2] abroad) on designing villas (p.66) for mainly English residents in the West Indies to where he had moved in 1965.

Before outlining his career in the theatre and introducing those who have most generously answered our request for contributions to this catalogue, one ought to define what kind of designer Oliver Messel was. This requires explanation for there has been a rapid and obvious change since the mid 1950s. The main items which have become largely outdated are the painted flat, the border, and back-cloth and these were what Oliver Messel was generally associated with in the popular mind – lavishly, tastefully designed sets with costumes, often richly coloured, of expensive materials. Such were the productions at Glyndebourne, always with an historical setting (for obvious reasons), and to which Messel could pay due regard, for he was assiduous in his study of styles, and knew very well how to mix these for dramatic results. In the Thirties and Forties, Messel could be relied upon to come up with such décors to suit Shakespeare, or almost any period play, and the ballet. There was another side to his theatre voice which got neglected in later years because either the fashion changed or he got no chance to use it except on the odd occasion. This side is more eerie, more imaginative and wilder, and he used it in several ways; either amusingly as for *The Little Hut*[3] and *Under the Sycamore Tree*,[3] or more threateningly, as in the films of *The Queen of Spades*[3] and *Suddenly Last Summer*[3] or in some of the masks of the Cochran Revues of the mid Twenties. This is not to suggest that Messel was some kind of Surrealist *manqué* lost to modern art. It is very doubtful if he was interested in contemporary art. He belonged to a generation too early to be influenced by radical teachers of modern art; that was to come later. There seem to be several reasons why Oliver Messel's type of theatre began to fade in the Fifties; the first is probably the expense of his productions, although those were nothing compared to costs today. Another reason is surely that in that period the commercial theatre began to change under the impact of innovators like Joan Littlewood, who encouraged her casts to improvise on stages with the least scenery to inhibit movement. But perhaps the most important change was the institution of the writer's theatre at the Royal Court[4] where décor was minimal so that the word could flourish. From there it is but a short step to our own day with its lack of interest in scenery, or certainly of the painterly kind where the brush strokes can be seen from the stalls.

✻

Oliver Hilary Sambourne Messel was born on 13th January 1904; he was the second son of Lt.-Col. Leonard Messel[5] of Nymans, Stapleford, Sussex. His mother was Maud Frances, the only daughter of the *Punch* cartoonist Linley

Fig. 2 Drawing probably of *aucubana japonica* (spotted laurel), pencil, 1920 (q.v. 11)

Sambourne.[6] Oliver's only sister Anne (now Lady Rosse), became the mother of Lord Snowdon (b.1930). To the latter, his nephew, Oliver Messel bequeathed the considerable collection of model sets, designs, costumes, photographs and personalia from which a selection has been made for this exhibition.

Messel tells us that by an early age he was making crocheted hats for his mother, thus exemplifying early one of his outstanding abilities, and on which commentators dwell, to make anything, from anything, with his hands (Fig. 2). An interest in craft work was encouraged by his father, who used to take his young son and daughter to the Victoria and Albert Museum.[7] 'I did nothing at school,' Messel has said.[8] 'I was no good at anything at Eton. It was just so much waste of time, but it was less horrible than private school, which was the nightmare of my life ...' Fortunately the Slade School[9] was more receptive. W. A. Propert, a friend of his father and who ran the Claridge Gallery[10] suggested the Slade, so Messel went there in January 1922. He did not find it a stimulus. However, a fellow-student was Rex Whistler,[11] and because study mainly consisted of life-drawing, which they found boring, they turned to making masks. This is easy to understand for the making of masks was very much in the air at this time.[12] However, the masks made by Messel, and certainly not those by Whistler,[13] had nothing of the primitivism of Picasso's creations. William Gaunt has described[14] how Messel's masks were made: 'First model in wax the head whose features you wish the mask to bear. Then take some brown paper and cut it into pieces about six inches square. Mix some sticky flour paste and wet the paper with it, squeezing the paper until it is itself paste-like. Lay on the model successive layers of the paper to the number of four or five layers. Work the surface until it takes the desired form and texture. Leave it to dry and when dry it will come away from the model head – a mask. Additional ornament and detail can then be applied with gesso and sticky paper. Cover with a copal glaze so binding the gesso and then paint on ruby lips and long lashes either with oil or watercolour.'

Judging from this it seems a reasonable assumption that mask-making (Fig. 3) had been a going thing at the Slade for some time; so it is natural that Messel, with his flair for handiwork, his ability to turn things into other more exotic things, should have turned to making masks. This was probably at much the same time he found that he was homosexual. '... I never thought of having anything to do with the theatre. I merely trained as a painter at the Slade. The curious thing was that in my time there were no such things as schools for the theatre or design, or anything like that. We just went to study to paint, and if anyone was given a job to do for the theatre they did it or didn't....'[15]

The jobs which students would have done would have been the painting of flats, those stationary pieces of scenery on the stage, or, though less likely, cloths for the front or back of the stage. Messel's love of portrait-painting,[16] which he practised all his life, led to his apprenticeship to John Wells[17] on leaving the Slade in 1924.[18] W. A. Propert had seen the masks Messel and Whistler had made and exhibited them at his Claridge Gallery. Let Messel continue;[19] '... I had some masks I'd made on exhibition at the Claridge Gallery, in London. It was an exhibition of young artists and they also had all the designs for an early Diaghilev ballet.[20] The impresario (Cochran) saw my masks and asked me to do some work for him ... Thus everything seemed to happen at once. Diaghilev asked me to do some masks (Fig. 26) for a ballet with designs by Braque called *Zéphyre et Flore* (Nos. 17, 18), and Boris Kochno took me under his wing and arranged I should have star billing for designing the masks. Cochran then, instead of being put off by my refusing to work for him, sent for me within a few weeks to go to his office. He was very kind and encouraging and eventually became like a second father to me....'

Fig. 3 Mask of a Faun, papier mâché painted (q.v. 13)

The year 1925 marks the start for Messel of a career in the theatre which lasted over fifty years – until 1976. Yet, it had a slow beginning, Messel's masks becoming a familiar feature of Cochran's annual Revues in the last half of the Twenties. They attracted favourable critical comment and were often reproduced in magazines[21] when Cochran's shows were reviewed (Fig. 28). In Gaunt's opinion[22] they charmed rather than scared and aptly conveyed a certain restlessness in the air at this time. From such a start Oliver Messel was to develop the characteristics which the middle-class public would become familiar with for many years – a playfulness, and a whimsicality purveyed with charm and taste. These elements came dynamically together for the first time in *Helen*,[23] the first of his solo-designed shows for Cochran, and probably the most wildly successful (p.84). To the public the whole thing was an unexpectedly pleasant surprise, but it was probably less of one to Cochran, who had known Messel's work for six years, and who had a discerning eye for undiscovered talent, as the programmes of his shows bear witness. Looking back some twelve years later Cochran[24] had this to say: '...with his *Comus*[25] at Sadlers Wells, Oliver Messel reminded me of James Agate's article on him in the *Sunday Times*[26] apropos of his work in my '1930' Revue: "It is a pity Oliver Messel is an Englishman; if he had been a Roossian or a Proosian presenting décor on the marges of some Czechoslovakian crocodile-infested swamp, we should long ago have hailed him as a great scenic artist. As he is merely a Londoner the play-going world is content to be completely ravished once a year at the London Pavilion, and to forget all about this fine artist until Mr Cochran next reminds us." Since then I have "reminded" London several times,

◀ Fig. 4 Tilly Losch as the Fu Manchu Marchioness in *Wake Up and Dream* (q.v. 28), 1929. Sasha

Fig. 5 Oliver Messel by Cecil Beaton (*c.*1927) ▶

and it was not long before I was proud to give Oliver Messel two opportunities for the display of his genius, of which he took full advantage and which put him far beyond any further need of a "reminder" from me to the public. *Helen* and the Lyceum version of *The Miracle*[27] established him as the only British designer who can 'steal the notices' from actors and author. . . .' Study of the *Helen* sets reveals that Messel had evidently found inspiration in the much earlier Baroque concept of the permanent set with arcading, columns, and triumphal arches to be found in most European theatres towards the end of the seventeenth and at the beginning of the eighteenth century. Such settings are seen at their brilliant best in the prints published by the Bibiena.[28] There is also the point to make that Messel was essentially a pastiche-maker from historical styles. He was not a theorist of the theatre like Appia or Craig, who were driven to innovate scenic design to express their theories. As Carl Toms has said (p.27), Oliver Messel was a great student of period. The boxes of Alinari photographs of Quattrocento paintings in the Snowdon Collection, acquired when Messel was designing costumes for the film *Romeo and Juliet*[29] (Fig.6), are not exceptional. There are other sources in the same collection including material on French early eighteenth century painters,[30] and prints of the sixteenth and seventeenth centuries for use as costumes sources, eighteenth century pattern-books as a basis for furniture designs (No.85), and architectural prints of all periods and countries. This does not make Messel a copyist for he successfully subsumed his source-materials[31] into a manner which was essentially personal by 1940. What are thought of now as colours typically Messelian – a claret-pink, sage-green, turquoise, ultramarine, a feverish yellow and pearly grey, can be found also, to a greater or lesser degree, in the work of his contemporaries, such as Burra, Piper, Richards, Nash and Whistler. These tones were characteristic of that period. However, it was in the very personal way Messel used them (establishing before he began to design a production which could be successfully put together, which could not), that in the end gave his work its

Fig. 6 Set design for the film *Romeo and Juliet* (MGM), 1936. From Messel, 1936 (q.v. Bib. 1)

painterly look, and a unity of mood on the stage which is more poetic, nostalgic, than that of his contemporaries.

'Painting is the thing I like doing more than anything else.'[32] Whether his style evolved by chance or, through determination, from the darker pre-war tonality to the clearer, more harmonious tonality evidenced in *The Sleeping Beauty*[33] and *The Lady's Not For Burning*,[34] is impossible to say. Most of such artistic developments are not rationalised ones but occur deeper. During the Fifties and Sixties Messel's sets reached their apogee in brightness and tenderness of colour, and he seems to have done this most artfully for his productions at Glyndebourne. Behind this of course there are frequent homages to Renoir, Manet, Watteau, Tiepolo, Veronese, Goya and others. Messel's critics found his work fussy, sugary, overdecorative and out of keeping with the spirit of a work on occasions, but that is to concentrate perhaps too much on the painterly aspect. That is important, but a designer has also to be continually conscious of the strengths and limitations of particular stages. None is alike; nor is the designer free to compose as he wills; he still has to come to terms with the script and the strategy of the director. Examination of the models in this Exhibition should confirm how Messel developed his skill in deploying his scenery at a time when it was still the fashion to have permanent sets or flats throughout a production. He has said:[35] '... When I'm designing, which is always terribly hard, I wrap a cold towel around my head and I have an awful headache because I think "Oh God, I mustn't repeat this! I can't repeat that". That's the terrible thing about the theatre – you have to be like a chameleon, always changing and trying to think of something that hasn't been done before.... With the theatre you're submitted to the author's point of view. You must illustrate what is there and not yourself.' The designer has not only to come to terms with a tiny space (like the one at Glyndebourne) but he often has by some trick of perspective to create the illusion, for the audience's benefit, that the space is bigger than it really is. That is why the perspective on the models exhibited sometimes looks awry, but the reason is that economies of space and the differing sightlines from every part of the house have been taken into consideration. The designer's model is not a toy, like a doll's house, but a scaled down version of the set.

※

The making of theatre is a collaboration between many skills. The respect of Oliver Messel's former colleagues for his professionalism is amply evident in the written contributions they have made to this catalogue. They cannot be thanked highly enough for the speed and enthusiasm with which they have delivered. As many views as would represent the theatre in action were sought and put into the framework which follows; thus one may learn something here of the process of inception and gestation of a production. In all cases it must begin with a writer, and here the most fitting is Christopher Fry,[36] the distinguished playwright and translator:

> If Oliver Messel's set-designs hadn't been tethered by practical commonsense they might have lifted off the stage altogether – at least that could certainly be said of his design for *Ring Round the Moon*,[37] the most successful of the designs for the three productions in which I was concerned; the most successful because in this his Muse or Genius seemed to have appeared on the stage in person without human aid. The delicacy, wit and 'visible music' of his art appeared without effort, both in the set and in the costumes. Noël Coward told me, after seeing a performance, that he had found a perfection of collaboration in the fusion of Anouilh's play, Messel's designs, Richard Addinsell's music and Peter

Brook's production (not to mention the happy casting. Claire Bloom still glides across the stage in my memory, as she seems to do in the painting of her by Theyre Lee-Elliott which hangs beside my desk).

The year before (1949) I had been given the good fortune of his designs for *The Lady's Not For Burning*[38] (Fig. 7). The set was enchanting; the inventiveness of it stays in the mind – the hanging birdcage, the shelf behind Tyson's desk, the way to the garden, the feeling of Spring. It was all a bit grand and ecclesiastical for an impecunious Mayor of a small country town, perhaps. But the charm of it, and particularly the space of sky, by sunlight, rainlight and moonlight, outweighed any such reservations.

With the third of the productions, *The Dark is Light Enough*,[39] the viewpoints of designer and author weren't so interlocking, through no fault of Oliver's. I had been late completing the script, and had been too close to it to be able to be clear about how it should be presented. The drawing-room of an Austrian Countess in 1848 would seem naturally enough to ask for an early Victorian richness, both in décor and costume, and this Messel provided in a masterly way, while still giving the light and air which was his hallmark. But I realised too late that this winter comedy needed only suggestion, rather than imaginative actuality; all that was required was a staircase and a window looking on to snow, the rest to be left to the words. Our two explorations were getting in each other's way – though this was not true of the set for the second act, the simplicity of the stables, where all seemed right again; and there's little doubt that if I had given Messel a clearer lead towards what I was trying to create, his genius would have supplied the answer – and how magical that would have been!

The relationship between a theatre designer and the director is a complex one and there seems to be no set way how it works. It is not only the director and designer who are principally concerned with interpreting the text; the author's requirements are of the utmost importance as both Messel and Fry have said, above. Some authors – a good example is Shaw – are very precise, textually, about the set; others, Shakespeare would do here, are rudimentary, but both cases might need as much discussion. Where director and designer have often worked together it is often the case that a lot of preliminary discussion becomes unnecessary, as through force of precedent, both will come up with similar concepts. Peter Glenville,[40] the director of plays and films, who often worked with Messel, says:

> For the most part theatre directors are not greatly interested to discuss casting, subtlety of character, or of script with a costume and set designer except in so far as these aspects directly concern the visual realization of the production. With Oliver Messel this attitude would certainly have been mistaken. His understanding of all aspects of a theatrical production was always sophisticated and intuitively sure. His views on casting, not really his direct concern, were always both persistent and canny. He would immerse himself in the overall mood and thrust of a play and the director's interpretation of it, and then he would proceed to create the background which would most perfectly realise it. He preferred to work on the settings by building his own models. His materials were often surprising and inventive; plastic putty, pipe-cleaners, matchsticks, strips of material, would all be collected together, and then gradually an extraordinary miniature décor would emerge in his studio. The model would be in great detail, the mechanisms clear, the painting exact, so there would be no subsequent need of reinterpretation by construction managers. Indeed, although highly classical in his tastes he always fought against old-fashioned conventions in set-building which in his day were much more hidebound than they are now.

Fig. 7 Costume design for Alizon in *The Lady's Not For Burning* (1949), (q.v. 56)

Fig. 8 The set for Act 3 of *Ring Round the Moon* (1950) (q.v. 57). Houston Rogers

One of the finest sets he ever created was for a production of Anouilh's *Ring Round the Moon*,[41] (Fig. 8), brilliantly cast and directed by Peter Brook. His idea was to suggest in theatrical terms a soaring Winter Garden, or hothouse, with plants and trees (adjoining a country house, off-stage). The leading scene builders of the day insisted that it had to be constructed from great hoops of wood – the inevitable building material in the theatre at that time. Oliver stoutly maintained that the proper effect could only be fashioned by hand from some form of iron or metal. His persistence won out. He discovered a new and little known scene builder who was willing to carry out Oliver's idea. The result was a classic – a triumph of elegance and originality.

Once I directed a play[42] with Oliver's designs which was a satire on the human condition. In the script, the locale of the action was described as taking place in the maze of rooms and corridors of a vast modern hotel. The *dramatis personae* were a swarm of ants behaving more or less as ants could comically be perceived to behave. The text was funny and imaginative. I discussed a possible production with Oliver and he agreed to work on the play if, instead of a hotel, the action could take place in a real ant colony below ground; and if all the characters could be dressed to suggest humanised ants; and so it was done – naturally with the author's consent. Alec Guinness was a splendid hero ant, and the final visual effect was a feast of fancy and of wit.

I also worked with Oliver on the theatre version of *Rashomon*[43] in New York. He devised a revolving Japanese forest, through which the leading female character was led on horseback by her husband through glades and trees that glided gently by as the couple progressed towards their fateful encounter with the bandit. Nearby was a ruined temple later to be battered by a tempestuous rain storm. It was a formidable challenge for a designer, magnificently mastered.

When Oliver designed *Romeo and Juliet*[44] for me in New York it was his first work in the theatre to be initiated on Broadway. Consequently he was required to join The Designers Union which involved taking all the technical tests and examinations demanded of new members. These were usually young men starting their careers. The fact that Oliver was ready to submit to this laborious process was a tribute to his practical good sense and determination. He was, after all, already a celebrated European designer of innumerable ballets, operas, films and plays. However, trouble arose when, as part of the examination process, he was required to paint a backcloth on canvas from a given standard size design. Oliver was a gifted painter so this was a task at which he could excel and indeed, enjoy. However, when the design was handed to him he was appalled at its form, colour and concept – in other words at its lack of taste. He absolutely refused to perpetrate on a large scale what, in his opinion, was a monstrosity. There was general confusion exacerbated by the fact that, as later emerged, the creator of the offending design was the President of the Union itself! The officials then suggested that Oliver should himself make a design which he would then paint as a backcloth. He did so, and designed an intricate and detailed romantic pastoral scene which the Union officials then doubted could ever be achieved on a large scale. Needless to say, Oliver had a field day making a masterpiece of scene painting. It was admired and wondered at. The Union and its President then generously and rather proudly welcomed Oliver into their fold.

Though Oliver Messel was a prodigious worker he could not cope without help from one or more assistants. His first one was John Claridge. In the following extract Carl Toms[45] gives a fascinating account of Messel at work – the real nitty-gritty of what is involved when using one's hands in a certain way.

> I went to work for Oliver Messel as an assistant, originally for three weeks, and stayed for six years (1952–1958). It was one of the most rewarding experiences of my life.
>
> I worked with him on interior decoration projects like the suites at the Dorchester (No. 78) and on ballets, operas, plays and musicals, both here and in America. In the process he taught me more about painting, architecture, furniture and costume that I had ever learned before. His influence on me was very great indeed.
>
> When I have a problem I still find myself wondering what Oliver would have done about it. It was from him I learned to let my instincts rule. He had an amazing sensitivity and perception which wasn't in any way intellectual. Oliver could not, and would not try to explain why he had designed a show in a particular way; his language was entirely visual – and a very eloquent language it was.
>
> He seemed to find his way to the style of presentation of a piece of theatre very tentatively; an outside observer would have got the impression he didn't quite know what he was doing. He would endlessly discard what would seem like brilliant ideas to try yet one more, in case it was better. Books were pored over in a search for things to spark off his imagination. It would often be something unexpected – a corner of a painting, the design on a piece of china, a strange piece of architecture (like for instance the Portuguese railway station which

OVERLEAF Fig. 9 Set model for Act 1 of *Le Comte Ory* (1954), (q.v. 52, 68)

inspired *Ring Round the Moon*)[46] or the postcard of a Raoul Dufy painting (which became the basis for *House of Flowers*).[47]

He did endless small pencil sketches on one of his favourite pads of blue-grey paper. When he found that he returned to an idea or a set of shapes several times he would start to make bits of model in a model frame – working very sketchily on bits of cartridge paper with charcoal, snipped out with scissors and stuck together with brown gum strip paper, roughly bent and shaped, working rather like a sculptor. I never saw him start with a ground plan – he arrived at that as he worked. He tried always to keep the rough model fluid – he would say 'not cut and dried'. He always had a careful cut-out of a character from the play to scale so that he was relating everything he did to the human size.

When the rough model seemed to be what he wanted we would start to make a finished version, replacing the rough pieces with carefully made ones so that it transformed slowly into the finished design. He would draw out each piece on scaled tracing paper, always by hand – he hated rulers, set squares and compasses. This design was then transferred to paper which he then painted in water-colour or sometimes even in oil paint. I then made it into a sturdy piece of model with details like furniture and set dressings – all half inch to one foot scale. I think that this freehand technique was what gave his work that special elusive quality, and a direct freshness, individual to him. This process could be quite rapidly achieved in days or it would take weeks and no one was allowed to see it until it was finished. He had to have total conviction in it himself *before* it was presented to the director or the producer.

The costumes were not designed until the set was finished then he would more often than not stay up all night and design them all. I would arrive in the morning to find them scattered all over the studio, always chaotic, full of tumbled piles of books on chairs, and on the floor swatches of material in amongst the tea cups and abandoned sandwiches. The house then usually became full of technicians, wardrobe supervisors, some construction painters and prop-makers (usually having tea in the kitchen) his favourite place for a meeting.

Oliver was a most informal man, always charming, but he certainly knew how to get his own way. Many a dazed technician left Pelham Place not quite realising what they had agreed to do, but they always did it, nevertheless. In the same way many a spoiled diva would be flattered into submission by his deft diplomacy.

Although his beautiful costume designs would seem to be, on face value, somewhat vague, he knew exactly what they were to be made of, how they should be cut, and he would choose all the details very carefully. He often made head-dresses, jewellery and masks, himself, exquisitely.

He had a faultless sense of colour and texture and was fearless in the use of both; always inventive, practical and entirely theatrical. The final result was invariably stunning to look at.

From the designer's studio come the sketches not only for sets and costumes but also for the accessories, like wigs, or head-dresses which may be infinitely detailed and though looking delicate must be strong enough to survive constant wear and tear in performance. Stanley Hall (whose firm Wig Creations supplied many Messel productions), makes the point which many other craftsmen do – Oliver Messel's endless search for perfection:

> ... I had been very lucky working at Denham Studios in the Thirties, the halcyon days of Korda, creating make-up and wigs for such period films as *Rembrandt*,[48] *Queen Victoria*,[49] and *Thief of Bagdad*,[50] and after the War I met and worked

Fig. 10 Costume design for Lady Teazle in *The School for Scandal* (1958) (q.v. 73)

with Oliver on many productions. His talents amazed me and though his attention to the smallest detail may have meant remaking a wig, costume or head-dress three times, he improved on each small detail and the final result made his work-force proud of the achievement. He could make, or mock-up anything from wigs to costumes and sets. He would work alongside everyone making things for his productions.

In wig-making one uses a block, a non-specified head, but Oliver made a complete bust – with face and shoulders – in papier mâché so that one could see the final effect of the wig before fitting it. And he could also create curious elderly characters with their hair fuzzed out (to make the most of it), and then enclose it in a hair-net.

His feeling for romance brought the curtain for *Ring Round the Moon*[51] down, on his magnificent set, with a glorious firework display; and his predatory garden in the film *Suddenly Last Summer*[52] gave the right feeling of evil and claustrophobia. His desert island for *The Little Hut*[53] was exactly the reverse, with large dotty nodding exotic plants. This play ended with an amusing monkey (played by William Chappell), climbing down a palm-tree on the stage. Oliver asked me to make the monkey mask, which I created in life-like rubber, and Hugh Skillen to make the monkey's costume. But when Oliver saw my realistic mask and Skillen's costume he decided Hugh and I should change roles. Thus, *I* made the costume, by knotting hair into a leotard, and Hugh made a papier mâché mask which simply *stared* at the audience. And it worked. He didn't want a real monkey, but a fantasy one, to round off this witty play as the curtain falls.

Visitors to this exhibition may be struck by the cursory appearance of the costume designs. This is because Messel is using a kind of shorthand which he knows he can rely on the cutter to read and follow. When designing these costumes he was also concentrating on how they would appear at a distance[54] so the sketches are better seen from far back. It is the usual practice for the designer to staple onto the design swatches of the materials he wishes used, and we have shown these so that the two things may be compared.

Rosemary Vercoe[55] for some time wardrobe-mistress at Glyndebourne, and who, with Eleanor Abbey, had much to do with Messel's opera designs, has this to say:

> There was always a great sense of achievement in working on Oliver's costume-designs for the various operas he did for Glyndebourne. He made huge demands on his makers and the first sight of his beautiful but very free sketches struck terror in all concerned. But once on his wavelength, and with the essential help of his wonderful 'translators' Carl Toms and Eleanor Abbey, it all became clearer. There was always a great deal of colour selecting and matching and fabric dyeing. His colours were highly personal and very exciting in all his productions. There was a tremendous amount of finely detailed and hand-crafted decoration and trimming to be applied to each and every comparatively simply cut garment. He was very particular about precise cut and style but his tremendous strength was the fact that you knew that he could, if necessary, carry out each bit of decoration himself and was always ready to twist and turn the bits of wire and gold braid to make a prototype to be copied and mass-produced. He was highly practical himself. Usually the first roughly put together costumes were displayed to him first in his rather chaotic South Kensington studio (Pelham Place), before being completed in the Glyndebourne work-rooms.
>
> He liked best to use makers who had worked with him on several productions and could set to work without too many questions – and the cumulative final effect of many of his shows was stunning and exciting in its own style. He was a very demanding perfectionist but always deeply appreciative when the results were as he had intended.
>
> I always enjoyed working with him.

❊

One of the purposes of this exhibition – apart from that of giving pleasure – is to reassess Messel's achievement. The making of a reputation, good or bad, is inescapable for any artist in the public eye. As stage-designers are all too aware it is predominantly their work which the public sits looking at all evening. But often the most critical eyes (for a whole host of reasons), are those of a designer's competitors. It is in the nature of things that rivalries flourish even if they be one-sided. Cecil Beaton,[56] for one, saw himself as a competitor:

> *Broadchalke*
> Oliver Messel has been cast to play the role of my rival over a long period of years. At the beginning of my career I felt that he had everything I longed for – a niche in the theatre, and in London life, and a group of doting friends and lovers. We became friends. I adored him but I was always envious of his success. He was avid to guard every aspect of it, and in fact so ambitious for more that not only was he a dog-in-the-manger about wanting to keep jobs from others but tried to hang onto those that he was unable himself to fulfil. Recently I felt the competition was over and that it had been won decisively by me. It was, however, a wry stroke of fate that in my photographic career my only serious rival should be Oliver's nephew. Tony Armstrong Jones suddenly had enormous success – and indeed deserved it. For his photographs were vital and he himself was a young man of great liveliness and a certain charm. The fact that he moved in the second-rate world of magazines and newspapers sullied him, but I personally think that he survived with his freshness pretty well intact...

A more objective assessment published in 1940, and so about fifteen years after Messel's star had begun to rise, is the following extract by R. Myerscough-Walker.[57] It is interesting in several ways, not least in the comparison drawn between American and English styles of design on the stage during the Thirties. Messel's work was known in the States as early as 1928 and had been sustained by visiting English productions, and by his films.

> Oliver Messel I have described elsewhere in this book as an eclectic, and this word, which may infer a depreciation of his work, can be used only with the qualification that he is the most brilliant eclectic working on the English stage today. I have described Gordon Craig as the supreme idealist and a master at both the art and the craft of the theatre. Messel is an idealist, but of an entirely different standard. His mind, in dealing with the theatre, is concerned with the most exquisite form of mounting (both décor and costume) of which he is capable. Where Craig wants to produce the whole play and get back to the essential dramatic form which was typified by such civilizations as the Greek (in the process of which he runs contra to all the commercial managements throughout the world), Messel is willing to accept the contemporary state in which the theatre finds itself and to create backgrounds and dresses for these productions in the most imaginative way that can be done.
> The New York theatre, for instance, is more vital, more fundamental than the hybrid creature we have in England, and the New York designers such as Lee Simonson,[58] Joe Mielziner[59] and Mordecai Gorelik[60] are poles apart from the English designers such as Rex Whistler and Oliver Messel. In 1938 two plays were presented in London, one by the Lunts called *Amphitryon 38*[61] for which Simonson did the décor, and the other *Golden Boy*[62] by Clifford Odets for which Gorelik prepared the designs. Both these creations were of a lesser degree but of the same kind as Gordon Craig's.
> Now such productions are never a commercial success in England. They are, for a limited run, capable of producing tremendous enthusiasm from which one might infer that they might be commercially possible in this country. But without going into the methods of letting and sub-letting the London theatres with the resultant high rents, the star system with its enormous salaries, the

necessity of the long run, and so on, you may take it for granted that the success of these plays is strictly limited and that this is not a criticism of the plays so much as a reflection on the English theatre public and, even more, on the producers.

Oliver Messel is a long way removed from such men as Simonson and Mielziner; and his productions for such men as Cochran show him to be eminently capable of taking on the extremely successful productions which are created in this country and designing for those productions such sets and costumes as will dazzle the average person into applause. How right this is need not be gone into now. It is sufficient to say that some designers regard the background as being most successful when it is not noticed. Others regard the décor as a further possibility of expressing their own ego. Messel's métier, therefore, is one of brilliance which includes taste, imagination, tremendous knowledge, technique, and a sense of elegance. He was originally a painter and his paintings show the same desire to create something elegant rather than fundamental ... Messel's approach is one of virtuosity; he is a sort of Fritz Kreisler[63] of the décor world, and in this he is as eminent in design as Fritz Kreisler is in music.

He comes of a very well-known and old family and his social aura is one concerned with society; that is to say, the so-called 'Society Set' of the English upper class. I mention this because it accounts to a great extent for his attitude towards the theatre, particularly in his elegant and frequently extravagant use of methods and materials. It also makes it surprising that a person of this upbringing should be so industrious, for among artists and designers he is one of most hard-working and meticulous men I have ever known. Although he works with a tremendous sense of industry he does, in some curious way, appear to ride over those with whom he is working. A man like Edward Carrick,[64] for instance, is a friend and equal of the workmen and carpenters who build his sets. Messel is no snob but he appears very far removed from the executants with whom he works and that applies to the technicians as well as to the workmen.

I suppose his best-known work is that for Evelyn Laye's[65] vehicle called *Helen*, which Reinhardt[66] produced for Cochran at the Adelphi some years ago. You may remember the all-white bedroom scene, hung in draperies, which was a tour de force in Messelian technique. There is a set which would be described by all practical people as being too white and too fragile to withstand the changes and constant storage and reassembling. Nevertheless it made that particular scene and in it you will find the ultimate height to which Messel has gone in theatre design.

❊

The placing of an artist is due to the public's estimate of him, finally; but it is quite useful to bring to mind his contemporaries. Messel differed from them considerably; he was really the poet of the brush, when compared with Whistler's irony and superb draughtsmanship, Osbert Lancaster's humour, Piper's envisioned imagination, or Burra's acidity.

The last word in this part must go to Sybil Rosenfeld,[67] the theatre historian, who saw and can still respond delightedly to the memory of *Helen* staged over fifty years ago:

When Messel's first work for the professional stage was seen in 1925, the revolt against the excessive naturalism of the late Victorian Theatre was in full swing. It took two divergent paths; the abstract, architectonic designs of Gordon Craig and his followers, and in contrast the simplified painted scenery with formalised or highly decorative elements. It was the second path which Messel followed; he was not influenced by Craig or by abstraction, as a comparison between Komisarjevsky's[68] *Macbeth* (1933) and Messel's *A Midsummer Night's Dream*[69] (1937) makes obvious.

Messel's early work for the theatre consisted of masks, a form of theatricalism which was completely unnatural. His first was for the Diaghilev production in 1925 of the ballet *Zephyr and Flora*[70] with scenery by Braque, followed by a series of fantastic masks for Cochran's revues. The connection with Diaghilev recalls the sensation made in 1911 by his Russian ballet with décors by Bakst[71] and Benois. It seems likely that Messel was influenced by the fairy-tale quality of Benois, with whom he shared a poetic imagination and a sense of period fantasy.

Messel's first full production for Cochran was a spectacular adaptation of Offenbach's *Helen* (Fig. 11). This was produced by Reinhardt, whose *Sumurūn*[72] had also made a sensation in 1911 with its use of a revolving stage

Fig. 11 Model of the final scene of *Helen* (q.v. **34**). Theatre Museum, No. E. 184–1934

and its white backgrounds. Both these featured in *Helen* with three revolving stages and the famous White Bedroom. Another influence here was that of the Baroque with Bibienesque perspectives and colonnades, and the Rococo with bands of material draped over the scenes. The whole was eclectic as it also included Greek temples, the Empire style in the Blue Bedroom, and costumes from the Carrousel of Louis XIV, and thus early demonstrated the genius of Messel for absorbing various styles and evoking their quintessential flavour.

Though temperamentally romantic, his delight in the eighteenth century found scope in his designs for *The Country Wife*,[73] which included a formal garden lit by four chandeliers, and for *The Rivals*,[74] which astonished by its eighteenth-century type of scene shift in full view of the audience.

His gift for fantasy was admirably suited to opera and ballet and was realised in his work for Glyndebourne, and in the splendid recreation of the 17th century in the post-war revival of *The Sleeping Beauty*.[75] But it also beautifully matched some of the poetic and unreal contemporary plays. Such were his scenes and costumes for Fry's *The Lady's Not For Burning*[76] which suggested rather than depicted its medieval setting; his shimmering, fairylike conservatory in Fry's adaptation of *Ring Round the Moon*,[77] and his twisting pattern of roots in Spewak's *Under the Sycamore Tree*.[78]

His great contributions to the theatre of his time were his sensitivity to period, his gift for decoration and his consummate taste, influences which are still with us in successors such as Carl Toms,[79] Henry Bardon,[80] Nicholas Georgiadis[81] and others.

NOTES: OLIVER MESSEL AND THE THEATRE

1 *Twang!!* (1965) Lionel Bart. Opened in London after a critical savaging in Manchester. Closed 30th January, 1966. An account of the eventful months prior to the opening is *Down in the Forest Someone Stirred*, Queen; 19th January, 1966, pp. 53–60 (Fig. 12).
2 *Gigi* (1973) and *The Sleeping Beauty* (1976); for details of both see pp. 109, 171 and Cat. Nos. 73, 42.
3 *The Little Hut* (1950), see p. 117 Cat. No. 49 *Under the Sycamore Tree* (1952), pp. 117, 130 Cat. Nos. 50, 62 *The Queen of Spades* (1949), p. 122 Cat. No. 58 and video clip, No. 98 *Suddenly Last Summer* (1960), Cat. No. 108 and video clip No. 98.
4 Irving Wardle, *The Theatres of George Devine*, Cape, 1978.
5 *Burke's Landed Gentry*, 18th ed. 1965 vol. 1, pp. 498–9.
6 His house at 18 Stafford Terrace, W8 (National Trust), is one of the best surviving for Victorian artifacts and pictures.
7 Information from Thomas Messel.
8 Interview by Patrick Foster in HERS *Magazine*, vol. 1, No. 5, May 1976, St James Barbados. Hereafter referred to as *IHM, 1976*. By permission of Patrick Foster.
9 See biog. outline (p. 15) for dates. He paid 1 guinea, 12 and 11 guineas for each term's tuition.
10 Formerly at 52 Brook Street, W1. It seems to have opened in 1925.
11 (1905–1944) For a *cat. rais.* of his work, see Laurence Whistler and Ronald Fuller, *The Work of Rex Whistler*, Batsford, 1960.
12 The interest in masks in the early twentieth century was strong. Yeats and O'Neill used them (Cat. No. 19), and they play an important part in Analytical Cubism (Picasso, *Desmoiselles d'Avignon*, etc.).
13 Laurence Whistler has told me that Rex Whistler's masks were grotesques. He did not make them for long, and now all have been lost.
14 *Masks by Oliver Messel*, The Studio, vol. 96, 1928, pp. 249–255; ills. Quoted by permission of Studio International.
15 *IHM, 1976*.
16 Evidently an early love; see No. 12.
17 Portrait-painter, landscapist, exh. 1917–35.
18 There is nothing in the scanty records about his having taken the Diploma but such facts were usually not recorded.
19 *IHM, 1976*.
20 Unfortunately no copy of the Claridge Gallery Cat. seems to have survived.
21 *The Sketch, Play Pictorial, The Bystander*, are representative.
22 Gaunt (op. cit.).
23 *Helen* (1932) p. 84 Cat. No. 34.
24 *Showman Looks On* (p. 226) J. M. Dent Ltd., 1945. By permission of Dorothy Dickson.
25 *Comus* (1942) p. 105 Cat. No. 40.
26 *Sunday Times*, 30th March, 1930.
27 *The Miracle* (1932), p. 80 Cat. No. 33.
28 A famous family of scene designers in Italy; q.v. P. Hartnoll, *Concise Oxford Companion to the Theatre*, 1981, p. 56.
29 *Romeo and Juliet*, film (1936), see p. 56.
30 Mainly Watteau, his followers Pater and Lancret, etc.
31 Messel was shy about visitors seeing him working from sources; information from Carl Toms.
32 *IHM, 1976*.
33 *The Sleeping Beauty* (1946), p. 109 Cat. No. 42.
34 *The Lady's Not For Burning* (1949), pp. 117, 119 Cat. Nos. 45, 56.
35 *Oliver Messel talks to Maxime de la Falaise McKendry; Interview*, 26–18th May, 1976. Hereafter referred

Fig. 12 Design for a pouch for the musical *Twang!!* (1965)

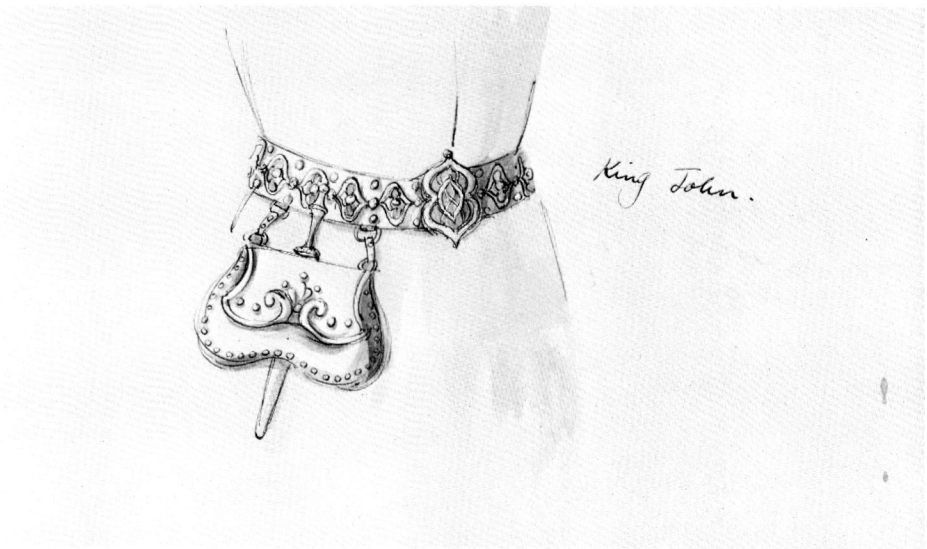

to as McKENDRY, 1976. By permission of the publishers.
36 b.1907; actor, playwright, producer, translator. His work is published by Oxford University Press. q.v. *Who's Who*, 1983.
37 *Ring Round the Moon* (1950), pp.117, 119 Cat. Nos.48, 57.
38 TLNFB, q.v. 34 above.
39 *The Dark is Light Enough* (1954), pp.117, 141 Cat. Nos.51, 66.
40 b.1913; actor, director, playwright; q.v. *Notable Names in the American Theatre*, James T. White & Co., New Jersey, 1976, p.770.
41 RRM; q.v. Nos.48, 57, pp.117, 119.
42 *Under the Sycamore Tree* (1952), q.v. Nos.50, 62, pp.117, 130.
43 *Rashomon* (1959).
44 *Romeo and Juliet* (1950), q.v. p.126 and Cat. No.60. Not to be confused with the MGM film Messel designed in 1936.
45 Carl Toms, OBE, designer; b.1927; q.v. *Who's Who*, 1983.
46 RRM; Nos.48, 57, pp.117, 119.
47 *House of Flowers* (1954), q.v. pp.149, 184 Cat. Nos.69, 99.
48 London Films (1936); dir. Korda; with Charles Laughton and Elsa Lanchester.
49 RKO (1938); dir. H. Wilcox. Anna Neagle was the Queen.
50 London Films (1940); dir. Korda; Sabu as the Thief; q.v. p.56.
51 RRM, q.v. Nos.48, 57, pp.117, 119.
52 *Suddenly Last Summer* (1960), q.v. p.56 and Cat. Nos.98, 108.
53 *The Little Hut* (1950); q.v. p.117 Cat. No.49.
54 McKENDRY, 1976: 'I always look at it through a long-distance glass in the fitting-room so that I can see what it looks like from far away. It's very important to have that balance, and I think it's a whole training – it's the important thing in theatre design. You must be able to gauge the proportion and whether it will be effective from afar.'
55 Vercoe; costume designer. Has done many productions with Patrick Robertson, notably for opera; part., English National Opera, from 1970s.
56 (1904–80); designer, painter, photographer, writer. This extract is from *Self-Portrait with Friends*, Weidenfeld & Nicolson, 1979, pp.335–6; by permission of the publishers.
57 Film and stage designer (dates not recorded). From: *Stage and Film Décor*, Sir Isaac Pitman, 1940, pp.172–5; extract quoted by permission of Pitman Books Ltd., London.
58 Lee Simonson; scene designer (1888–1967).
59 Jo Mielziner; scene and lighting designer, lecturer, theatre architect; b.1901. For biog. outline, q.v. *Notable Names in the American Theatre*, New Jersey, 1976, p.986. Probably the most prolific and influential New York stage designer.
60 Mordecai Gorelik; scene designer, director, playwright; b.1899; q.v. *NNITAT* (above) p.776 for biog. outline.
61 A comedy by Jean Giraudoux (1929) prod. Jouvet; Paris.
62 Group Theatre, New York, 1937.
63 (1875–1962) Austrian violinist. A great virtuoso with a warm ingratiating tone.
64 b.1905; film and stage designer. A son of Edward Gordon Craig. Is now generally known as Teddy Craig.
65 Actress, often in musical comedy; b.1900. The star of *Helen*; q.v. No.34, p.84.
66 Austrian actor, manager, director; (1873–1943). For further information see Cat. Nos.34, 33 for *Helen* and *The Miracle*.
67 See Bib. 9(e).
68 Theodore Komisarjevsky; Russian director; (1882–1954); in England after 1920; Stanislavsky theorist; directed Chekhov for a regular company at Barnes; later at Stratford and in West End. Wrote much. Died in America.
69 q.v. No.38, p.97.
70 q.v. No.18, p.71.
71 Léon Bakst (1866–1924); Alexandre Benois (1870–1960); both associated with the golden years of the Diaghilev ballet, for set and costume designs.
72 Presented by Cochran in 1911. *Samurūn* was a wordless play based on the *Arabian Nights*. In the same year, also under Cochran's management, Reinhardt directed *The Miracle* at Olympia – not to be confused with the Lyceum production (also Cochran's) in 1932. (Cat. No.33)
73 *The Country Wife* (1936); q.v. p.93 and Cat. No.36.
74 *The Rivals* (1945); q.v. p.106 and Cat. No.41.
75 q.v. No.42, p.109.
76 q.v. Nos.45, 56, pp.117, 119.
77 q.v. Nos.48, 57, pp.117, 119.
78 q.v. Nos.50, 62, pp.117, 130.
79 q.v. 45 (above).
80 b.1923; designer of Shakespeare, opera and ballet.
81 b.Athens; prolific designer for plays, opera and ballet.

CHRONOLOGY OF HIS INVOLVEMENT IN STAGE PRODUCTIONS

1. Theatres are in London unless stated otherwise. Titles are as they appear in programmes; likewise, performance dates, and casts, etc.

2. Abbreviations:

(B)   – Ballet
c   – costume(s)
CG   – Royal Opera House, Covent Garden
(EF) – Edinburgh Festival
(LIV) – Liverpool
m   – mask(s)
Met   – Metropolitan Opera House, New York
(NY) – New York
(O)   – Opera
(P)   – Play, with or without music
(Rev) – Revival(s)
(s)   – setting(s)

1925 Nov. 12   Coliseum, *Zéphyre et Flore* (B), (m, symbols).
1926 Apr. 23   London Pav., *Cochran's Revue (1926) (The Masks)* (c,m).
1927 June 19   Strand, *The Great God Brown* (P) (m).
1928 Mar. 22   London Pav., *This Year of Grace* (Cochran's 1928 Revue); *(Lorelei)* (c,s). *(Dance Little Lady)* (c,m); Nov. 7th Selwyn Th. (NY), (c,m).
1928 June 24   Arts Th. Club, *Riverside Nights* (P), *(Nigger Heaven)* (c,m).
1929 Mar. 27   London Pav., *Wake Up and Dream* (Cochran's 1929 Revue); *The Wrong Room in the Wrong House, Wake Up and Dream, The Dream* (s and c for these). *What is This Thing Called Love* (s, idol); *A Girl in A Shawl* (c,s).
1930 Mar. 27   London Pav., Cochran's 1930 Revue. *Piccadilly 1830, Heaven* (c,s).
1931 Mar. 19   London Pav., *Cochran's 1931 Revue; Stealing Through, Scaramouche* (c,s).
1932 Jan. 30   Adelphi, *Helen* (P), (c,s).
1932 Apr. 9   Lyceum, *The Miracle* (P), (c).
1933 Jan. 27   Gaiety, *Mother of Pearl* (P), (s).
1935 May 2   Drury Lane, *Glamorous Night* (P), (s).
1936 Oct. 6   Old Vic. *The Country Wife* (P); Dec. 1st, Henry Miller's Th. (NY), (c,s, both prods.).
1937 July 15   CG (De Basil Coy). *Francesca da Rimini* (B); Oct. 24th Met. (NY), (c,s, both prods.).
1937 Dec. 27   Old Vic. *A Midsummer Night's Dream* (P), (c,s).
1940 May 29   Old Vic. *The Tempest* (P), (c,s).
1940 Sept. 5   Arts Th. Club, *The Infernal Machine* (P), (c,s,m).
1942 Jan. 14   New, *Comus* (B), (c,s).
1942 May 8   His Majesty's, *The Big Top* (A Cochran revue), (c).
1945 Sept. 25   Criterion, *The Rivals* (P), (c,s).
1946 Feb. 20   CG, (Sadlers Wells B). *The Sleeping Beauty* (B), (c,s); Oct. 9th Met. (NY). (Rev: 1950 Sept. 14 Met. (NY), Los Angeles; 1955 NBC TV rel. (USA); CG, 1952, 1956, 1958, (BBC TV Act 3), q.v. 1960, 1976 below.

Fig. 13 Oliver Messel and his sister Anne; he is wearing one of Paris' costumes for *Helen* (q.v. 34) c.1932 by Cecil Beaton

1947 Mar. 20 CG, *The Magic Flute* (O), (c,s).
1949 May 11 Globe, *The Lady's Not For Burning* (P); 1950 Nov. 8, Royale Th. (NY) (c,s, both prods.).
1949 July 15 Adelphi, *Tough At The Top* (P); (c,s).
1950 Jan. 26 Globe, *Ring Round the Moon* (P), (c,s), Nov. 23 Martin Bech Th. (NY), 1951; Folkes Th. Copenhagen, (c,s, three prods.).
1950 Aug. 20 Kings Th. Edinburgh, (Glyndebourne Op. at EF); *Ariadne auf Naxos* (O), 1st vers.
1950 Aug. 23 Lyric (Shaftesbury Ave.), *The Little Hut* (P), (s); 1953, Oct. 7 Coronet Th. (NY), (s).
1950 Dec. 21 CG, *The Queen of Spades* (O), (c,s). Rev: 1956.
1951 Mar. 10 Broadhurst Th. (NY), *Romeo and Juliet* (P), (c,s).
1951 June 15 Glyndebourne, *Idomeneo* (O), (c,s). Rev: 1952, 1953 (EF), 1956, 1959, 1964.
1952 Apr. 14 Streatham Hill Th.; Aldwych, Apr. 23, *Under the Sycamore Tree* (P), (c,s).
             NOTE: At this point, Carl Toms joined Messel as assistant until 1958.
1952 June 18 Glyndebourne, *La Cenerentola* (O), (c,s). Rev: 1953 (EF), 1954 (Berlin), 1956 (Liv.), 1959, 1960.
1952 Oct. 10 Aldwych, *Letter From Paris* (P), (c,s).
1953 June 2 CG, *Homage To The Queen* (B), (c,s). Sept. 18 Met. (NY), then Detroit, San Francisco. 1958, Brussels.
1953 June 24 Glyndebourne, *Ariadne auf Naxos* (2nd vers.) (O) Rev: 1954, (also EF); 1957, 1958, q.v. 1962 below.
1954 Apr. 30 Aldwych, *The Dark Is Light Enough* (P). 1955 Feb. 23 ANTA (NY), (c,s, both prods.).
1954 June 10 Glyndebourne, *Il Barbiere di Siviglia* (O), (c,s). Rev: 1955 (EF), 1961.
1954 Aug. 22 King's Th. Edinburgh (Glynd. Fest. Op.). *Le Comte Ory* (O), (c,s), Rev: 1955, 1957, 1958; also Paris, 1958.
1954 Dec. 30 Alvin (NY), *House of Flowers* (P), (c,m,s).
1955 May 11 Th. Royal (Bath), *Zémire et Azor* (O), (c,s).
1955 June 8 Glyndebourne, *Le Nozze di Figaro* (O), (s). Rev: 1956, 1958, 1962, 1963, 1965.
1956 June 15 Glyndebourne, *Die Entführung aus dem Serail* (O), (c,s). Rev: 1957, 1961.
1956 July 19 Glyndebourne, *Die Zauberflöte* (O), (c,s). Rev: 1957, 1960.
1958 Mar. 26 Cambridge, then Duke of York's, *Breath of Spring* (P), (c,s).
1958 Sept. 19 Det Ny Th. (Copenhagen), *The School For Scandal* (P), (c).
1958 Nov. 15 CG, *Samson* (Oratorio), (c,s).
1959 Jan. 27 Music Box (NY), *Rashomon* (c,s), (P).
1959 May 28 Glyndebourne, *Rosenkavalier*, (c,s), (O). Rev: 1960, 1965.
1959 Oct.   Met. (NY), *The Marriage of Figaro* (reworked from Glyndebourne prod.) (O).
1960 June 10 CG, *The Sleeping Beauty* (B), (part-redesigned c. and s).
1962 July 19 Glyndebourne, *Ariadne auf Naxos* (1st vers.) (O).
1964 Sept. 18 ANTA (NY), *Traveller Without Luggage* (P), (c,s).
1965 Dec. 20 Shaftesbury, *Twang!!* (P), (c,s).
1973 May 15 San Francisco; St. Louis, Detroit, Toronto; Nov. 13 Uris (NY) *Gigi* (P).
1976 June 15 Met. (NY) (Am. Ball Th.) *The Sleeping Beauty* (re-worked from the CG, 1946 prod.) (B).

MESSEL'S *SLEEPING BEAUTY*

Oliver Messel was indignant at Cyril Beaumont's account of his production of *The Sleeping Beauty* (Sadler's Wells Ballet, Royal Opera House, 20th February, 1946) for my *Ballet* magazine. 'Why couldn't you have written about it yourself?' he asked. He felt that Beaumont's slow-stepping prose had given no impression of his own poetry; and he resented unfavourable comparisons with *The Sleeping Princess* designed by Bakst for Diaghilev at the Alhambra in 1921, a production he remembered. 'Mine is better than Bakst's,' he said. Indeed Messel had thrown himself heart and soul into this undertaking, the greatest of his life. (I never saw his all-white *Helen* for Cochran. I wish I had.)

Beaumont was blissfully unaware that to list the colours of dresses in a given scene ('court ladies', he wrote, 'in . . . pink and brown, green and yellow, pale blue and beige, and scarlet and grey') did not really give the reader a feeling either of the colour scheme or of the artist's individual touch. I must avoid this pitfall. On the other hand, comparisons with the Bakst production, the designs of which had long been familiar from the Levinson-Brunoff book, even before the costumes were sold so surprisingly by Sotheby's in the late Sixties, cannot altogether be abjured. It happened that I was asked to catalogue these sales, then, thanks to several friends of the yet unestablished Theatre Museum, I was enabled to buy nearly a hundred of them. It is odd that the Bakst costumes – which had 'slept' not for a hundred years but for forty, and not in a lilac-shrouded castle but in a Parisian warehouse – survived in good condition, whereas Messel's costumes, made a quarter-of-a-century later, have been subjected to such constant wear and tear, such adaptation for new interpreters and such frequent renovation, that few remain intact. Moth and dust are less corrupting than popularity and sweat.

Both Bakst and Messel looked back towards the seventeenth and eighteenth centuries: both borrowed as much as they invented. Alexandre Benois thought Bakst was shaky on architecture and perspective: I thought Messel even more so. Each designer sought inspiration from the fantastic palaces conceived by the Bibiena family of stage decorators, who, in the words of A. Hyatt Mayor, 'at their drawing boards, unhampered by the need for permanence, the cost of marble, the delays of masons, the whims and deaths of patrons, in designs as arbitrary as the mandates of the autocrats they served, summed up the great emotional architecture of the baroque'. Both Bakst and Messel mixed the periods of their costumes. Each had an overall vision which transmuted borrowed themes into personal statements. While Bakst aimed in his court scenes at the utmost splendour of colour and grandiloquence of baroque design, Messel's opalescent fairyland was seen through the dewy eyes of a love-sick poet.

The flattened arches and banded columns of Messel's Prologue, *The Christening*, through which could be seen a feathery park, were taken from Watteau's painting *Les Charmes de la Vie* in the Wallace Collection. On our first glimpse of the court we saw ladies with stiff vertical costumes and the tall head-dresses of 1690, but with Elizabethan ruffs above their exposed bosoms. Some had magenta skirts. The Master of Ceremonies wore Tudor uniform of billiard-table green, with red and gold trimmings, but a Charles II periwig. His plain white cloak

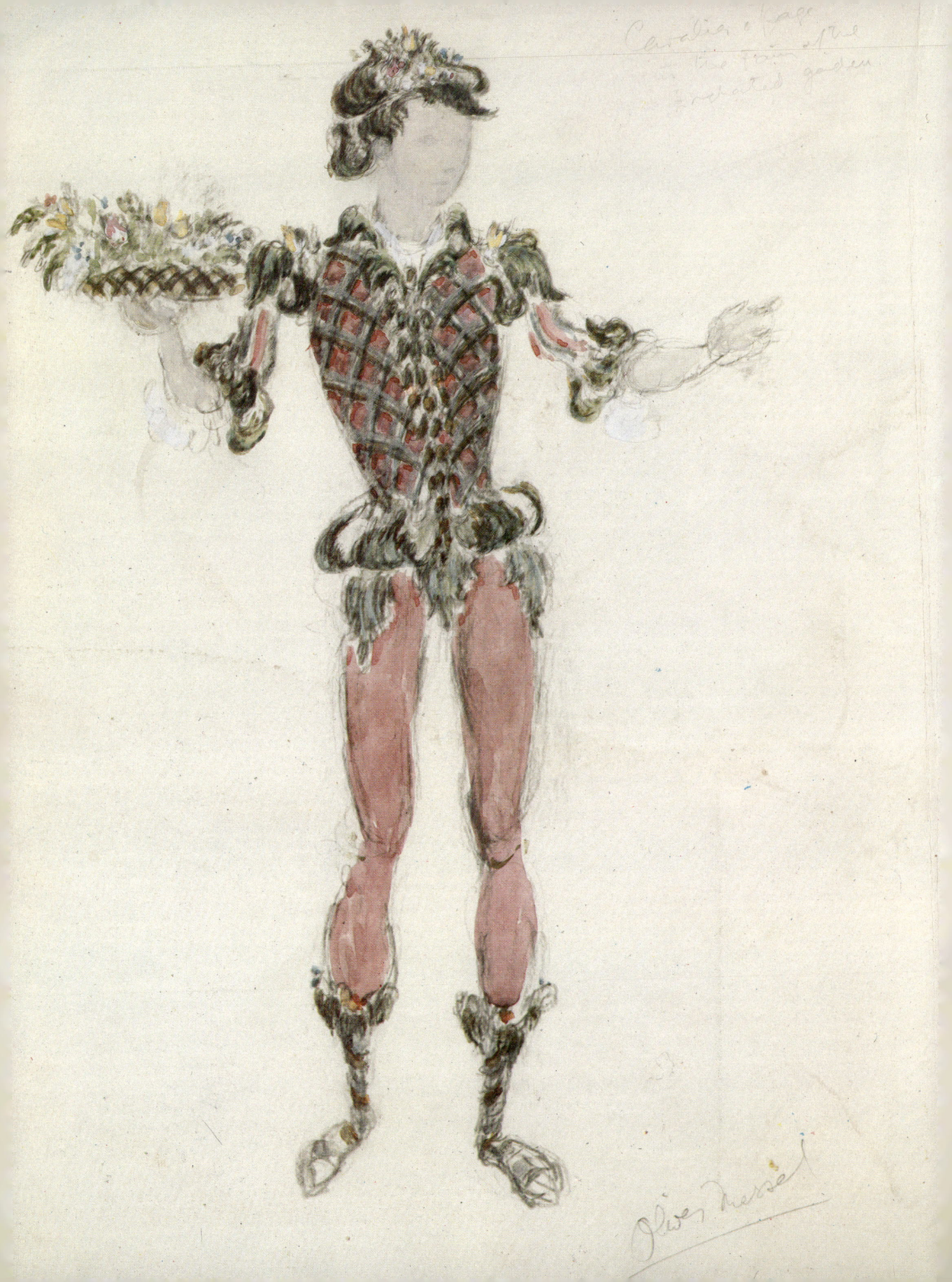

was an example of Messel audacity. The King in crown, cuirass and gauntlets, with effulgent gold lions' masks on his knee-caps and rosettes on his shoes, could perhaps have been designed by Bakst: so might the pink and silver costume of the Queen, whose wide-hooped skirt was of the Marie-Antoinette period, although its fringed overskirt, applied with baroque motives and heroically draped, harked back to the previous century.

It was in the costumes of the six visiting Fairies and their Pages (Fig. 14), and in the gifts borne by the latter, that Messel's green fingers had induced a highly personal efflorescence. The 'confections' of these ballerinas (for once the silly dressmaker's word, suggestive of sugared almonds or crystallized violets, seems *le mot juste*) presented a misleading air of negligence. Just as rustic lovers might emerge from a barn with straws in their hair, so these carefree godmothers appeared to have brought in with them from woodland and seashore – in the form of flowers, birds, water, vines or lilac – reminders of their journey. There were no stronger notes than in a bed of sweet peas: to the trimmings of head-dress and corsage, as to the filigree of proffered jewel-casket, birdcage, bouquet and cornucopia, had been devoted the delicacy of a Renaissance goldsmith or of a miniaturist such as Nicholas Hilliard. Nor should the rococo cradle of baby Aurora be forgotten, or that black, streamlined internal combustion-engine, the raven-guarded chariot of Carabosse.

In Act I, *The Spell* (Fig. 15), we were out in the garden, and a very thrilling one, too. Was the segment of a hemi-cycle of columns which loomed on the left a

◀ Fig. 14 Costume design for the Cavalier to the Fairy of the Enchanted Garden, *The Sleeping Beauty* (1946) (q.v. 42)

Fig. 15 Cut-out design for Act 1, *The Sleeping Beauty* (1946) (q.v. 42) ▼

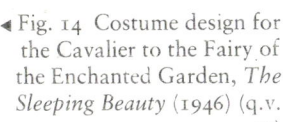

reminiscence of or a homage to Bakst, the curve of whose whiter columns, in his garden scene, stood out against darker trees? I do not know: I only just thought of this. Messel's trees were unreal like the later Gainsborough's: those of Bakst were carved walls of Boboli box with the punctuating obelisks of Tùscan cypress. Above Messel's colonnade we had a glimpse of the palace, rearing on its cliff. Two single jets of (painted) water rose skyward.

The Queen and her ladies were now dressed in the Henrietta Maria style. The Garland dancers had a kind of French peasant costume, mainly in rural green and scarlet – like those of Bakst. Their raised and lowered loops were of Morning Glory. Of the four visiting Princes, two periwigged and one from Poland with a fur cap, the dark-skinned Oriental was favoured with the most Messeline attire, an open-work white turban, vermilion-lined sleeves and white legs tapering to golden boots with curly toes. For her first entrance, Aurora at sweet sixteen wore traditional rose-pink, with transparent sleeves. There was the suggestion of a Velasquez Infanta about the bunched tulle flowers at the sides of her coiffure and the highlights of silver on her skirt.

For Act II, which begins with the hunters' picnic and ends with the Prince's *Vision* of Aurora, Bakst clearly set out to plan an autumnal tapestry of tawny colours and varied blues and greens, with his Prince and jilted Countess outstanding in military scarlet and a Veronese-yellow riding-habit. Messel tried to be different. His gloomy grotto might have been acceptable, but its distant view of bleak hills was not. He had dared to invent a landscape and failed. Why were there no clumps in those distant valleys? The effect was depressingly lunar. Some of the ladies' wide-hooped Louis XV dresses were of the most improbable colours and material for a midnight outing in November. I recall one particularly glaring lemon-yellow skirt. I thought the Countess's vivid pink was unsuitable, too.

On the other hand, once the flashy court had left the Prince alone (to wish he was in Paris, perhaps), the incursion of ice-blue fairies was sheer joy. Fonteyn's dress had the melancholy appeal of her music. Her diadem looked as if it were made of gossamer stretched on frosted twigs; it had Ionic volutes at the sides. Then came the unfolding gauzes of the Panorama; and we followed the Prince's voyage in the Lilac Fairy's butterfly-wafted boat. What mysterious meanderings, now distant, now as if in a close-up, seen between the legs of enormous spiders!

The Awakening was, from the point of view of design and lighting, the most beautiful moment in the ballet. To the hushed and eerie music the lights came slowly up, behind gauzes, to reveal a fairy architecture which would surely have enchanted Perrault and Tchaikovsky. ('Myself when young did eagerly frequent' the edition of Fitzgerald's *Rubaiyat of Omar Khayyam* illustrated by Edmund Dulac, and was fired by the vision of an Orient I found therein. How many young people in the 'forties and 'fifties must have been launched by Oliver Messel's invention into a happy demesne of dreams!) Messel's cut-cloth of middle-distance arches were first perceived in silhouette; and what high-soaring arches they were, springing by Messeline megalomania from clusters of *three* Corinthian columns! The designer had set out to out-Bibiena the Bibienas, and, so far as improbability was concerned, he succeeded. With the brightening day, our eyes were beckoned on incredible explorations up the *perron* painted on the backcloth, to climb a staircase more stupendous than those of Persepolis, Caserta or Tsarskoe Selo, between switchback balustrades. What an intoxication – even if the blasé critic, after a thousand and one nights, became increasingly unwilling to suspend his disbelief in Messel's perspective!

It was easy to spot Messel's favourite among the dancers of the *divertissement* at the Act III *Wedding*: on the tunic of Florestan, who danced the swinging *pas de trois* with his two white-clad Sisters, the designer had lavished his favourite discord of orange-vermilion and cyclamen pink. As one fairy-tale character succeeded another Messel's fancy never flagged: but I thought his attempt to give the Bluebird rightful prominence led him to provide fine feathers (painted and appliqué) of too strong a blue. For the *Grand Pas de Deux* the Prince and Aurora naturally wore white and gold: their crowns, which had to be light in weight, were nonetheless marvellously encrusted.

Paint-brush in hand, with a mouth full of pins, begging, borrowing – for clothes coupons were scarce in 1946 – badgering and bullying, Oliver Messel had done his conjuring-trick. The Royal Opera House was open again. Our Ballet, soon to become Royal, was installed there in fitting splendour. Margot Fonteyn had balanced in the Rose Adage, and not been found wanting. The war was over.

Richard Buckle

OUTSIDE THE THEATRE
FILMS · PAINTING · DECORATIONS
DESIGNS FOR DECORATIVE ARTS
INTERIOR DECORATION
VILLA AND PUBLIC BUILDING DESIGNS

Films

Messel provided designs for costumes, décor or both, for eight films (see p. 56 for details), and worked on at least two more which failed to materialise. Undoubtedly it was the success of *Helen* which led to his being asked by Korda to design the costumes for *The Scarlet Pimpernel* and *The Private Life of Don Juan*. Both are typical period pieces which proved vastly popular, particularly the first (which was re-issued, 1942). Messel was then asked to Hollywood to work on the film of Shakespeare's *Romeo and Juliet*. Existing evidence in the form of photographs of Quattrocento paintings, of Renaissance embroidery, of furniture and other artifacts show that, as he usually did, he researched the period in preparation. Nowadays it is unlikely that so much historic detail would be used in a Shakespeare film; or such a film might not have a period setting at all. But in the Thirties historical accuracy was always aimed at. Despite the attractiveness of Thirties film lighting these films were in black and white, and it was not until *Caesar and Cleopatra* that it was possible to see any of Messel's film designing in colour. For this film he did his usual painstaking research and the result, in two set-pieces – Cleopatra's bedroom and music-room – are costumes and settings which show the designer at his best in combining period-flavoured artifacts with the liberty that a 1940s audience would understand. It is difficult to realise, looking at the film now, that almost all the materials used were hard to get hold of in a period, (1944) when rationing was still in force. To counter this Messel used all his ingenuity in making supposedly valuable things from almost anything to hand, as Marjorie Deans has described.[1] Messel's second post-War film was again very different from its predecessors and was made in circumstances as awkward as the Shaw film, as Thorold Dickinson,[2] the director of *The Queen of Spades*, explains:

> Oliver Messel designed and built the film *The Queen of Spades* (1949) while another director whose name I forget was under consideration. When I arrived at the Welwyn Studios the sets were almost complete. Messel was obviously a man of the theatre with little film experience. He couldn't understand what scales you can use in film. He built a coach which was so big once you got it moving, it could only move ten feet before it was going through the studio wall. That made it virtually useless as all the sets were built indoors. I don't think we ever used it. I accepted the film because Walbrook[3] and I had got on well once we had started, and also because I had visited Russia several times on my organisational work for the Film Society of London during the 1930s. No Englishman had made a Russian subject before.
>
> Oliver's sets were handsome and full of character and Dame Edith Evans[4] was wonderful company but needed delicate persuasion on this her first feature film. The film abounded in problems, as with that of her make-up, for instance. Looking back I believe Oliver was well chosen for the job. Another art director would have had difficulty with achieving the necessary foreign atmosphere so close to the end of the War.

The studio itself was tiny and not soundproofed properly. We were continually having to wait while a train went by or because the hooter on the Shredded Wheat factory was blowing for meal breaks.

Like most designers, Messel had his share of films which got no farther than the drawing-board. One such was *Arms and the Man* (Fig. 80), which would, (judging from the finished sketches (No. 71), have introduced a Balkans flavour into Messel's work for the first time. It seems that he may have been involved, to some degree, in making designs for *Cleopatra*, in which Elizabeth Taylor and Richard Burton were to star, but the facts are obscure. He is not credited with any work in the titles. The most significant feature of Messel's last film *Suddenly Last Summer* was the jungly, creepy garden,[5] which was based on something similar in Barbados. Unfortunately the film was shot in black and white.

Painting

To be a painter was Messel's intention when he went to the Slade, and he painted portraits throughout his life and had regular exhibitions (see p. 58). 'Painting is the thing I like doing more than anything else. I adore the theatre and all the fun of opening, but I hate the fact that in the end everything's thrown away. I'd like to spend the last years of my life on something that might remain . . . Painting though gives me much more satisfaction. You only have yourself and your interpretation. I love the human face. I realise that portrait painting is despised nowadays, but to me there's endless variety and scope in painting people's[6] faces.' . . . The critical reception to Messel's portraiture has been polite rather than enthusiastic and there

Fig. 16 Oliver Messel painting a mural at Flaxley Abbey, Gloucestershire, *c*. 1962

is no doubt that his output was uneven. At his best, his portraits have a spontaneous, evanescent quality but with little of the assurance of his mentor in this field, Glyn Philpot the portrait painter, who was also his godfather. Unlike Rex Whistler, Messel seldom executed murals though two have been recorded (Fig. 16 and p. 64).

Decorations

Messel had a feeling for, and doubtless enjoyed, grand occasions like the gala evenings at Covent Garden, lavish marriage receptions (q.v. No. 96), and balls. He would usually dress such settings with some form of tenting to disguise the customary lines and accentuate the new figuration with flowers, special lighting effects, and festooned fabrics. Bill Lorraine[7] recalls an occasion of this kind – a ball at the American Ambassador's house in Regent's Park (p. 62). For this Messel and Lorraine spent much time in Kensington Church Street to hire as many chandeliers as they could. Ultimately these were fitted with candles, and the result was striking, if tiresome to maintain.

Designs for Decorative Arts

These cover three fields, textiles, furniture and perhaps metalwork. *Textiles:* Messel's first commission here was the printed silk scarf, designed for Cresta Silks Ltd., to commemorate the Coronation of Queen Elizabeth II. It was printed in gold. For the Silver Jubilee, twenty-five years later, the same design was used by Berne Silks to market a similar scarf with the design printed in silver. In the early Fifties, Messel began several years of association with the silk-making firm, Sekers, of Whitehaven, Cumberland. Lady Agi Sekers[8] recalls:

> Miki, my husband (the late Sir Nicholas Sekers), studied textiles in Germany and was in charge of a silk-mill in Budapest before he accepted the offer of the British government to set up a silk-mill in West Cumberland. Hungarian experts trained the unemployed in a disused undertaker's shop while the building went up. By 1939 these men and women wove the finest parachute silk for the RAF. Meanwhile Miki experimented with using nylon and he was the first to develop drip-dry easy care fabrics with a look of sumptuousness, ideal for the theatre and ballet. He was a great supporter of the theatre and he regularly supplied Covent Garden and Glyndebourne with fabrics. He met Oliver there. They shared a passionate belief in excellence down to the smallest detail. The very best was not good enough. Yet to many Oliver seemed over fussy, but Miki understood that he was a perfectionist not tolerating mediocrity. Oliver himself was a craftsman and he could rely on Miki with regard to textures, but he was astonished when his simple sketches of oak-leaves could be turned by Miki and his Jacquard looms into rich-looking brocades at the time of the Coronation (1953).
>
> In the early post-War period Miki had the then new idea of establishing the Friends of Glyndebourne. Oliver would give marvellous lunch-parties to a mixture of would-be patrons – friends, industrialists, music-lovers, socialities. The tables were garlanded with fresh flowers, antique china, glass, silver, and food out of this world. He could be hilariously funny, a wonderful mimic; or he could dreamily draw you into his world of illusion. When he was about to design an opera-set he would play the music and attempt to enter the composer's mind – how *he* would have visualised the background.
>
> The theatre at Rosehill (Fig. 17), near Whitehaven, was designed[9] by Oliver and opened in 1959 by Peggy Ashcroft reading a special poem by Christopher

Fig. 17 The interior of the theatre at Rosehill, Whitehaven, opened in 1959. 80. Rosehill Arts Trust Ltd

Hassall. It was a very simple place but gave the illusion of great luxury – a glowing jewel-box, crimson, white and gold. The walls were lined to the ceiling with slubbed silk. The chairs were silk and the ceiling was white with a simple moulding. Gold paint would *not* do for Oliver. As we could not afford gold-leaf we had to cut out little circles of gold paper and stick them on by hand. The foyer was the typical Messel sea colour and the carpets uniformly plain claret.

The Royal Shakespeare Company visited, so did casts from Covent Garden. Solti conducted. We had Joan Sutherland, Schwarzkopf, Gielgud, Britten and Rostropovitch. The latter was so delighted with the concert (this was before his London début) that he invited the entire audience to come back an hour later as his guests, for a second concert *free of charge*. To our surprise, everyone did!

The brocade patterns can be seen in the exhibition (Nos. 90–92). It is also worth pointing out that this enterprising firm also commissioned from other leading designers at this time (p. 58). As Lady Sekers says, the building of the Whitehaven Theatre (No. 80), was a most uncommon occasion, and though over twenty years old now it may still be the most recently privately sponsored theatre in the country. It is now maintained by a trust and continues to prosper in an area where theatres are few. There is some evidence (No. 88), that Messel may have been commissioned, or was at least thinking of ideas towards cutlery making, but it has proved impossible to determine if these designs were manufactured.[10] In an interview[11] he gave shortly before his death Messel stated that Wedgwood had asked him to design plates but it seems that no designs were ever received at Barlaston.

Interior Decoration

The firm of Sekers was also involved in Messel's largest decorative commission in London – the two commissions he undertook for the Dorchester Hotel in Park

OUTSIDE THE THEATRE · 51

Lane (No. 78). These dated to 1953 and 1956. The earlier consisted of a suite which later became known as the Oliver Messel Suite. It is on the seventh floor and faces onto a garden terrace reached from a sitting-room which with its floral chintzes and furniture evokes a countrified Regency setting, and the intention here was to give a comfortable and luxurious apartment without coldness and formality. The double bedroom vaguely recalls the Adam style and is hung with yellow silk while the ceiling and much of the furniture[12] was coloured a pinkish-purple; original colour designs for *The Sleeping Beauty* (1946), are framed on the walls. The chintzes[13] and carpets[14] were designed by Messel. Also in 1953 he completed the Penthouse, on the eighth floor, largely consisting of a dining-room (Fig. 18), which is one of the most charming and perhaps his most successful interior. The room leads onto an ornamental garden with a fountain surmounted by Leda and the Swan.[15] What area is not occupied by burgundy curtains in this room is mirrored with a figuration of gilded leaves and branches, and the whole design was brought together by the use of a moss-green carpet also individually designed.

The second commission completed three years later was for a room suitable for parties and is known as the Pavilion Room. This incorporated Etruscan elements as they are found in French décor of the early nineteenth century. Settings for *The Magic Flute* are painted on the walls. This room is a cunning mixture of formality in its classical ornamentation and informality in the use of mainly green walls and red tones in the upholstery. This room adjoins the Penthouse and both are good foils to each other. Messel has said[16] that his aim overall was to produce something, unlike the usual dull hotel room, and in which he could feel at home.

Messel's next undertaking was his largest, and was entirely different from the Dorchester commissions. The project (executed 1960–2), at Flaxley Abbey,

◀ Fig. 18 View of the Penthouse dining-room, the Dorchester Hotel, London, *c.*1953. **78b**. Norman Parkinson

Fig. 19 The screen in the bow drawing-room at Flaxley Abbey remodelled *c.*1962. **82**. *Country Life* ▼

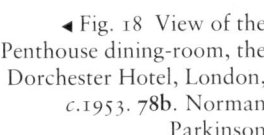

Gloucestershire, was to make habitable a large house which had begun as a monastic building in the twelfth century.[17] In the way of old buildings the Abbey had acquired seventeenth and nineteenth century extensions, the latter disguising earlier, more distinguished, work. There was also a large area of garden which needed pulling together and styling. Messel's aims at the house seem to have been to act as a restorer of former glories rather than as a remodeller; to revive what there might be of the seventeenth century, compatible with modern living, and to remove nineteenth century disfigurations. Also, he introduced certain features into the eighteenth century part of the house (Fig. 19), to accord with the style and spatial context. In this work Messel was probably one of the earliest at this time to undertake what has now become commonplace – the restoration of an ancient building with historical accuracy. But the results at Flaxley are difficult to assess in a few lines, as it is a house not open to the public. An interim opinion must be that Messel's work is the most important he did of this kind of restoration.

Different to Flaxley is the next large commission, to redecorate the Bath Assembly Rooms which he undertook, between 1961 and 1963, when asked to do so by the National Trust. The Rooms had been bombed in the War and were re-erected by Sir Albert Richardson and Partners and were finally opened by the then Duchess of Kent in 1963. Messel's brief included the wall colours, mirrors for The Octagon and Ballroom (Fig. 20), furniture for the Tea Room, and a bar for The Octagon. The results were greeted generally favourably,[18] although there were minor criticisms. The Rooms as seen by the curious public in 1963 were not quite what Messel had envisaged for his furniture for the Tea Room was not undertaken, nor was his charmingly light-hearted design for the bar for The Octagon. Money had run short, and the substituted furnishings were most inappropriate. Messel's scheme remained *in situ* until 1978 when a new scheme was commissioned[19] from David Mlinaric.

Villa and Public Buildings Designs

It may seem strange that such a successful designer should have spent his last fourteen years (1964–78) designing villas in the West Indies, but there are several reasons why. For most of his life Messel had suffered from arthritis. Despite the well-being look of his numerous photographs he was often ill. As early as 1958 he had found relief in the Barbados sun. When *Twang!!* failed in 1965 there was to be no further stage commission until that for *Gigi* (New York), eight years later. As has already been noted (p. 17), a quiet but inexorable revolution in theatre décor and forms of presentation was taking place in England during those eight years. Now domiciled (*c*. 1964) in Barbados, Messel began to design buildings in two main locations – on Barbados, and on the adjacent island of Mustique[20] in the Grenadines. This small island now has, at a conservative estimate, some seventeen villas and at least two public buildings (see p. 66 for details), all of which were designed by Messel. As he had had no training as an architect his sketches were 'realised' by Arnë Hasselquist,[21] a Swedish architect. On Barbados Messel designed some sixteen villas, at least two public buildings, and there are a few scattered elsewhere. Sensitive to locality he has said,[22] of his buildings on Mustique, which constituted the first development there: '... it was originally a French island so I've tried to create a West Indian style with French Provincial influence – it has a slight feeling of the Camargues region of France. ... In St Vincent there's a French influence you see in all the arcaded streets. Each island has its own sort of atmosphere which is great fun...' According to David Pryce-Jones[23] the Mustique villas have certain common factors like shingled surfaces, are light in colour, are magnificently sited, and the largest part is a living-room from

Fig. 20 View of the Ballroom of the Bath Assembly Rooms before 1978 when the Rooms were redecorated by Mlinaric. 81. The National Trust, Bath Assembly Rooms

which extends either to north or south, bedroom wings enclosing a garden or patio. For the house which he built for himself in Barbados,[24] Messel made use of the local coral stone and capitalised on what he is always conscious of, at the Mustique sites, fine views of the sea and the brilliant tropical light. In his own place he ran the entrance portico across the breadth of the house in order to frame a distant prospect. Here one gets an echo of Messel the stage-designer but generally these villas are not in any way theatrical judging them from photographs.

To survey his work in this medium and discover the principles on which he worked necessitates a visit to the West Indies as the very first step. Who knows but that Oliver Messel's fame may eventually be based on his ability as an architectural designer, although a considerable amount of explorative work remains to be done on the subject.

NOTES: OUTSIDE THE THEATRE

1 Marjorie Deans, *Meeting at the Sphinx; Gabriel Pascal's Production of Bernard Shaw's Caesar and Cleopatra,* (col. ills., incl. Messel ints), MacDonald, 1946.
2 (b.1903); CBE; film director, Professor, Film, Slade School.
3 (1900–1976) Austrian actor.
4 (1888–1976) a leading actress, particularly in comedy roles. She made her first film at 61.
5 Messel said of this sinister garden: '... I couldn't find anyone to make the garden so I used this wonderful person who makes all the head-dresses for Margot Fonteyn productions and he made the insect eating plants and all sorts of exotic, larger-than-life plants. I myself made banana leaves with waxed crinkle-paper and then mixed them all in real plants. I made all the vines from paper twisted round in coils and then covered with pale green flock.' ... pp.18–19 from *McKENDRY, 1976.*
6 *IHM*, 1976.
7 b.1908; lighting expert; worked many times with Messel from the Cochran Revues onwards to Glyndebourne. He told me how Cochran, his wife and Oliver Messel would sit in the stalls to watch a lighting rehearsal. When Lorraine asked them how it looked they would invariably answer; 'If it's all right with you Bill, it's all right with us.'
8 Widow of Sir Nicholas Sekers. No longer associated with the firm.
9 That is, the interior. All this work was executed and co-ordinated by John Claridge, an early assistant to Messel.
10 Neither Fiona MacCarthy, nor Robin Gooden had heard of any Messel cutlery designing.
11 *McKENDRY*, 1976. Mrs Gater of the Wedgwood Museum says that no designs were ever received, but the idea was talked about.
12 This is mainly antique.
13 The original ones were made by Sekers; they have since been changed.
14 Made by Luforma Ltd of Castle Northwick; and possibly, some work by Donegal Carpets, Ireland.
15 Made in cement by W. Goor, an artist who is not recorded.
16 In the Dorchester hand-out for 1953; q.v. (Bib.8).
17 James Lees-Milne, *Flaxley Abbey, Gloucestershire, Country Life,* March 29, pp.842–845, April 5, pp.908–911, April 12, pp.980–984; all ill. 1974.
18 John Cornforth, *The Bath Assembly Rooms Restored, Country Life,* January 9, pp.56–59, 1964.
19 For later events since the Cornforth article (op. cit.) see Dudley Dodd, *Bath Assembly Rooms,* The National Trust, 1979. The only Messel feature which remains is the ceiling of the Ball Room.
20 Mustique=moustique, (Fr), mosquito.
21 David Pryce-Jones, *Architectural Digest Visits Princess Margaret,* Arch. Dig., October 1979, pp.112–119, 164; ills. col. Ibid. p.118.
22 *McKENDRY*, 1976.
23 David Pryce-Jones, *On Mustique, the Tropical Charm of The Gingerbread House,* Arch. Dig. July/August 1980, pp.58–63.
24 David Pryce-Jones, *Mango Bay a House of Tropical Allure in Barbados,* Arch. Dig. May 1981, pp.98–103.

FILMS

1. The year given is that when the film was first shown.

c = costume(s)
s = setting(s)
Dir = director
ints. = interiors

1934 *The Private Life of Don Juan,* London (UA) Dir. A. Korda, (c).
1935 *The Scarlet Pimpernel,* London (UA) Dir. A. Korda, (c).
1936 *Romeo and Juliet,* MGM, Dir. G. Cukor (s with Gibbon, c with Adrian).
1940 *The Thief of Bagdad,* London, Dir. M. Powell, (c with Armstrong and Vertes). This won two Academy Awards for Technicolor and special effects.
1946 *Carnival,* Two Cities, Dir. S. Haynes, (c for Sally Gray).
1946 *Caesar and Cleopatra,* IP Pascal, Dir. G. Pascal, (c and ints).
1948 *The Winslow Boy,* London BLPA, Dir. A. Asquith, (c).
1949 *The Queen of Spades,* World Screenplays, Dir. T. Dickinson, (c,s).
1955 *Arms and The Man,* Korda, Dir. Peter Glenville, (c,s). Partly designed then film dropped.
1960 *Suddenly Last Summer,* Horizon, Dir. J. L. Mankiewicz, (c,s) (Fig. 21).
1963 *Cleopatra* (?). It seems there may have been some involvement by Messel on this film but it is difficult to establish what.

Fig. 21 Elizabeth Taylor in *Suddenly Last Summer* (Horizon), 1960. **98, 108**. Ken Danvers. Columbia Pictures Industries Inc.

EXHIBITIONS

London galleries unless otherwise stated.

For Catalogues: see, Bib. sect. 5, 6.

1925 ?	Claridge Gallery, *Character Masks*.
1933 Dec.	Lefèvre Gallery, *Drawings, Maquettes, and Masks for the Theatre, by Oliver Messel*. (Designs, models for *Helen, The Miracle*, masks (incl. No. 14); a design for *Ballerina*. *Ballerina* by John Murray Anderson (1886–1954) was never produced.
1936 July	Leicester Galleries, *Film Designs for Romeo and Juliet*.
1938 Dec.	Leicester Galleries, *First Exhibition of Paintings by Oliver Messel*, (portraits).
1938 Feb. 3–26	Redfern Gallery, *Designs for the Theatre* (incl. some by Oliver Messel).
1938 Dec. 19–31	Carol Carstairs Gallery (NY), *Paintings and Designs by Oliver Messel*. (*Romeo & Juliet* film designs; portraits).
1947 Mar. 20	*The Magic Flute*, Royal Opera House, Covent Garden.
1948 Nov.	Leicester Galleries, *Designs by Oliver Messel for the Film of Pushkin's The Queen of Spades*.
1951 Nov. 29–Dec. 29	Redfern Gallery, *Designs by Oliver Messel for a Cochran Production. (Tough at the Top)*.
1959 July 8–28	Sekers Ltd. (Bruton Street), *Paintings and Drawings for Fabric Designs; Cecil Beaton, Oliver Messel, Graham Sutherland*. (9 Messel designs shown).
1959 Nov.–Dec.	Sagittarius Gallery (NY), *Paintings and Designs*.
1962 July	Chichester Antiques, Chichester, *The Painter and the Stage* (some Oliver Messel *Die Zauberflöte* designs), also model sets Nos. 44, 45, 50 in this present exhib.
1962 Oct. 25–Nov. 10	O'Hana Gallery *Oliver Messel, Exhibition of Paintings* (Portraits).
1963 Summer	Linley House (Bath). *Drawings for the Bath Assembly Rooms Redecoration*.
1966 Oct. 5–22	Wright Hepburn Gallery. *Theatre Designs by Oliver Messel*.

Fig. 22 Oliver Messel working on his mask of Queen Elizabeth I, c.1933 (q.v. 2) shown in the Lefèvre Gallery exhibition, 1933 (Planet News) UPI

DECORATIVE ARTS COMMISSIONS

1952   Silk scarf commissioned by Cresta Silks Ltd; also a tie-case bearing a rose to commemorate the Coronation of Elizabeth II (1953).

1952   Covers for the Glyndebourne Festival programme; also for 1953, 1954, 1956.

1953   Silk brocade patterns for Sekers; the 'Coronation Collection'.

1956   'Doll's-house' for International Paints Ltd advertising campaign; rep. in *House and Garden* for May, p.28/9.

1959   Further designs for Sekers; exhibition that year (see p.58, Fig.23).

1963 (pre-1964)   A design, or designs for Donegal Carpets, Dublin. Some cutlery designs exist but there is no record of their having been produced. (See No. 58.)

c.1977   Messel talked (see p.49) of being asked to design plates for Wedgwood but the designs (if they were executed), did not reach the factory.

Finally, not true commissions, but nonetheless probably extensive are the suites of furniture and in the main, wooden artifacts made from Messel's designs for him by local craftsmen in connection with his house-designing in the West Indies (No.88).

Fig. 23 Oliver Messel, Graham Sutherland and Cecil Beaton at the Sekers Exhibition, London, 1959. Keystone Press Agency

TEMPORARY DECORATIONS FOR FESTIVE OCCASIONS

London venues unless otherwise stated.

1939 The Georgian Society Ball.
1950 Lady Marriott's party.
1950 Covent Garden gala evening in honour of President Auriol, of France.
1951 Festival of Britain project, unrealised; supper boxes and stage in the style of 18th century Vauxhall Gardens.
1953 Covent Garden gala evening (auditorium and Royal box decorated) for *Homage to the Queen* (ballet to celebrate the Coronation) (Fig. 24).
1953 Dorchester Hotel exterior during Coronation week.
1954 Covent Garden gala evening (Royal box) in honour of the King of Sweden.
1954 Justerini and Brooks, wine merchants.
1954 Dorchester Hotel; suite; for the wedding of Sir Berkeley Ormerod.
1959 Party given by John Aspinall.
1960 Ball at the American Ambassador's residence, Regent's Park.

Fig. 24 View of the Crush Bar at the Royal Opera House, on the night of the Coronation Gala, 1953. 95. Louis Klementaski

INTERIOR DECORATION COMMISSIONS

1932(?) London, Bagatelle Club (Devonshire House).
1937 London, San Marco Restaurant (q.v. Bib. 4).
1939 Santa Barbara, Calif. Mural for Wright Luddington (q.v. Bib. 4).
1946 Glyndebourne, Sussex; new proscenium, and curtains.
1953 London, Dorchester Hotel; suite and Penthouse, the former becoming known as the 'Oliver Messel Suite' (q.v. Bib. 8).
1956 London, Dorchester Hotel; the Pavilion Room (q.v. Bib. 8).
1957 Paris; Reader's Digest building; restaurant, etc.
1957 London, boardroom for L. Messel & Co.
1957 (? place) a room for Mr and Mrs E. Ivens.
1957 (? place) a room for Mr Billy Wallace.
1959 Whitehaven, the Rosehill Theatre.
1959 New York, the National Theatre, (Billy Rose Theatre).
1959 London, Rayne shoe shop (including minor decorative features like toy monkeys, etc., for show-cases) (Fig. 25).
1960–3 Westbury (Glos.), Flaxley Abbey; major redecoration scheme (q.v. Bib. 8).
1961–3 Bath; the Assembly Rooms (q.v. Bib. 8).
1961 London, Green Street Club.

Fig. 25 View of the façade of H. and M. Rayne shoe-shop, Old Bond Street remodelled, 1959. 79. Peter Waugh

INTERIOR DECORATION COMMISSIONS * 65

DESIGNS FOR HOUSES AND OTHER BUILDINGS IN THE WEST INDIES

(a) *Barbados* – All houses redesigned on existing sites, with the exception of Mango Bay, his own house.
 (i) *Houses* (with dates where known): (*c*.1961–1978). Alan Bay, Cockade House (1974), Crystal Springs (1968), Fustick House (1968), Heron House, Leamington (1963), Maddox, (his own house; 1964–5, q.v. Bib.8); Mango Bay, (his second house 1968–9, q.v. Bib.8), Mirabell House. Other houses for: C. Baskowitz Esq., Lord Bernstein (1961), Mr and Mrs Brecht, Peter Moores Esq., Mr and Mrs Packard, R. Wilson Esq. And these public buildings: the Garrison Museum (unfinished), the Queen's Park Theatre and Sandy Lane Hotel.
(b) *Mustique* (an island in the Grenadines).
 (i) *Houses* (with dates where known): (*c*.1969–78). For Princess Margaret (1971, q.v. Bib.8), Mrs Clarke, Serge Continot Esq., G. Dalla Valle (1974, Mr De Bevis, Sr. Egas Fuente, 'Nadiaville' for Charles Gordon Esq., (1974), Lord Lichfield, Dr C. Manning, Mr Hans Neumann, George Phillips Esq., Mrs De Strakish, Lady H. Svedjar, Hon. Colin Tennant (1977). Also, The Pagoda House, The Gingerbread House No.83, (*c*.1972; q.v. Bib.8), The Jacaranda House. And the village school, provision shop, and small hotel.
(c) *Santa Lucia* – a house for Mr and Mrs Van Geest.
(d) *Dominica* – a house at Pont Carib for Mark Gilbey Esq. (1969).
(e) *Guyana* – a house.

CATALOGUE

NOTE TO THE CATALOGUE

The principle in selecting from the Snowdon Collection has been to represent Oliver Messel's work in all its parts. Where the Collection is weak, as, for instance, in the Cochran *Revues* period, the material has been supplemented from the Theatre Museum (Enthoven and Beaumont Collections, and later acquisitions). The exhibition is arranged chronologically and begins with family portraits, Messel's interest in making masks at the Slade, then debouches into the first Room (71), where the concept of making is carried further by a representation of the artist's studio. In this kind of setting Messel created most of his post-War productions including such items as the costume from *Zémire et Azor* newly made afresh from the original design. The productions in this first Room include the Cochran *Revues, The Miracle, Helen,* and break off with *The Sleeping Beauty* (1946), and *The Magic Flute* (1947).

Room 72 is entered through a group of model-sets lit as they were in the artist's home. The remaining space is occupied by graphic work for productions until 1955, and with costumes and head-dresses.

The last group of productions follows along the right-hand wall of Room 73. The Room also contains representative examples of Messel's architectural work, and interior and decorative arts designs. Stills and selections from three films designed by Messel, are to be seen on video, and slides of those productions not represented in the Rooms can be seen on the slide-tape.

Graphic Work: this is all on paper generally the bluish-grey sketch-pads he liked. Abbreviations used for the media are: p. – pencil, ch. – charcoal, w. – watercolour, g. – gouache.

S.C. – Snowdon Collection.

Dimensions are stated thus – height × length × breadth in inches.

Photograph sizes are as originally published.

Model sets: as these are made of the same common materials a generalised description will suffice: the superstructure, container and proscenium are of wood, the latter being painted in most cases. All the sets were glazed, seemingly on a permanent basis when made, so they can, unlike most contemporary stage models, be viewed only from the front. The stage, tabs, borders, and back-cloths are of stout and painted card joined (where necessary), by brown gummed paper. The props are of various materials: these include balsa wood for the furniture, velvets and silks for furnishing fabrics, plaster for mouldings, pipe-cleaners for plants, etc., metal foil for mirror-glass. All of these features are painted, to a greater or lesser degree.

Finally, the lighting of the galleries, in which there are textiles, follows the requisite light levels for conservation.

The music-over, in the exhibition, has not been catalogued but includes some from the Cochran *Revues, Helen,* and Tchaikovsky's *The Sleeping Beauty* in Room 71; and, from Mozart, Rossini and Strauss in Room 72.

Catalogues numbers 1 to 23 are in Room 70, numbers 24 to 43 in Room 71, numbers 44 to 70 in Room 72 and numbers 71 to 108 in Room 73.

Room 70
TENTED ROOM

1 **Three mirrors:** mirror-glass and fibre-glass frames (46 × 66)

   Made for The Octagon and Ball Room of the Bath Assembly Rooms; designed about 1962 for the opening in 1963. See No. 81(f) for the design. Lent by the National Trust.

2 **Mask** of Queen Elizabeth I: papier mâché, false hair, net, pipe-cleaners, chandelier and mirror glass ($34\frac{1}{2} \times 34\frac{1}{2}$)
   Exhibited at the Lèfevre Gallery, 1933 (q.v. p. 58) Cat. No. 6. Ill. in *The Sketch* 13th December, 1933, p. 477 (Fig. 22).

   This mask was probably made for the exhibition of 1933 where it was offered for 200 guineas, but remained unsold. It is more ingeniously made than might at first appear; the ruff is of wire net, with a painted design, and the jewellery in the hair and the earrings, are pieces from a chandelier, with mirror-glass. The source is probably the 'Armada Pattern' portraits of 1588 of which two are close in having similar ruffs and features; one, in 1963, was owned by G. Tyrwhitt-Drake, Petersfield; the other attributed to Gower was acquired by the National Portrait Gallery in 1879 (no. 541); both are discussed by Roy C. Strong, *The Portraits of Elizabeth I*, Oxford, 1963; p. 74; ill.

3 **Titania and Bottom,** oil painting (44 × 38)
   Executed probably about 1937 when Messel designed the décor and costumes for the Old Vic production (q.v. No. 38).
   Lent by F. Baden Watkins, Esq.

4 **Two lamps,** in the form of gilded bird-cages, with glass sides and a figure holding the lamp (15 × 9) c. 1953.
   On loan to the Theatre Museum from HM Queen Elizabeth the Queen Mother.

5 **Wooden garden bench,** walnut, carved in relief ($37 \times 60 \times 26\frac{1}{2}$)
   Probably Spanish; early eighteenth century. Formerly in the hall of Oliver Messel's house in Pelham Place.

FAMILY PHOTOGRAPHS, DRAWINGS, PAINTINGS

6 **Black and white photograph** of Lt.-Col. Leonard Messel, OBE, TD, in the uniform of The Buffs (Royal East Kent Regt.). Probably taken in 1919 when he was awarded the OBE. Father of Oliver Messel ($8\frac{1}{4} \times 6$); by Van Dyke, London.

7 **Black and white photograph** of Mrs Leonard Messel (wife of Col. Messel); d. 1960. Mother of Oliver Messel. Taken in 1951 ($11\frac{3}{4} \times 9\frac{1}{2}$) by Tony Armstrong Jones.

8 **Black and white photograph** of Anne, Countess of Rosse (Anne Messel, sister of Oliver Messel); mother of Lord Snowdon. c. 1932 ($14\frac{1}{2} \times 10\frac{1}{2}$) by Norman Parkinson.

9 **Black and white photograph** of Anne, Countess of Rosse and Mrs Tom Renshaw in the garden of Nymans, Stapleford; c. 1950. ($9\frac{1}{2} \times 11\frac{3}{4}$) by Tony Armstrong Jones.

10 **Black and white photograph** of Oliver Messel and Miss Nancy Beaton, probably in Cecil Beaton's studio.
   Inscribed 'from Cecil'. Late 1920s.
   ($11\frac{1}{2} \times 10\frac{1}{4}$) by Cecil Beaton.

11 **Drawing of a Shrub;** probably *aucuba japonica* (spotted laurel).
   Pencil on paper; (10 × 9) 1920.
   Drawn by Oliver Messel at the age of 16 (Fig. 2).

12 **Oliver Messel** as a youth. Self-portrait, oil on canvas.
   Inscribed on the reverse 'A sketch I did when I was 19 (?)/To Tony with fondest love, Oliver'. (19 × 17) (framed).

   This was probably executed when Messel was at the Slade, following the tradition of student self-portraiture there; a fine example elsewhere is the Stanley Spencer, of 1913, in the Tate, (6188). *Frontispiece.*

MASKS AND PHOTOGRAPHS OF MASKS

13 **Mask of a Faun,** papier mâché, painted hair, painted and glazed. (11 × 8) c. 1924 (Fig. 3).

   This mask was made by Messel probably during his last year at the Slade. 'It was shown to C. B. Cochran (possibly at the Claridge Gallery) and subsequently led to all my work in the theatre.' – note pasted inside in the Mask in Messel's handwriting. This mask is to be seen lying on a table in the film *Suddenly Last Summer*, 1960.

14 **Black and white photograph** of a mask called Jehanne. Probably papier mâché, and other materials, c. 1925.
   Shown in the Claridge Gallery Exhibition of 'Character Masks' 1925. Dimensions not known.

This 'medieval' mask has since disappeared but it is illustrated in Laver's book (q.v. Bib. 1, p.6) where it is shown in side view.

15 **Black and white photograph** of a front view of the same mask.
Illustration from *Robes of Thespis* (q.v. Bib. 4) pl. LXXX.

16 **Black and white photograph** of a mask called 'Hyacinth', papier mâché, feathers and fabrics. Probably about 1925. Dimensions not known. Possibly shown in the Claridge Gallery Exhibition referred to above.
Illustrated in *Robes of Thespis* (op. cit.), pl. LXXVII.

17 **Two masks** to be worn as hats on the side of the Muses' heads in the Diaghilev ballet *Zéphyre et Flore* probably first used in the Paris run of the ballet opening on 28th April, 1925.
(16 × 26 × 4) (mounted). Lent by the Museum of London No. 74.69 A & B.

18 **Black and white photograph** of Tamar Gevergeva with a 'mask' as for No. 17 (above) in *Zéphyre et Flore*.
Photograph by Claude Harris, from the 1926 souvenir programme of the Théatre de Monte Carlo. Enthoven Collection (Fig. 26).

Messel's professional career had an unsensational but prestigious beginning. In 1925 he provided 'masks and symbols' for Léonide Massine's ballet *Zéphyre et Flore*, which the Diaghilev Ballet had premiered in Monte Carlo in April 1925. Since 1909 *Les Ballets Russes de Serge Diaghilev* had dominated the European dance scene, not only in choreography but in the approach to music and design. Diaghilev selected his designers from the most distinguished names in theatre and painting – Benois, Bakst, Gontcharova and Larionov had been succeeded by Picasso, Derain, Matisse, Sert, Laurencin, Gris and Braque; to be linked, even in a minor capacity, with the Company gave an artist great prestige.

Zéphyre et Flore was intended to recreate a mythological ballet as performed by a serf company in early nineteenth century Russia. Failing to find a suitable Russian designer, Diaghilev had commissioned Georges Braque, though the only Russian touch in his designs were the simplified *kokochniks* (traditional Russian head-dresses, often pointed or round), worn by the Muses; these were, however, stylistically at odds with their 'twenties sack dresses', and according to Lydia Sokolova, one of the original Muses, were 'torture' to dance in. The ballet was not a success and Diaghilev ordered revisions in choreography and design before it was seen in Paris and London later in 1925.

Fig. 26, 18

Messel was introduced to Diaghilev by one of his father's friends, Dr W. Archibald Propert, Director of the Claridge Gallery and author of *The Russian Ballet in Europe, 1909–1920*, and the friend who had arranged for Messel to study at the Slade, in preference to University, when he left Eton. Like all who met him, Messel never forgot Diaghilev's compelling, almost mesmeric personality, which had enabled him to gather around his company a matchless group of collaborators.

At the insistence of Diaghilev's secretary Boris Kochno, programmes for the London première in November 1925 acknowledged 'Masks and symbols

Oliver Messel' – his first credited work in the professional theatre. James Laver, in his introduction to *Stage Designs and Costumes* by Oliver Messel, refers to the task being 'to decorate with masks some of the scenery' but the masks were, in fact, worn by the Muses – *The Queen* for 18th November, 1925, reported 'the Muses ... wear Mycenian gold masks on the tops of their heads as though they were Watteau hats'. According to Dame Alicia Markova, these masks were in use by the Paris première in June 1925, although Messel is not credited on the Paris programmes. Just what form the symbols took is hard to determine; Messel, in a letter (1974) to Kay Staniland of the Museum of London, referred to 'grotesques popped about the décor', but no photographs of the complete setting as used in Paris or London seem to exist.

19 **The Great God Brown**
Four scenes illustrated in *Theatre World* for April 1926 from the first American performance of Eugene O'Neill's play, which was about the ambiguities caused by the masks everyone wears unaware (metaphorically), in every day life, and centred around the relationships of two young couples. The play was also presented for two performances by the Stage Society[1] at the Strand Theatre commencing on 19th June, 1927, the leads being played by Mary Clare, John Gielgud, Moyna MacGill and Hugh Williams. Nothing remains of Messel's masks that is known of, and O'Neill's play which the London critics found heavy-handed in its symbolism and unconvincing theatrically has scarcely been revived. (Fig. 27)

20 **'Modern caricature mask'** worn by Oliver Messel to parties ($11 \times 5\frac{1}{2}$) *c*.1927.
Papier mâché, painted and glazed. Pasted inside is a label reading, 'mask that Noël Coward saw and gave the idea for *Dance Little Lady*' in Messel's handwriting. Ill. in Laver (q.v. Bib. 1; p. 40) whose description, above, is used here.

21 **Black and white photograph** showing Oliver Messel in party clothes wearing the Mask No. 20. Reproduced from Laver (op. cit.) pl. 3.

22 **Mask** probably used in the sketch 'Nigger Heaven' presented as part of the entertainment 'Riverside Nights'. Papier mâché, painted and glazed (11×10), *c*.1928.

This early mask which is illustrated in a Cecil Beaton photograph of Oliver Messel lying face upwards, his head surrounded by masks, dating before 1929, was probably used in the sketch in *Riverside Nights*, written and arranged by A. P. Herbert and Nigel Playfair; given at the Arts Theatre on 24th June, 1928. This is copied, probably from a photograph, from a Nubian (Sudanese), tribal dancer with face whitened by clay.

23 **Black and white photograph** showing Oliver Messel's head amongst masks.
Inscribed 'from Cecil' ($11 \times 8\frac{1}{2}$). Before 1929, by Cecil Beaton.

THEATRE MAGAZINE, APRIL, 1926

William Brown (*William Harrigan*) with his two personalities, the two masks which he wears to hide his real self—one the mask of Dion, the other his own

Margaret (*Leona Hogarth*) in love with a personality, the mask of lover, Dion (*Robert Keith*), fails to recognize him when he shows his naked face

The mask is no newcomer to the theatre, but the use of the mask as employed by Eugene O'Neill in his latest play offers an original contribution to modern drama. The mask in "The Great God Brown" is the protagonist of the play. It is the embodiment of an identity, a distinct personality. This outer face represents an assumed character-reputation which screens from the world the individual who wears it. As the characters themselves develop and change so the mask changes. It resembles not only the naked face of the actor, but bears a likeness to some familiar figure like Pan or Mephisto, as in the case of Dion, one of the principal characters, whose mask shows four different stages of development

Photos by Bruguière

Margaret with the mask of her dead husband, Dion. The real man she never knew, but his mask, what she thought him to be, is loved by her always

The four principals, Dion (*Robert Keith*), Margaret (*Leona Hogarth*), Brown (*William Harrigan*), Cybel (*Anne Shoemaker*), with one of their masks, which they wear at the Greenwich Village Theatre

"THE GREAT GOD BROWN" AT THE GREENWICH VILLAGE THEATRE
Eugene O'Neill restores the old Greek masks in a drama of modern life

Room 71
C. B. COCHRAN AND HIS REVUES

C. B. Cochran[2] (1873–1951) was the most adventurous and in many ways discriminating[3] impressario of his time. Although he entered most areas of entertainment he became best known in the Twenties and early Thirties for revues, a special form of entertainment consisting of songs, sketches and chorus numbers very popular in this period but, as a form, under a cloud presently. As the subject of this exhibition is Messel, not Cochran, more about him will have to be gleaned from his autobiographies (q.v. Bib. 3). It has already been related (p. 18) how Messel entered Cochran's orbit. His work for Cochran was to cover[4] many years; it began in 1926 at the London Pavilion where these Revues were staged.

1926

24 **Cochran's Revue**, 1926.
Revue in two parts consisting of seventeen scenes by Ronald Jeans. Lyrics by Donovan Parsons, Sissle and Blake and others. Music by Pat Thayer, Sissle and Blake and others. Staged by Frank Collins. Musical numbers by Max Rivers and Léonide Massine. Designed by Doris Zinkeisen, William Nicholson, Oliver Messel, André Derain and others. Directed by C. B. Cochran and presented at the Palace Theatre, Manchester, 17th March, 1926, and London Pavilion, 23rd April, 1926; with Laurie Devine, Léonide Massine, Spinelly; etc.

a **Black and white photograph** showing dancers wearing masks and costumes designed by Messel for scene no. 8 *The Masks* ($5 \times 8\frac{1}{4}$)
Photograph in *Queen*, 5th May, 1926 (Fig. 28).

b **Black and white photograph** of an 'eighteenth century mask' shown at centre stage in (a) above. (8×6) Rep. in Laver (op. cit.) pl. 7.
Photograph by Lenare.

As with most Cochran shows the 1926 revue had a try-out period at the Palace Theatre Manchester, where any adjustments or changes would be made. Each revue invariably caused the national press to focus on a particular performer, designer, or scandal, and in 1926 the British début of the French actress and dancer Spinelly received a great deal of coverage. Scene 8, *The Masks* opened the second part of the show, with a dance fantasy in which masked figures appeared representing dancers through the ages. Oliver Messel designed and executed twelve masks which showed the full range of his talent in this medium (q.v. Bib. 6(b). *The Sketch*, 17th March, 1926). Of particular interest was the eighteenth century dancer whose enormous head-dress foreshadowed Messel's device of treating hair in a stylised way, and of making wigs of metal and paper which were stiffened and painted.

Fig. 28, 24a

Fig. 29, 26b

25 **Costume design** for a Highlander; p. and w. (14 × 10). Signed; dated 1927.
Inscribed in pencil: 'these bands of yellow on cuffs, collar, and hat to be done in gold'.

This design does not seem to have been used; alternatively it might have been for a party outfit. It is one of two, both are faded.
Theatre Museum.

1928

26 **Cochran's 1928 Revue;** *This Year of Grace*.
Revue in two parts consisting of twenty-four scenes. Book music and lyrics by Noël Coward. Dances and ensembles by Max Rivers and Tilly Losch. Designs by G. E. Calthrop, Doris Zinkeisen, Oliver Messel and others. Directed by C. B. Cochran and presented at the Palace Theatre, Manchester, 28th February, 1928; London Pavilion, 22nd March, 1928; Maryland Theatre, Baltimore 31st October, 1928; Selwyn Theatre, New York, 7th November, 1928.
With Maisie Gay, Sonnie Hale, Tilly Losch, Jessie Matthews, etc.

a **Mask** worn by the chorus in *Dance Little Lady*. Papier mâché, painted, crinkled waxed paper (11 × 10)

b **Black and white photograph** showing Lauri Devine and the masked chorus in *Dance Little Lady* by Noël Coward, a song which is still remembered (Fig. 29). Photograph (5¼ × 8¾) in *Dancing Times*, May 1928.

c **Black and white photograph** of Laurie Devine and William Cavanagh on the set for *Lorelei* (Fig. 30). Photograph (6½ × 9½), in *Theatre World*, June 1928. Oliver Messel did the décor and costumes for both scenes.

This Year of Grace was a triumph for both Cochran and Noël Coward.[5] The revue opened with a cast headed by Sonnie Hale, Maisie Gay and Jessie Matthews. Making her début on the London stage was the newly arrived Tilly Losch, who received a great deal of enthusiastic praise for her dancing and choreography in *Arabesque*. Messel was this time responsible for designing two scenes, the costumes and set for *Lorelei* and the masks and costumes for *Dance Little Lady*, in which there was no scenery,

Fig. 30, **26c**

the action taking place in front of black curtains. The young Australian dancer Lauri Devine featured in both scenes. Her reputation had been founded on her remarkable abilities as a contortionist dancer and in *Lorelei* she danced the part of a Rhine Maiden who lured ships and sailors to their destruction. It was, however, in *Dance Little Lady* that she was able to show her mimetic talents and suppleness to a greater effect. Set to the clever lyrics and music of Coward, it was the show's greatest success. It took a satirical view of contemporary manners, with Sonnie Hale singing the song of jazz obsessed 'moderns' who sacrificed everything to the great god 'Jazz', and Laurie Devine as the dancer who 'jazzes' herself out of all semblance to humanity until she becomes a mechanical doll with a strange mask instead of a face. The extraordinarily vapid masks and costumes by Messel added a sinister insight. Messel had previously made a grotesque 'ghost-like' mask for his own amusement and from it evolved the idea for the whole scene (Laver, op. cit.); Gaunt (q.v. Bib. 3), has described how the masks were made (p.18).

Prompted by the show's success Cochran and an American associate Archie Selwyn opened a second one in New York, with Noël Coward and Beatrice Lillie in the leading roles.

27 Mask, also early, and dating from *c.*1928. Possibly made for a Cochran Revue. Papier mâché, painted and glazed (11×10)

This mask appears in the same photograph referred to in No.23 but, otherwise, has not been recorded.

1929

28 Cochran's Revue *Wake Up And Dream.*

Revue in two parts consisting of twenty-seven scenes. Book by John Hastings Turner. Music and lyrics by Cole Porter. Dance and ensembles by Tilly Losch and Max Rivers. Staged by Frank Collins. Designed by Oliver Messel, Rex Whistler, Paul Colin, Meraud Guinness, Norman Wilkinson and others. Directed by C. B. Cochran and presented at the Palace Theatre, Manchester, 5th March, 1929 and London Pavilion, 27th March, 1929. With Sonnie Hale, Tilly Losch, Jessie Matthews, George Metaxa, etc.

a Black and white photograph of Tilly Losch as the Fu Manchu Marchioness, in *China* (part of *Girl in a Shawl*).

Photograph (9×7) by Sasha (Fig. 4).

b **Black and white photograph** of Tilly Losch as the Bluebird in the dream sequence, the second number, ($6\frac{3}{4} \times 5\frac{1}{2}$)
Howard and Joan Coster, published *Vogue*, 15th May, 1929 (Fig. 31).

Wake Up And Dream is perhaps Cochran's most bewildering revue. Lacking the mordant satire and biting 'philosophy' of Coward's writing it was essentially a dancing revue with only the first three scenes having any relation to the author's original work. The opening scene showed a room occupied by a couple in caricature masks, representing a hardened financier and his wife, who had everything except a sense of humour. *The Atom*, played by a small boy, releases the spirit of humour from Pandora's box. This spirit, in the form of George Metaxa, declares in his song that the audience should wake up and dream. The dream which follows brought forth a panorama of figures from history, arts and fairyland, among them Bluebeard, Columbine, Queen Elizabeth, goblins and the Lady of the Moon. This and the subsequent visions, were masterpieces of staging enabling the designers, costumiers, and scene painters, to display their imaginations to the full. Of the five scenes given to Messel, the opening sequence of three were the most taxing. He enlisted the help of his sister, Anne Armstrong-Jones to make the costumes for Tilly Losch, Alanova and Edwin Lane. With the costumes Messel excelled; the material used for the chorus dresses was a 'white Argentine' which looked like glazed butter muslin, and the bodices were sewn with hundreds of large mica spangles. The effect was that of frosty icicles in black, blue and silver dancing against a black background with the crackling of ice in movement. Tilly Losch appeared as the Bluebird in a towering head-dress reminiscent of the strange structures Messel had created for the Claridge Gallery, and for the 1926 revue. Some of the silk crinoline dresses in the first act, edged with treble rows of lace, measured four yards across, which posed problems. The London Pavilion stage was almost the smallest in London, with only one narrow entrance, so that the dress worn by Alanova (as the 18th century Lady) had to be suspended from the flies and then brought down for her to step into before she appeared. The scene *What is this Thing Called Love* was much more restrained. The dance of forsaken love took place against a backcloth of futuristic design, with the eerie symbolic movements of Tilly Losch and Toni Birkmayer watched over by a towering idol, both of these designed by Messel.

In the dances comprising *A Girl in a Shawl*, a Venetian gondolier, a Chinaman, and Englishman in Chicago, and a Spaniard, all sang of their love for a particular girl. Oliver Messel was responsible for the first sequence, *China*, in which Tilly Losch appeared

Fig. 31, 28b

as a Manchu Marchioness. The setting was effectively simple, showing a red, rustic Chinese bridge contrasted against a huge blue curtain draping the stage. Messel experimented for weeks to achieve the right effect for Tilly Losch's robe. He wanted something with a glazed surface which had to hang in folds like a heavy silk. Dissatisfied with American cloth, he had a fabric specially woven which enabled him to paint on a fine layer of rubber which would not over-stiffen the fabric. The head-dress was also of rubber decorated with delicate rubber scrolls. The costume of William Stephens as the coolie was similarly contrived. The costumes were again executed by Anne Armstrong-Jones.

1930

29 **Cochran's 1930 Revue.**
Revue in two parts consisting of thirty scenes. Book by Beverley Nichols. Music by Vivian Ellis, Beverley Nichols, Lord Berners and Henri Sauget. Dances and ensembles by Boris Kochno, George Balanchine, Serge Lifar, and Ralph Reader. Staged by Frank Collins. Designs by Doris Zinkeisen, Oliver Messel,

Fig. 32, 29a, b

Rex Whistler and others. Produced by Charles B. Cochran, at the Palace Theatre, Manchester, 4th March, 1930, and London Pavilion, 27th March, 1930, with Joan Clarkson, Maisie Gay, Ada May, Lifar and Nikitina, etc.

a **Black and white photograph** showing the set of *Piccadilly 1830* and *Heaven*, both scenes with settings and costumes designed by Messel ($3\frac{1}{2} \times 6$) (Fig. 32).
From Laver (op. cit.) pl. 10. Photograph by Sasha.

b **Black and white photograph** showing costumes designed for the above mentioned scenes ($5\frac{1}{2} \times 7$)
From Laver (op. cit.) pls. 25, 27 (Fig. 32).

Cochran's 1930 revue depended less on witty lyrics and theme than any of the previous Pavilion revues. The all singing and dancing show astounded audiences with lavish, and sumptuous costumes and settings. The two Messel scenes *Piccadilly 1830* and *Heaven* were in the middle of the show and gave scope for his remarkable talent for creating elaborate effects out of unusual materials. Believing that people came to his productions as much to see the costumes and settings as they did to see the show, Cochran this time gave full scope to the skill and fantasies of his entourage of designers. In an interview with *Dress* magazine, he described working with Messel on this review: 'Every time I saw him before the production he would pull something new out of his pocket – usually something used for domestic work – which he proposed to employ to give the illusion of some other fabric. His fantastic imagination is really marvellous.' The fabrics Messel had shown Cochran were floor swabs, sponges, dusting-mop fabric, painted sacking and rubber sheeting. In *Piccadilly 1830* (while Lifar and Nikitina were miming the adventures of a pair of lovers trying to evade the watchful eye of an elderly invalid) who would have noticed that the fur on the gentlemen's coats and the girls' muffs was made from dusting-mops, or that the dresses which gave the illusion of rich lace with bold design were, in fact, made from curtain fabric painted to give the effect of lace; and that Eric Marshall's costume as the Singer was made from rubber sheeting. Similarly, in *Heaven*, representing the celestial 'all-white' meeting of famous historical celebrities including among others, Nell Gwynn, Gladstone and Nelson. Ruth Weeks as Lola Montez wore a dress inset with squares of charlady's swabs. *Heaven* was to be a very important stage in Messel's development. This daring use of an all white set would, in 1932, exert some amount of influence on fashion and interior decoration after the production of *Helen*.

1931

30 **Cochran's 1931 Revue.**
Revue in two parts consisting of twenty-two parts. Music by Noël Coward and others. Dances and ensembles by Billy Pierce, Buddy Bradley and Georges Balanchine. Staged by Frank Collins. Designed by Doris Zinkeisen, Rex Whistler, G. E. Calthrop, Oliver Messel and others. Produced by Charles B. Cochran, and presented at the Palace Theatre, Manchester, 18th February, 1931, and the London Pavilion, 19th March, 1931. With Clark and McCullogh, Ada May, etc.

a **Black and white photograph** of Cochran's Young Ladies in metal head-dresses in *Stealing Through*. Photograph ($4\frac{3}{4} \times 7\frac{1}{4}$) in *The Sketch*, 25th February, 1931, by Sasha.

b **Black and white photographs** of Eve, the contortionist, in *Scaramouche* from *The Sketch*, 1st April, 1931 (5×4). Photograph by Keystone.

c **Costume design** for a Venetian clown probably made for *Scaramouche*. Reproduced in colour from Laver (op. cit.) pl. 28.

This was Cochran's last revue at the London Pavilion; despite Coward's music and the humour it was a failure, as Cochran admitted. It ran twenty-three days. The two scenes which Messel designed – *Scaramouche* and *Stealing Through* – were praised. In the former, the Cochran Young Ladies appeared in Brünnhilde type helmets and long chiffon sleeves portending similar ones in *Helen*. The more ambitious piece *Scaramouche* was a take-off of the Italian *Commedia dell'Arte* of the eighteenth century, to Pergolesi, a composer virtually re-discovered by Stravinsky (*Pulcinella*, 1920). Overall, the biggest hit of this show was Eve, an eighteen-year-old Scot whose contortions, in a serpent costume, got rave notices.

All photographic material from the Enthoven Collection (Theatre Museum).

31 **Section of Oliver Messel's Studio (Pelham Place).**
Carl Toms describes elsewhere (p. 27) what Messel's studio was like, and as we felt that the Exhibition should have a didactic purpose as well as being a retrospective it seemed fitting to make an atmosphere, if not a replica, of the Pelham Place studio. This Mr Toms has kindly done, and filled it with the sorts of things which are indispensable to any theatre designer (not only Messel).

Some of the things shown here are: brown gummed paper, balsa wood, charcoal sticks, charcoal fixing spray, swatches of materials, sketch-pad, brushes in pots with ends wrapped in loo paper, paint-box, scissors, a Stanley knife, easel with a painting of the Countess in *The Queen of Spades* film, when young; a painting of the Old Vic interior, c.1946; a partly completed model for *Der Rosenkavalier* (Act 1), (q.v. Nos. 55, 75); an altar of paper made when Oliver Messel was nine and lent by his sister Anne, Countess of Rosse; etc.

a **Fancy dress costume** worn by Oliver Messel; late Twenties.

Fitted skirted jacket of black sateen, with stand-up collar, fastening to neck; the long sleeves are partially attached at the back armhole, hanging behind the set-in bishop sleeves of off-white crêpe marocain. The bold stiffened epaulettes are covered with off-white crêpe marocain and edged with a roll of off-white felt, from under which fall black coq and scarlet feathers. Hanging from the left epaulette and passing under the sleeve are scarlet cord and plaited aiguillettes, ending in brass ferrules. The jacket is painted with white clouds, scrolls and stars.
  Black wool tights.
  Black leather military boots.
  The costume was worn by Messel at a party given by Nicholas de Gunsberg in the Bois de Boulogne. The design was painted onto the jacket while Messel was wearing it by Jean Cocteau, the stars being in the form of the Cocteau 'signature'.
  From this setting came many hundreds of designs of all kinds, amongst them one for a costume for Zémire.

32 **Costume** for Zémire (*Zémire et Azor*).

Oliver Messel designed this for the Bath Festival, in 1955. To give visitors some idea (other than by print) of the intermediary processes between the designer and costumed singer, we have been most generously assisted by Monty Berman who has had re-made a costume originally made by his firm, Berman's, for this production. This costume is made of silk paper taffeta with gilt embroidered decoration. Also see No. 70.

1932

33 **The Miracle.**

A wordless spectacle (1911) in seven episodes by Karl Vollmoeller with music by Engelbert Humperdinck, presented by Charles B. Cochran at the Lyceum Theatre, on 9th April, 1932, directed by Max Reinhardt. For this production music by Anton Rubinstein, Frederick Schirmer and Einar Nilson was added. Dances and ensembles were by Léonide Massine; scenery and decorations were by Professor Oskar Strnad, and the costumes were designed by Oliver Messel. With Tilly Losch as the Nun, Maud Allan as the Abbess, Glen Byam Shaw as the Cripple, Léonide Massine as the Spielmann, and Diana Manners (Lady Diana Cooper) as The Madonna, etc.

a **Black and white photograph** of the stage of the Lyceum Theatre as it looked on the opening night (see above) with the permanent set, designed by Oskar Strnad, to represent The Cathedral where Act 1 takes place, and to where the sick go seeking miracles from The Madonna, on the pedestal (to the right) (10×17)

Amplified photograph which originally appeared in *The Morning Post*.

b **Black and white photograph** of the crowd watching spellbound as The Cripple (Glen Byam Shaw) is made whole. Act 1. ($8\frac{1}{4} \times 11\frac{1}{2}$) (Fig. 33).
Photograph by Betram Park.

c **Black and white photograph** of the Madonna comes to life and puts on the discarded robe of the Nun who has been tempted by the Knight ($10 \times 8\frac{1}{2}$)

d **Black and white photograph** of a wood nymph (Diana Gould) dancing in the Forest episode in the second Act where the Knight and the Nun celebrate ($10\frac{1}{2} \times 8\frac{1}{2}$) (Fig. 34).
Janet Jevons (*The Sketch*, 27th April, 1932).

e **Black and white photograph** of the Nun, whose lover (the Knight) has been murdered, is forced into a mock marriage with the Prince (Glen Byam Shaw). Act 2, third episode ($9 \times 7\frac{1}{4}$) (Fig. 35).
Janet Jevons (*The Sketch*, 27th April, 1932).

f **Black and white photograph** of the King (Lyn Harding), murdering his son the Prince, disguised as a robber; Act 2, episode 3.
($4\frac{1}{4} \times 5\frac{1}{4}$) from *Play of the Moment*. (In *Theatre World*, 9th April, 1932.)

g **Black and white photograph** of roundel portrait of the Nun in the Coronation scene (Act 2, fourth episode), where the mad King makes her his Consort. ($3\frac{1}{4}$ diameter) from *Play of the Moment*.

h **Black and white photograph** of the Spielmann bribing the Nun's gaolers after she has been imprisoned as a witch (Act 2, fifth episode). ($4 \times 6\frac{1}{2}$) from *Play of the Moment*.

All photographic material from the Enthoven Collection (Theatre Museum).

Fig. 33, 33b

j **Lady Diana Cooper,** as the Madonna; p. and w. on card ($12\frac{1}{4} \times 8\frac{1}{2}$)
By the Duchess of Rutland; 1932.
Lent by Lady Diana Cooper.

k **Costume design** for the Nun.
Inscribed 'Tilly for dancing in Banqueting Scene'; p. and w. (23×17). Signed; 1932.
Lent by Marianne Ford.

When this opened it became Cochran's fourth production to run concurrently in the West End, and it was his second production of Vollmoeller's drama. The first has been staged by Cochran at Olympia in 1911, and was also directed by Max Reinhardt. Like Craig Reinhardt was an important innovator; he introduced the theatre of the crowd, of massed spectacle, set often in large spaces other than in theatres; or, when he worked in theatres he would project the stage into the auditorium, and employ that as an adjunct to the stage. Thus, in the Lyceum production the processions used the aisles, and the scenery, built as architecturally real as possible, contributed to the overwhelmingly mystic effect. This feeling, as Agate pointed out in his notice in the *Sunday Times*, was not intrinsically in the mime, dancing and musical accompaniment, but was projected by the audience onto the production, which was always difficult to get seats for. The notices,[6] which in 1932 were almost three times the length they are today, were uniformly good. Tilly Losch, as the Nun on whom the action focuses,

▲ Fig. 34, 33d   Fig. 35, 33e ▶

brought innocence, radiance and energy to the part and was a foil to the 'compassionate grace' (Ivor Brown, the *Observer*), and serenity of Lady Diana Cooper's Madonna. Speaking[7] very much later Oliver Messel remarks on her costume and her organising ability. Of the costumes Cochran mentions[8] that some eight hundred were designed and generally these were thought put to best use in the second act when the action is away from the Cathedral. Agate, looking for wit, still influenced by *Helen*, did not find any though he found much invention, and Ivor Brown said that 'Mr Messel has dressed it all with a fine sense of the heraldic world as he has recently shown for the mock-classic' [in *Helen*]. All in all the success of *The Miracle* further increased Messel's fame although it was a very different kind of production. As a form *The Miracle* left no very firm impact on the course of the London theatre, although it anticipates the Hollywood pageant cinema of the mid-Thirties.

1932

34 Helen

An 'opera bouffe' (in three acts, nine scenes), based on *La Belle Hélène* (1864) by Meilhac and Halévy, music by Jacques Offenbach. Presented by Charles B. Cochran at the Adelphi Theatre on 30th January, 1932; the music arranged by E. W. Korngold. Directed by Max Reinhardt. Dances and ensembles by Léonide Massine; scenery, costumes and accessories designed by Oliver Messel. With Evelyn Laye as Helen, wife of Menelaus of Sparta, Bruce Carfax as Paris, Prince of Troy, George Robey as Menelaus, Yetta as Venus, W. H. Berry as Calchas, Roy Russell as Achilles, Victor Dill as Hector, Stafford Moss as King Priam, Désirée Ellinger as Orestes, Joy Spring as Pylades, Sepha Treble as Leaena, Iris Browne as Parhenis, Orests' girls friends, and Mr Cochran's Young Ladies, men dancers, Greek chorus, worshippers, etc.

S.C. 1 costume, 8 masks.

a **Model** for the Walls of Troy; Act 3, scene 3 (28 × 25 × 22¼)
Theatre Museum E.184–1934 (Fig. 11).

This is for the final scene by which time cuckolded Menelaus is about to fight Paris, watched from the wall above by Helen and Priam. Just when Menelaus, unusually, has the advantage Venus appears and takes Paris away. Helen then descends and takes the crestfallen Menelaus off home in a ship which can be seen at the back of the stage. As she does so she throws the captain an enticing glance, and it is obvious that Menelaus' troubles are not yet over.

Shown in the Lefèvre Exh. (q.v. p.58), Cat. No. 54 (75 guineas); rep. in Laver, 1933 (q.v. Bib. 1) pl. 15, photograph by Sasha. Given by Oliver Messel, in 1934.

b **Costume** for Paris in Act 3, scene 3.

One-piece costume in the style of classical Greek armour, of off-white heavy flannel. The tunic is cut straight across the front; over the shoulders, forming sloping sides to the neck, are appliquéd broad round-ended 'straps'. From under the curved lower front edge emerges a band cut into lappets, under which is fixed the kilt, formed of individual graduated strips. Beneath the kilt is an asymmetrically cut skirt, edged with heavy white twisted cotton fringe. Fixed across the neck at centre front is a winged cherub head of papier mâché. On either shoulder and over the top sleeve is a paper mâché mask of an upper face and hair; the top side of the elbow length bell sleeve is pleated into the lower edge of the mask, leaving the outer arm bare.

The costume is appliquéd with narrow strips and studs of lightly padded white leather, simulating an embossed design. All edges of the tunic and kilt are bordered with narrow strips of white leather. On the chest are motifs and foliated arabesques. At the waist is a stylized flower and, continuing around the back, simulated strappings with curlicue ends below which are outlines simulating overlapping scales. The simulated strappings at shoulder and waist have a central row of small studs. The 'scales', with occasional central studs, are repeated on the kilt strips. The skirt has a border of outline ovals with small ovals at the centre, between lines of white leather.

The tunic is padded and lined with white cotton and fastens on an extension down the back with hooks, bars and eyes. On the left front shoulder and right back shoulder are heavy bar fastenings. The lining is marked with make-up.

Large semi-circle of off-white heavy duty flannel with a fringe of heavy white twisted cotton, arranged to fit around the left arm and fall in elegant folds as a cloak. On the left shoulder is a stylized ram's head of gilded and antiqued rubber composition. The cloak has heavy hooks to fix onto the bars on the tunic.

The costume seems to be the one originally worn in *Helen* by Bruce Carfax as Paris in the final scene outside the walls of Troy, when he is rescued from Menelaus by Venus. Messel was photographed in the costume by Cecil Beaton (Fig. 13) and Peter Glenville (for whom the costume was probably enlarged) wore it to Lady Jersey's ball at Osterley in 1939.

The costume originally had short ostrich plumes emerging from under the half masks, over the sleeves.

c **Letter** from C. B. Cochran to James Laver referring to the Introduction of Laver's book referred to above (q.v. Bib. 1). Laver was at this time in the Department of Engraving, Illustration and Design at the Victoria and Albert Museum, a Department now known as Prints and Drawings. Cochran makes interesting references to *Helen* and Reinhardt's share as director of it.
($10\frac{1}{2} \times 8\frac{1}{4}$). Enthoven Collection.

d **Costume design** for an Amazon.
P, w, Signed; 1932.
Inscribed in top left-hand corner 'S.K. – B – 41' and in the bottom left-hand; '1. Jackson, 2. Fey, 3. Hulley, 4. Gillespie, 5. Barton, 6. Wilson, 7. Barnes' – some of Mr Cochran's Young Ladies.
No. 13 in the Messel Exhibition, 1933 (q.v. p. 58) (23×17).
Lent by Marianne Ford.

e **Costume design** for members of the Greek Chorus.
P, w, gold paint. Signed ($11\frac{1}{2} \times 7\frac{1}{4}$) 1932.
This may have been No. 18 in Messel's Exhibition, 1933 (q.v. p. 58) Theatre Museum; Cyril Beaumont Collection.

f **Costume design** for Helen, in Act 1.
P, w. Signed, 1932 (23×17)
No. 1 in the Messel Exhibition, 1933.
Lent by Marianne Ford.

g **Black and white photograph** of Yetta, as Venus ($9 \times 6\frac{1}{2}$)
Camera portrait by Bertram Park; publ. in *The Sketch*, 10th February, 1932.

h **Double page spread** in colour of costume designs for *Helen*; publ. in *The Sketch* for 3rd February, 1932, pp. 202–203.
Shown are; costumes for Laeana, for a Trojan warrior, Venus, Juno, Minerva, a Spartan warrior, Parthenis, Paris, Menelaus, Helen and Achilles.
Laver (op. cit.) also reproduces some of these, with others. Other designs from *Helen* were in Messel's exhibition referred to above.
($12\frac{1}{2} \times 19$) (Fig. 36).

These designs are the best witness of the colourfulness, yet at the same time delicacy, of *Helen* which was intended to suggest the Ancient World.

Fig. 36, **34h**

j **Black and white photograph** of the outer court of the Temple of Jupiter, at Sparta. Act 1, scene 1. Helen having grown tired of Menelaus wishes for a lover. ($6\frac{1}{4} \times 8\frac{1}{2}$) (Fig. 37).
Photograph by Bertram Park.

k **Black and white photograph** of Evelyn Laye (b.1900), as Helen of Troy ($5\frac{1}{4} \times 8\frac{1}{2}$)
Published in *The Sketch* for 3rd February, 1932.

l **Black and white photograph** of Helen, in her bath (Act 2, scene 1), attended by her maids, watching the contortionist Eve, who was billed in *Helen* as 'the Foreign Dancer'. She had had a great success in Cochran's 1931 Revue (see No. 30) and this scene, where there was little furtherance of the plot, was a good spot for her.
($7 \times 9\frac{1}{2}$)
Photograph by Bertram Park.

m **Black and white double page spread** of the Orgy Scene, Act 2, scene 2. By this time Paris, having awarded the apple to Venus (in the judgment scene for beauty), is promised Helen. After the orgy Paris manages to distract Orestes, who has been keeping an eye on Helen, and makes his way to her.
From *The Sketch* for 17th February, 1932 ($12\frac{1}{2} \times 19$)

The Orgy Scene takes place after a peace conference established between the warmongering Greeks and the Trojans.

W. A. Darlington, in his notice for 1st February, was particularly impressed by it and said, in the *Daily Telegraph*, '. . . it is the Orgy scene that will draw the town. Professor Reinhardt and M. Massine have here contrived that rare stage miracle, a scene of revelry in which you really do feel that the revellers are, in far from sober fact, enjoying themselves. It is gay, this scene, with a gaiety that seems spontaneous and is really a work of the highest artifice. . . .'

n **Black and white photograph** of Helen's Chamber (Act 2, scene 3), shortly before Paris joins her. Photograph by Sasha published in *The Studio*, special Winter number *Settings and Costumes of the Modern Stage*, p. 17.
($7\frac{1}{2} \times 5\frac{1}{4}$) (Fig. 38).

▼ Fig. 37, 34j   Fig. 38, 34n ▶

This is the white bedroom which, with the orgy scene, is one of the best remembered set-pieces of *Helen*. Darlington (op. cit.) speaks of, '...the unrelieved dead white of Helen's Chamber in which the only note of colour as the curtain rises is struck by Evelyn Laye herself (as Helen) lying among her white pillows under a white coverlet. A more perfect setting for her fresh, clear beauty cannot be conceived....'

o **Black and white photograph** of Orestes' girl friends, Parthenis and Leaena, played by Iris Browne and Sepha Treble, respectively. (8 × 7)
Photograph by Dorothy Wilding; published in *The Sketch* for 19th March, 1932 (Fig. 39).

p **Black and white photograph** showing Menelaus (George Robey) discovering Helen and Paris (Bruce Carfax) together, Act 2, scene 3. Seizing this chance to stress his importance Menelaus calls in the Kings but the outcome is ignominius for him. They laugh, the lovers escape, and the Greeks declare war on Troy.
(7 × 9½)
Photograph by Bertram Park.

q **Black and white photograph** of the final scene, Act 3, scene 3, when Helen appears on the walls of Troy causing the opposing Greek and Trojan armies to unite and do her homage.
(7 × 9½)
Photograph by Bertram Park.

r **Page of black and white photographs,** by A. C. Cooper, published in *The Sketch* for 10th February, 1932, showing six of the model sets made for the production. The sets are: those for Act 1 on the left-hand side reading down the page; for Act 2, the middle and bottom panel on the right-hand side; and from Act 3, the top right-hand one. Unfortunately all these models were accidentally destroyed shortly after this record was made, according to the letter-press. This seems difficult to explain as three of them were shown in the Messel Exh. (q.v. p. 58) of 1933; Cat. Nos. 50–52; although it is possible that they were remade. (11 × 8)

All photographic material from the Enthoven Collection (Theatre Museum).

s **Mask** (one of seven surviving) used by the Chorus, probably illustrated in (e) above, and based on an ancient model.
Papier mâché and probably, flat oil paint. (11 × 10)
1932.

Helen could hardly have had better notices. All the critics were charmed. Yet there was minor fault-finding in so far as not many of the words of the songs were audible, and George Robey, though amusing, seemed rather wasted as Menelaus. But there is no doubt, reading the reviews now, that the critics, and, of course, the public – who came in droves – were bowled over. The combined talents of Reinhardt, Massine, Messel, and Evelyn Laye were formidable. They were very diverse talents, and as A. P. Herbert said, were held together by the heterogeneous reins of Cochran.

La Belle Hélène was written as satire on the morals of the Second Empire, and was not new to Reinhardt who had directed it three times previously. What was new about *Helen* was the book which had been completely rewritten by A. P. Herbert in his best debunking style; with such instances as Paris insisting on having a boiled egg before going out to fight Menelaus, or, the latter drunkenly eating Helen's face cream while she and Paris are in bed close to. It was this bedroom which is most remembered. Like all the scene-changes it received applause when revealed. Of a dazzling white it was a monumental conception based on the baroque; in its large scale it brings Vanbrugh to mind. It is not strictly true to say that Oliver Messel introduced white into the décor of the Thirties. It was already on the way in by 1932, along with pastel shades.

Cochran had been waiting (a characteristic which paid off handsomely in more than one venture), to produce a version of *La Belle Hélène* because he was looking for singers who could act rather than putting up with actors who could sing a bit. In Evelyn Laye he found a stylish, fair, (like so many leading-ladies of the period) and intelligent practitioner of musical comedy; and, in his leading-man, Bruce Carfax, someone whom Agate (the *Sunday Times* notice) considered could never have a better part. Reinhardt, whose reputation had been established partly on providing spectacle, did not disappoint, as Darlington's comments (above), about the Orgy Scene bear out. Perhaps to our eyes such ensembles look overcrowded, still in the tradition of the crowded stages of the late nineteenth century. However, it was one of the various stengths of the décor, that by a judicious use of light colours for the costumes, Messel achieved an effect of weightlessness for the crowd scenes. When all is said and done it is the décor of *Helen* which was its most remarkable feature. Perhaps Agate (op. cit.), put it as its best when he asked, '...if this show is not Mr Messel's, whose is it?... [It is] a triumph of wit, fantasy and ravishment' and Herbert Farjeon, writing at the same time, put it, '...Yet the artist who most deserves a smile and perhaps something more from Helen is none of these but Oliver Messel who has so ravishingly designed the scenes and costumes'. Messel never had quite the same opportunity again to invent costumes which poked fun at the conventions of the eighteenth and nineteenth centuries, and with more than a side glance – in the short skirts of Leaena and Parthenis, for instance – at one of ours.

Helen established Oliver Messel as the leading designer of the period and as regards future work he was home and dry.

The names of two other rising stars can be seen among the 'Men dancers' in the programme; Walter Gore, who was to become an important choreographer, and dancer for the Ballet Rambert, and William Chappell, who also danced, and was to become a designer for the Rambert, and a director of plays (q.v. Nos. 49, 51).

Fig. 39, **340**

Erratum

Please note: on page 144 entries k and l should follow entry 107f on page 189.

Fig. 40 The set of *Mother of Pearl* designed by Oliver Messel for Cochran in 1933. *Illustrated Sporting and Dramatic News*

1935

35 **Glamorous Night**
A musical play, in two acts, written and composed by Ivor Novello, lyrics by Christopher Hassall; presented by Leontine Sagan at the Theatre Royal Drury Lane, on 2nd May, 1935. Settings and some costumes by Oliver Messel; dances invented and arranged by Ralph Reader. With Ivor Novello as Anthony Allen, Mary Ellis as Militza Hajos, Barry Jones as King Stephen, and Lyn Harding as Baron Lydyeff, etc.

a **Black and white photograph** of the open deck of the SS *Silver Star*, as she sinks after yet another attempt to kill her famous passenger Militza; curtain on Act 1.
($13\frac{1}{4} \times 11$) Stage Photo Co.
Enthoven Collection.

b **Black and white photograph** of the ballroom in the Palace of Krasnia, Act 2
($4\frac{3}{4} \times 6$) A. Console. Published in *The Sketch* for 15th May, 1935 (Fig. 41).
Enthoven Collection.

The title *Glamorous Night* is of the operetta within Novello's Ruritanian fantasy of a young English inventor who saves Militza Hajos from assassination attempts by political enemies. Although the plot is silly beyond belief, some of the music is now in the light music repertoire and most of the critics were content to forget about the plot. The shipwreck (only a matter of going down two feet, according to Agate), was organised by a gang of forty. The *Silver Star* weighed four tons and carried a cast of two hundred. Messel's settings and costumes were quite liked although Agate in the *Sunday Times* was chilling: 'Mr Messel's décor suggests that he has succumbed to the notion of designing down to a popular audience. It is certainly less imaginative than usual except in the case of one of the colossal Studio figures whose left hand has five fingers and one thumb!' Nevertheless, Ivor Brown thought that Messel retained a sense of comedy amid all the glamour and the grandeur. This was the only collaboration between Messel and Novello whose Ruritania could only have had a limited appeal to Messel's more subtle imagination.

Fig. 41, 35b

1936

36 The Country Wife
A comedy (1674), in three acts, by William Wycherley. Presented at the Old Vic by Lilian Baylis in association with Gilbert Miller on 6th October, 1936; directed by Tyrone Guthrie. Settings and costumes by Oliver Messel, with music by Frederick Austin and Herbert Menges. With Michael Redgrave as Horner, Edith Evans as Lady Fidget, Ruth Gordon as Mrs Pinchwife, Ernest Thesiger as Mr Sparkish, etc.

S.C. 4 models, 3 set details.

a **Model:** the piazza of Covent Garden (Act 3, scene 7).
($22 \times 21\frac{1}{4} \times 17$)

b **Black and white photograph** of Horner and Mrs Pinchwife, meeting in a garden near Horner's lodging.
(10×8) (Fig. 42).
J. W. Debenham.

c **Black and white photograph** of Mr Harcourt (Alec Clunes), Mr Sparkish, and Alithea (Ursula Jeans); Act 3, scene 1.
(10×8)
J. W. Debenham.

d **Black and white photograph** of Lady Fidget and Mrs Pinchwife.
(10×8) (Fig. 43).
J. W. Debenham.

e **Black and white photograph** of Ruth Gordon as Mrs Pinchwife (the Country Wife) fresh to London.
(10×8)
J. W. Debenham.

Wycherley's frank and heartless comedy of deceived husbands and unfaithful wives brought the American actress Ruth Gordon to the London stage for the first time, and she was well received, although there were some reservations about her accent. The correspondence columns[9] of the *Daily Telegraph* and the *Sunday Times* were enlivened shortly after

◀ Fig. 42, 36b   Fig. 43, 36d ▼

the opening by a debate about the 'cultural value' of *The Country Wife,* since it was being presented at the Old Vic which was exempt from Entertainment Tax. This was complained of by Sydney Carroll[10] of the Ambassador's Theatre. It brought a retort from Lord Lytton,[11] chairman of the Old Vic Governors, who held that the play exposed immorality for ridicule rather than for admiration. He then went on to suggest that if Bernard Shaw had written *The Country Wife* it would have been published as one of his Unpleasant not his Pleasant plays. Carroll pretended to be astonished by this and the fight was joined by Agate,[12] who dismembered both correspondents and summed up the situation in a number of maxims, one being 'Both [correspondents] are wrong if they think that a play with an obscene subject cannot be a work of art.'

Apart from the acting, which attracted high praise, so did the production by Tyrone Guthrie.[13] W. A. Darlington, in the *Daily Telegraph,* spoke of the playing as like a good rugby team in action, and of Messel's contribution as giving 'the last touch of style to a fine theatrical achievement'. On the other hand, Agate found the sets a little too fussy, though *The Times* critic saw them as 'gaily decorated'. What is obvious from the remaining photographs and models is that Messel was fully in accord with the mood of the play. In a sense it was the first 'serious' work he had done in the theatre.

The play had a different cast when it went to New York. It was the first Messel décor, in substantial form, to be seen on Broadway.

1937

37 Francesca da Rimini
Ballet in 1 Act and 2 Scenes.

Choreography by David Lichine. Music by Pyotr Ilyich Tchaikovsky. Libretto by David Lichine and Henry Clifford, partly drawn from Dante. Presented on 15th July 1937, at the Royal Opera House, London, by Col. W. de Basil's Ballets Russes, with Lubov Tchernicheva as Francesca, Paul Petroff as Paolo and Marc Platoff as Malatesta.

Synopsis: Francesca, betrothed to the brutal and ugly Malatesta, loves his brother, Paolo. They read of other ill-fated lovers, and a vision of Lancelot and Guinevere appears to them. They are discovered by Malatesta who murders Paolo; Francesca, grief-stricken, throws herself on Malatesta's sword.

a **Head-dress** for Francesca in Scene 1.

A stiffened wired circle padded with cellophane entwined with a rope of gilded organic fibre, the upper wire circle rising at centre front to support the decoration. The head-dress is covered with intertwined leaves, berries and flowers of gilded leather, each flower having a pearl centre, gold wire stems and random large pearls, some of which are partially gilded. At centre front is a lantern-shaped stone, cut and silver backed, around which are three cupped faceted studs, the backs painted silver, framed with gilded leather covered wire. Above is a small ball of diamanté studs. Much gilded decoration is missing from the sides.
Made by Barbara Karinska.

b **Black and white photograph** of Lubov Tchernicheva as Francesca, Paul Petroff as Paolo, and Tatiana Riabouchinska as Angelic Apparition. ($6\frac{1}{4} \times 4\frac{3}{4}$) (Fig. 44).
Photograph by Gordon Anthony.

c **Black and white photography** of Scene 1, with Lubov Tchernicheva as Francesca. (8×10) (Fig. 45).
Photograph by Gordon Anthony.

d **Black and white photography** of Scene 2; the vision (12×16)
Photograph by Gordon Anthony.

e **Set design** for Scene 2; costume designs for Malatesta and Francesca in Scene 2 (Fig. 46).
Published in the official souvenir for Col. W. de Basil's *Ballets Russes* season at the Royal Opera House, London, June 1938.

Lubov Tchernicheva (1890–1976) had been with the Maryinsky Imperial Russian Ballet in St Petersburg before joining Diaghilev in 1911. Married to his *régisseur,* Serge Grigoriev, they remained with the company until Diaghilev's death in 1929, after which they joined the de Basil Ballets Russes, she becoming their Ballet mistress. An extraordinary beautiful woman, she continued to appear in certain roles, notably as Zobeide in *Schéhérazade,* and the role of Francesca, which was created for her. Many ballet-goers still remember her as Francesca (at the end of the ballet), when, in an agony of passion and grief, she flung herself upon Malatesta's sword.

Doubtless Messel owed the commission for *Francesca da Rimini* to his work on the film *Romeo and Juliet* which had been released in 1936, and these were his first designs for a full ballet. Arnold Haskell acclaimed his work in the *Daily Telegraph* for 16th July, 1937: 'One cannot praise the general make-up too highly. Oliver Messel's décors and costumes are not merely beautiful, but expert from a theatrical point of view – a rarity at present!' Messel was certainly well served by his scene painter and

SCENERY BY OLIVER MESSEL FOR "FRANCESCA DA RIMINI"

COSTUMES BY OLIVER MESSEL FOR "FRANCESCA DA RIMINI"

costume maker. The scenery had been realised by Prince Schervachidze, who had worked for Diaghilev and been responsible for the execution of designs by the greatest living artists, including the great drop-curtain for *Le Train bleu* by Picasso. The costumes were the work of Russian-born Barbara Karinska, one of the greatest makers of ballet costumes of the twentieth century. The combination of Karinska and Messel was perfect. Her interpretation of his designs, both in the making and ornamentation, gave the ballet great style, and, comparing *Francesca da Rimini* with later work, it can be seen how often Messel's ethereal, romantic concepts for ballet were to suffer at the hands of lesser costume makers. In a letter to Kay Staniland of the Museum of London, in 1975, Messel paid tribute to Karinska's 'taste and brilliance of cut . . . her tunics and bodices were cut in such a way to fit like a glove, yet by a special method of setting the sleeves in high there is perfect freedom of movement.'

1937

38 A Midsummer Night's Dream.

Comedy (c.1595) in five acts by William Shakespeare. Presented by Bruce D. Worsley at the Old Vic on 27th December, 1937, directed by Tyrone Guthrie. Settings and costumes by Oliver Messel; choreography by Ninette de Valois. Music by Mendelssohn. With Kirby's Flying Ballet. With Gyles Isham as Theseus, Stephen Murray as Lysander, Anthony Quayle as Demetrius, Alexis France as Hermia, Agnes Lauchlan as Helena, Ralph Richardson as Bottom, Vivien Leigh as Titania, and Robert Helpmann as Oberon, etc.

S.C. 67 set details, 19 costume designs, 2 head-dresses.

a **Costume design** for Oberon; cr, w, g, gold paint. (15 × 10) Signed.

◀ Fig. 46, 37e   Fig. 45, 37c ▼

A MIDSUMMER NIGHT'S DREAM * 99

b **Black and white photograph** of Vivien Leigh as Titania.
($12 \times 8\frac{3}{4}$). By 'Anthony'.

c **Black and white photograph** of Titania and Oberon.
($12 \times 8\frac{3}{4}$). By 'Anthony', (Fig. 47) BBC Hulton Picture Library.

d **Black and white photograph** of a group of Titania's fairies dancing to Mendelssohn.
($6\frac{1}{4} \times 8\frac{1}{4}$) (Fig. 48). J. W. Debenham.

e **Black and white photograph**, Athens. (left to right): Theseus enthroned (Gyles Isham), Hippolyta (Althea Parker), Hermia (Alexis France), Helena (Agnes Lauchlan), Demetrius (Anthony Quayle), and Lysander (Stephen Murray).
($6\frac{1}{4} \times 8\frac{1}{4}$). J. W. Debenham.

f **Black and white photograph** of 'The Rude Mechanicals' in the play scene: Starvelling (Jonathan Field), Flute (Frank Napier), Quince (Frank Tickle), Snug (Frederick Benett), Bottom (Ralph Richardson), and Snout (Alexander Knox).
($7\frac{3}{4} \times 9\frac{3}{4}$). J. W. Debenham.

g **Head-dress** for Titania worn by Vivien Leigh.
Heavy wire circle concealed by brown paper tape covered with flowers of off-white velvet with silver faceted bead centres, alternating with flat roses of bright pink ribbon with gold braid centres; these are surrounded by green French enamel varnished silver leaves backed with green organdie, faceted silver-backed stones, the larger having rough cellophane bows behind them, and occasional pearls and silver faceted sequins on wire supports. Above the flowers stand wires, each supporting a large pearl alternating with longer wires each supporting a silver backed rhinestone surrounded by a tuft of shredded cellophane. Fixed at the back of the head-dress is a large flat bow of gauze silver strip ribbon with long tails. From below the flowers on the front third hang short wires each ending in a small circle of silver faceted beads around a central pearl; from below the remainder emerge the loops of a serpentine wire covered with gold metal mesh. From the sides hang long fringes of individual strings threaded with oval silvered beads separated by horizontal silver scallop-edged flower sequins from lines of three faceted silvered beads; at the bottom of each string hangs a large vertical faceted silver sequin. Made by Thérèse Clement.

◀ Fig. 47, 38c   Fig. 48, 38d ▼

In the programme Guthrie explains that he is setting the play in the early Victorian period to suit the architecture of the Old Vic (1833), and Mendelssohn's music. Whether or not this warranted explanation was a point made by the critic of *The Times* (in company with others), who said that Shakespeare and Mendelssohn were beyond 'fashion'. The production was generally well received; the Athenian lovers, and the clowns (with Richardson as Bottom), receiving much more than a duty mention. The costumes of Oberon and Titania (**b**) and (**c**), were commented on as being particularly attractive, as also were those of the fairies. This was not the first time Robert Helpmann had appeared as an actor[14] and his Oberon was praised, for speaking, slightly above that of Vivien Leigh, who, as can be seen from the photographs, looked enchanting. Of the costumes and décor a review signed H.H. (Harold Hobson?) in *The Observer*, for 2nd January, 1938, says, 'Mr Oliver Messel is an artist who moves with freedom on the stage, and finds inspiration in its technical limitations. One feels at once that he approached this task with enthusiasm and carried it through with zest. His woods and palace interior are contrived and painted with what suggests a double delight in pictorial bravura and practical ingenuity. His period sense is keen. The costumes he has designed, particularly those of the fairies, are charming in themselves and as Victorian pastiche...'

The writer touches here on two elements, which by this date have obviously become settled in Messel's artistry – a keen period sense, and the ability to create light-hearted pastiche.

1940

39 The Tempest

A romantic comedy (c.1611) in five acts by William Shakespeare, presented by Tyrone Guthrie at the Old Vic on 29th May, 1940; directed by George Devine and Marius Goring. Setting and costumes by Oliver Messel; dances arranged by Suria Magito and the music arranged by Berthold Goldschmidt from classical composers. With John Gielgud as Prospero, Alec Guinness as Ferdinand, Jessica Tandy as Miranda, Marius Goring as Ariel, and Jack Hawkins as Caliban, etc.

S.C. 5 costumes.

a Costume for Sebastian worn by Andrew Cruickshank.

Late Elizabethan-style costume. Boned doublet of brown rough wool with pointed front and stand-up collar; attached to the collar, high to the back, is a ruff of coarse boned crin, edged with a double row of pipe-cleaner strip. From the collar to the point at lower edge is a narrowing 'V' of black velveteen edged with gold metal thread cord and white cotton covered piping, with down the centre, five large oval rhinestones in gold metal mounts surrounded by looped pipe-cleaner. Around the bottom of the doublet, fixed on the right, is a bold belt of white cotton overlaid with rows of white cotton covered thick piping painted gold alternating with rows of black silk braid.

The sleeves, full topped and narrowing to the wrist, are of off-white silk taffeta, stitched and gathered to give the effect of latticed quilting, and decorated with large faceted chandelier drops surrounded by gold serrated-edge paper simulating metal mounts; under each drop is a piece of blue metallic paper mounted on a larger piece of brown paper set on a larger circle of cheap gold lamé on a larger circle of pinked-edge black felt; over the bass, surrounding the drop, is looped white pipe-cleaner. Over the shoulder point is a padded roll of heavy off-white wool bound with crossed lines of narrow black velvet ribbon, bound with strips of the same wool bound with lines of narrow black velvet ribbon; below this, off-white cotton stockinette is rolled into four tubes bound with black plaited plastic millinery 'straw'. The doublet fastens down the left side, from ruff to centre front, with press studs and hooks and eyes; the belt on the left is attached to the doublet with hooks and eyes. The doublet is lined with off-white cotton; fixed from the side seams is a separate front lining of off-white cotton fastened down the centre front with hooks and eyes. Breeches of brown rough wool fastening with straps and buckles below the knee, front fly fastening and buttons for braces. The breeches are slightly padded beneath the off-white cotton lining.

Long-sleeved coat with stand-up collar, worn as a cloak, of scene flax lined with calico and, down the front edges, book muslin, quilted in vertical lines, making the front fall stiffly and hold shape. The edges are outlined in thick piping cord roughly wrapped in white cotton tape and bound with narrow black tape. The coat is roughly dyed pink and randomly sprayed blue, forming mauve patches

Fig. 49 Prospero and Miranda in *The Tempest* (1940). **39**. By 'Anthony'. BBC Hulton Picture Library

where the dye is thinly applied. The coat is attached to the doublet with large hooks and bars.

b **Black and white photograph** of Prospero and Ariel. Inscribed in ink (perhaps in John Gielgud's handwriting) 'Thou shalt be as free as mountain winds/only exactly do all points at my command' Act 1, scene 2; this is the point where Prospero makes Ferdinand and Miranda fall in love.
($11\frac{3}{4} \times 8\frac{3}{4}$)

By 'Anthony'.

This was the second time John Gielgud had played Prospero; he first appeared in the role in 1930. The production was one of the first[15] to be directed by George Devine who was to become one of, or, *the* major figure in the London theatre of the 1950s and later. It is interesting that the décor should have been undertaken by Messel rather than by Motley with which firm Devine had been professionally and personally associated for some time. Nonetheless *The Tempest* provided Oliver Messel with the opportunity to treat the décor with a freedom which would not have been permissible in a work later than Shakespeare. In this production Messel returned to using masks, which he had not employed for some years, and made effective ones for Caliban and for Ariel. It is possible that the idea of using masks may have come from Devine who was particularly interested[16] in their effect on the actor. Messel also used gauzes which were considered old-fashioned in 1940.

Despite the War the play attracted large audiences and was able to run its term of six weeks without enemy interference. Gielgud's Prospero was well received, as were the Ariel of Marius Goring and Jack Hawkins' Caliban hidden behind a mask truly monstrous.

Reactions on the part of the critics to the décor and costumes were contradictory, notwithstanding the fact that, to us, the set looks specially bleak for Messel; it appears functional and with a flavour of the contemporary. The bleakness was noted by *The Observer* as being unrepresentative of Prospero's island which should have looked verdant. On the other hand *The Times* critic found the set over-elaborate and Victorian in spirit, while the *Daily Telegraph* critic felt that the décor owed something to El Greco, and that it was (including the beauty of the masque scenes), the best he had seen of the play.

Fig. 50 Advertisement for *The Infernal Machine* by Jean Cocteau, presented at the Arts Theatre in September 1940 and for which Messel executed costumes, masks and sets. Arts Theatre

"THE INFERNAL MACHINE"
PLAY by COCTEAU

THE SPHINX from one of the designs by OLIVER MESSEL

THURS. 5th SEPT.

THE ARTS THEATRE & BALLET CLUB

SEPTEMBER—OCTOBER 1940

6 & 7 GT. NEWPORT ST., LEICESTER SQ., W.C.2

1942

40 Comus.

A Masque in one act after Milton. Choreography by Robert Helpmann. Music by Purcell, arranged by Constant Lambert. Presented on 14th January, 1942 at New (now Albery) Theatre, London by the Sadler's Wells (now Royal) Ballet. With Margot Fonteyn as The Lady, Robert Helpmann as Comus; etc.

Synopsis; Comus captures The Lady and tempts her to drink the potion that will transform her into one of his creatures, but she is rescued by her brothers. To release her from the enchantment, the Attendant Spirit summons up Sabrina, the River Goddess, and the Masque ends with the Triumph of Chastity over Vice.

a **Model** for Scene 2, Comus' Palace.

Backcloth, four cut cloths and false proscenium of charcoal, pencil, watercolour, acetate with miniature banqueting table and figure of Comus in wood, gesso, modelling clay painted in oils, white and gold paint. At the top of the false proscenium is painted drapery and a border of silver fringe; at the sides are pink-mauve velvet covered strips.
($17\frac{3}{4} \times 22\frac{1}{2} \times 13\frac{3}{8}$) set in case with architectural surround.

b **Black and white photograph** of Margot Fonteyn and Robert Helpmann. (10×8) (Fig. 51). By Gordon Anthony.

c **Black and white photograph** of Scene 1, Comus attended by his Rout. ($6\frac{3}{4} \times 8\frac{3}{4}$) (Fig. 52). By Gordon Anthony.

d **Black and white photograph** of Comus' Palace. (20×16) By Gordon Anthony.

e **Black and white photograph** of Hugh Skillen with masks for the Rout. ($7\frac{1}{4} \times 6\frac{1}{4}$) By Germaine Kanova.

Although the programme described Comus as 'a Masque' it was in fact a ballet with mimed episodes

◀ Fig. 51, 40b   Fig. 52, 40c ▼

and two interpolated speeches from the original Milton masque. For this his first ballet, Helpmann turned to Messel, with whom he had first worked professionally when playing Oberon at the Old Vic in 1937. He must have been aware of Messel's talent for period design (rare in the British theatre at that time) and his sympathy with the English masque tradition. Messel's settings were beautiful, though his costumes did not, perhaps completely solve the problem of evoking period and at the same time be suitable for dancing.

It is on Comus that Messel is first credited as working with the mask and head-dress maker Hugh Skillen. Skillen had given up a stage career in 1938 to become a mask and prop maker with Thérèse Clement. He was to work frequently with Messel in the years to come, and though Messel retained absolute control over the realisation of his designs, the recognisable 'Messel' style in head-dresses lies as much in Skillen's characteristic choice of materials and way of making as in the original design.

Later productions on which Skillen was to work included; *The Sleeping Beauty*, the film and opera of *The Queen of Spades*, *The Little Hut*, *Ring Round the Moon*, *Under the Sycamore Tree*, *La Cenerentola*, *The Dark is Light Enough*, and *Homage to the Queen*.

1945

41 The Rivals

A comedy (1775) in five acts and an epilogue by Richard Brinsley Sheridan. Presented by Tennent Plays Ltd and C.E.M.A.[17] at the Criterion Theatre on 25th September, 1945; directed by William Armstrong and Edith Evans, assisted by Tyrone Guthrie. With Edith Evans as Mrs Malaprop, Anthony Quayle as Captain Absolute, Audrey Fildes as Lydia Languish, and Peter Cushing as Mr Faulkland, etc. Settings and costumes by Oliver Messel; incidental music adapted by Leslie Bridgewater from William Boyce.

S.C. 4 models, 34 set details.

a **Model**; Captain Absolute's lodgings, Act 2.
($17 \times 17\frac{1}{4} \times 10$)

b **Black and white photograph** of Julia (Jean Wilson) and Lydia, conferring in Act 1, scene 2 about their respective romances.
(8×10)

c **Black and white photograph** of Captain Absolute and Mrs Malaprop, with his letter addressed to Lydia which has been found. Act 3, scene 3.
(8×10)

d **Black and white photograph** of Lydia, Fag (Michael Gough, with hat), Mrs Malaprop and Julia.
(8×10)

e **Black and white photograph** of Lydia, Mrs Malaprop, Sir Anthony Absolute (Morland Graham), and the Captain; Act 4, scene 2. The Captain has called on Lydia at a critical phase in his relationship with her.
(8×10)

f **Black and white photograph** of Mr Faulkland (Peter Cushing) and Julia; probably Act 4, scene 3, at a moment in their tortuous love affair.
($6\frac{1}{2} \times 4\frac{3}{4}$)

g **Black and white photograph** of Julia, brooding on her difficult affair with Faulkland.
($6\frac{1}{2} \times 4\frac{3}{4}$) (Fig. 53).

h **Black and white photograph** of Bob Acres (Reginald Beckwith), and Sir Lucius O'Trigger (Brefni O'Rourke), in the duel scene, Act 5, scene 2, set in King's Mead Fields.
(8×10)

Photographs by Houston Rogers, London.

With *The Rivals*, his first post-war production, Messel was back with a familiar and, on his part, well-liked period – the eighteenth century. In general here he got better notices than the cast, who, with the middling exception of Edith Evans, were blamed by *The Times* critic for lacking style and conviction. Some of that may have been due to the complicated directorial situation applying at the rehearsals – Edith Evans and William Armstrong being, in the main, in charge, with assistance by Tyrone Guthrie. But it is difficult to imagine Guthrie content to play the part of assistant. Beverley Baxter *(Evening Standard)*, thought that the acting was too modern, too like that of a Coward play. This raises the interesting question as to how an eighteenth-century comedy can properly be played now. What is a style to be based on? Although Messel's notices were favourable, Brown *(The Observer)* drew an interesting parallel between Messel's style and another, earlier, '. . . [he] seems to have decided to avoid the clear, clean, glittering Lovat-Fraser eighteenth-century décor, which all of us know and most of us like. His alternative is heavier in colour, less trim, and much handicapped by the tiny stage for which he works . . .'.

Fig. 54 Princess Aurora and Prince Florimund, Act 2, *The Sleeping Beauty* (1946). **42**. Edward Mandinian

1946

42 The Sleeping Beauty

Ballet in three acts. Choreography by Marius Petipa; additional choreography by Frederick Ashton and Ninette de Valois. Produced by Nicholai Sergeyev. Music by Pyotr Ilyich Tchaikovsky. Libretto: Marius Petipa and Ivan Vsevolojsky after Charles Perrault. First performance of a new production; 20th February, 1946 by Sadler's Wells (now Royal) Ballet; revised and remade 1952, 1959 (Royal Ballet Touring Company), 1960 (Royal Ballet at Covent Garden).

Synopsis: based on the traditional Fairy Tale. Prologue: The Christening. Act 1: The Spell. Act 2: The Vision. Act 3: scene 1, The Awakening; scene 2, The Wedding.

a **Design** for the backcloth and cut-cloth for Act 1.
Ch, p, w. Chinese white, varnished. Inscribed: Act I, Act I.
($32\frac{3}{8} \times 21\frac{3}{4}$), cut cloth ($30 \times 22\frac{3}{8}$) (Fig. 14).
Attached are the remains of cellophane covering, marked up for the scene painters.

b **Design** for the gauze for Act 3 scene 1.
Ch, p, 2, oil paint; on tracing paper laid down on blue background. Covered with cellophane marked up for the scene painters. ($29\frac{3}{4} \times 18$)

c **Costume design** for the Vision of Princess Aurora in Act 2.
Ch, p, Chinese white. Signed. Inscribed on reverse mount: 'Princess Aurora Costume for Margot Fonteyn Act 3 (sic)/$19\frac{1}{2} \times 12 \times 12$/Sleeping Beauty/' (Customs stamp dated 28th September, 1949). ($14\frac{7}{8} \times 21\frac{1}{2}$). Although most of the dancers performing Princess Aurora had a head-dress trimmed as in the design, Fonteyn's was trimmed with a double pendant frill from the lower edge, in the manner of the head-dress for a Friend of Princess Aurora in Act 1 and **w** below. (See illustration below.)

A number of *The Sleeping Beauty* designs have a Customs stamp dated 28th September, 1949; this implies that they are for the 1946 production and were exhibited in New York to coincide with the first visit by the Sadler's Wells Ballet in 1949. Messel's work on *The Sleeping Beauty* played a large part in the Company's success in New York and on subsequent American tours. The ballet was performed on the opening night of the first New York season and created a sensation, and established the Sadler's Wells Ballet as a major international Company.

d **Costume design** for Prince Florimund in Act 2.
Ch, p, w, gold paint. Signed. Inscribed on reverse mount: 'Forest Hunting scene/The Prince/Red Velvet/Paltenghi Halpmann (crossed out/Helpmann' (in Ninette de Valois' writing). ($14\frac{3}{4} \times 22$)

Robert Helpmann and David Paltenghi shared the role of Prince Florimund during the 1946 season, when the ballet was performed seventy-eight times; owing to Helpmann's illness, Paltenghi took the lion's share, with fifty-seven performances to Helpmann's twenty-one.

e **Costume design** for King Florestan XXIV in the Prologue.
P, w, chinese white, gold and silver paint. Signed. Inscribed on reverse mount: Prologue/SK27/1 King/Blue/gold. ($14\frac{7}{8} \times 22\frac{1}{8}$)

As far as can be ascertaned, the crown was never trimmed with ostrich plumes. (See **r** below.)

f **Costume design** for the Queen in Act 1.
Ch, p, w, gold and silver paint. Signed. Inscribed on reverse mount: 'Feathers & jewelled ribbons for hair Hugh Skillen/The Queen Act 1/Bodice like silver moiré jacket Rosencavalier (sic)/Blue velvet applique/all the edges to neck with lurex horsehair!/skirt/net over brilliant silver/velvet ribbons/edge of skirt ruched Taffeta/29' ($14\frac{7}{8} \times 19\frac{7}{8}$) (Fig. 55).

g **Costume design** for the Lilac Fairy.
Ch, p, w, chinese white. Inscribed: 'The Lilac Fairy'. Signed. ($14\frac{7}{8} \times 19\frac{7}{8}$). This would seem to be a later revised design; the original 1946 costume was much heavier and the head-dress much bolder.
(See **t** below.)

h **Costume design** for Cattalabutte in the Prologue.
Ch, p, w, chinese white, gold paint. Signed. Inscribed on reverse mount: 'Prologue/Cantalabutte (sic)/3'. ($14\frac{7}{8} \times 21\frac{1}{8}$)

i **Costume design** for the Fairy of the Enchanted Garden in the Prologue.
Ch, p, w, chinese white, silver paint. Signed. Inscribed on reverse mount: 'Prologue/Enchanted Garden/$18 \times 12\frac{1}{2}$/9/' (Customs stamp dated 28th September, 1949). ($14\frac{7}{8} \times 19\frac{7}{8}$)

j **Costume design** for the Cavalier to the Fairy of the Enchanted Garden in the Prologue.
Ch, p, w, chinese white, gold and silver paint. Inscribed: 'Cavalier & Page/to the Fairy of the/Enchanted garden'. Signed. On reverse mount: 'SK2/Enchanted Garden/19×13/ 16/' (Customs stamp dated 28th September, 1949). ($14\frac{7}{8} \times 19\frac{7}{8}$) (Fig. 14)

k **Costume design** for a Nymph in Act 2.
P, w, chinese white, gold paint. Inscribed on reverse mount: '16 Nymphs/Act 2 Nymphs/horsehair panniers/pale lavender/swags/$18\frac{1}{2} \times 12\frac{1}{2}$/ 55/'

THE SLEEPING BEAUTY · 111

(Customs stamp dated 28th September, 1949); attached to reverse mount net and lurex novelty fabric samples. ($14\frac{7}{8} \times 21\frac{1}{2}$)

Though the Customs stamp indicates that this design dates from 1946, the fabric samples are clearly for a much later revival, probably the 1976 production by American Ballet Theatre.

l **Costume design** for the Wolf in Act 3.
Ch, p, w, chinese white, gold paint. Signed. Inscribed on reverse mount: 'The Wolf/Auroras Wedding/1 Wolf/SK24/18 × 14/4/' (Customs stamp dated 28th September, 1949)/Thomas Messel stamp). ($14\frac{7}{8} \times 19\frac{7}{8}$)
Lent by Thomas Messel.

Aurora's Wedding was the name given to Act 3 of *The Sleeping Beauty* when divorced from the whole and given as a separate ballet. Messel would have been used to seeing it under this title during the late 1920s and 1930s danced by the Diaghilev or de Basil Ballets Russes.

m **Costume design** for a Court Lady in the Prologue.
Ch, p, w, chinese white, gold and silver paint. Signed. Inscribed on reverse mount: '4 Court Ladies No. 2/Prologue/4/2 Court Ladies/SK12/(illegible) not open in front/No. 33.' ($14\frac{7}{8} \times 21\frac{3}{4}$)

n **Costume design** for a Court Lady in Act 3.
Ch, p, w, chinese white, gold paint. Signed. Inscribed on reverse mount: 'The Spell and (crossed out)/Court Ladies Mazurka/Act III/6 Mazurka Girls/SK22/ir 10?/white taffeta/stripes painted & enhanced with gold lurex stripes/lurex/yellow net over gold gauze/lurex bands, etc./ 63/6/' (Thomas Messel stamp). ($14\frac{7}{8} \times 21\frac{3}{8}$)
Lent by Thomas Messel.

o **Tunic** for the Queen's Page.
Short tunic of grey cotton painted silver with round neck, puffed sleeves and, added to lower edge, a border cut into lappets; the tunic is appliquéd with arabesques of greenish slate velveteen. Halfway across the shoulders is fixed a turn-back collar of mauve artificial taffeta lined with greenish slate velveteen. Over the puffed sleeves are small cap sleeves of bands of grey cotton painted silver, mauve artificial taffeta and, at the edge, greenish slate velveteen. Loose over the puffed sleeves are narrow strips of greenish slate velveteen simulating slashing; from the lower edge to the elbow fall loose open-topped sleeves of mauve artificial taffeta with a gold composition stud at the top edge, within which are open-topped sleeves of pleated white cotton. Each lappet is edged with greenish slate velveteen accented by narrow gold braid, and has a central small gold-painted composition stud. Down the centre front is a line of large gold-painted composition studs. The costume is lined with white cotton and fastens at the back with hooks and two rows of eyes.

The costume must be one of the very few remaining from the original production. It was worn on the opening night of the production in February 1946 by Peter Clegg, who was then a student at the Sadler's Wells Ballet School. He was later to become a leading soloist with the Company and eventually Ballet Master to the Royal Ballet New Group (now Sadler's Wells Royal Ballet) and to Northern Ballet Theatre.

Theatre Museum. Given by Peter Clegg, Esq.

p **Head-dress** for Princess Aurora in Act 1, worn by Moira Shearer.

Wired headband with upstanding band of brown painted net, overlaid with motifs of gold metal ribbon covered wire backed with large copper sequins. From lower edges curve wire framed wings, covered with paper painted gold and antiqued. At the centre front is a mount of sequins and bright gilt beads. Down the right side is a 'plume' of frilled gathered crin ribbon trimmed with iridescent sequins.

The original head-dress was heavier and the plume much fuller, though it seems that, from early on, dancers scaled the head-dresses to suit their individual requirements and hair styling. This head-dress was worn by Moira Shearer, and thus the 'plume' which was usually pink, to match the dress, was changed to white to avoid clashing with her red hair. The plume is much smaller than that originally worn by Fonteyn. Shearer was one of the four Auroras in the 1946 production, with Margot Fonteyn, Pamela May and Beryl Grey, and she danced the role until 1953.

Lent by the Archives, Royal Opera House, Covent Garden.

q **Head-dress** for the Vision of Princess Aurora in Act 2, worn by Moira Shearer.
Miniature coronet of acetate painted silver and antiqued, each point supporting a heavy metal wire from the top of which hangs a crystal bead *tremblant*. The base is encircled with heavy silver metal braid. From either side curves a large shell-like mount of acetate, the outer edge cut in deep curves, painted in off-white, pale blue and pale green to simulate a shell; on the inner curve are two rows of silver metal cord embracing a row of oval rhinestones; above the cord is a line of large baroque pearl studs. From inside the curve rise four 'stems'

Fig. 55, **42f**

threaded with iridescent beads topped with a large oval cut crystal bead.

The head-dress is recognisably that worn by Moira Shearer, as the tape-ties to secure the head-dress to the head, are reddish-brown to tone in with her hair. The side frill is missing. For Shearer it was as in the original design (see c above) fitting around the back of the side curves.

Lent by the Archives, Royal Opera House, Covent Garden.

r **Crown** for King Florestan XXIV.
Crown with base of a double twisted rope of gold lurex fabric metal strip. From the base rise six three-quarter length figures with outstretched touching wings of gilded and antiqued papier mâché; the details of the loin-cloth, wings and hair enhanced are with gold lurex braid. Rising from the base between and behind the figures, are six ogee-moulded ribs of buckram covered with gold tinsel brocade, each decorated with four gold lurex covered wires and, at base, centre and top, pairs of wings centred with a rhinestone stud. The crown is topped with a large finial in the form of a stylized sunburst, centred back and front with a large oval rhinestone set in a gold lurex covered wire frame; at the base of the finial is an upward and larger downward facing ring of stylized foliage in gold lurex covered wire.
(See e above.)

Theatre Museum. Given by the Royal Academy of Dancing.

s **Head-dress** for the Queen in the Prologue and Act 3.
Wired triangle, the sides curved to fit; loosely covered with cotton net interwoven with cellophane strip; the wired edges continue down the side, each end trimmed with a small dark red velvet ribbon bow, the tails hung with gilt drop beads trimmed with amber beads and tiny filigree mounts. Across the front of the frame, mounted on wires, is a triangular structure: on the lowest wire are three very large oval pearlised studs surrounded by gold lurex cord and an outer row of tiny crin loops, the base of each set with a rhinestone; on either side of the centre mount is a tiny deep red velvet tab; at either end of the row is a small gold oval stud surrounded by gold lurex cord which continues over the top into wired extensions each supporting a gold drop and amber bead *tremblant*; at the centre of the second wire is a large oval rhinestone surrounded by gold metal braid and an outer row of tiny crin loops; on either side is one of the gold metal stud mounts; on the third wire are two of the large oval pearlised stud mounts; on the fourth one of the small gold oval stud mounts, drop rhinestones *tremblant* replacing the gold drop beads. At either end of every row and forming the apex of the triangle is a flat double bow of latticed metal braid with a central rhinestone quatrefoil above which are loops of crin ribbon interwoven with three rows of gold metal strip and two rows of white thread. Up the back of the head-dress are three off-white ostrich feathers which curl over the top, and two high flat loops of broad crin ribbon edged with iridescent cellophane strip, the tails falling to the waist.

The red bows and tabs indicate that the head-dress dates from before 1959, though the feathers seem to be a later replacement.

Theatre Museum. Given by the Royal Academy of Dancing.

t **Head-dress** for the Lilac Fairy.
Double wire band fastened over the head by an elastic extension with a hook and eye; the lower band rises to link with the upper at centre front. To either side, slanting towards the back from centre front, is a row of velvet shapes cut and painted to simulate lilac leaves, each with a central vein of wired pale green chenille; between each leaf rises a wire supporting a rhinestone drop *tremblant*. At the centre front is a high ruche of off-white tulle surmounted by a tuft of pink-mauve tulle set with small tufts of white cellophane strip, scattered sequins and wires supporting rhinestone drops and beads *tremblant*. Either side of the head is an elongated tuft simulating lilac clusters of pink-mauve tulle scattered through with small twists of pinkish red dyed sponge and tufts of off-white crin with iridescent edge, sequins and wires supporting rhinestone drops and beads *tremblant*. Towards the back of the head-dress are two similar smaller lilac tufts of pinkish-mauve tulle.

The original Lilac Fairy head-dress was much heavier and higher, overemphasising the head, but over the years it was reduced in size. The exhibited head-dress was worn by Sadler's Wells ballerina Anya Linden (now Lady Sainsbury), who danced the role between 1956 and 1960.

u **Head-dress** for Carabosse.
Long straggly greying wig with fringe. Attached over the head is a double-crescent wire band, to the top of which are fixed four long intertwined serpents of narrow tubes of black crin inside which is bold silver lurex covered wire, with tongues and tails of silver lurex covered wire bound with dark thread and rhinestone eyes. From either side of the serpent rise two high black 'antennae' covered with sellotape which curve sharply and descend to the wig as large 'bat-wings' the frames of which are silver lurex covered wire filled with black net; the wing 'membranes' are simulated by vertical silver lurex covered wire, with horizontal curves painted in

French enamel varnish. From the back of the wire band, down the hair, hangs a ragged hood of black net trimmed with random black-dyed chicken feathers.

The head-dress was worn in the Touring Company production by Ronald Emblen. The design for the Royal Opera House production had, from 1946, 'wings' set facing the sides, reminiscent of a medieval head-dress.

Theatre Museum. Given by the Royal Academy of Dancing.

v **Head-dress** for the Cavalier of the Fairy of the Golden Vine in the Prologue.
Double wire circle linked across the back by tape extension. The frame is covered with fake leather vine leaves, painted in shades of brown, green and gold, with veins of lurex covered wire, and stylized bunches of grapes formed of faceted transparent plastic studs painted with blue French enamel varnish, each stud surrounded by lurex covered wire which extends into long stems. Among the leaves are stems and corkscrew-twisted tendrils of gold lurex covered wire.

Theatre Museum. Given by the Royal Academy of Dancing.

w **Head-dress** for a Friend of Princess Aurora in Act 1.
Wire headband, the centre section covered with gold lurex thread 'figure of eight' loops; the sides are of upstanding crin mesh overlaid with points of white lace, with, against the face, a stiffened ruche of brown loose meshed lace, ending at eye level in loops of gold lace ribbon surmounted with a baroque pearl edged with loops of gold lurex. From the lower edges hang pendants of loose meshed brown lace trimmed with rosettes of gold lace each with a central iridescent faceted jewel.

Lent by the Archives, Royal Opera House, Covent Garden.

x **Head-dress** for the Blue Bird in Act 3.
Fantastic head-dress on wired base fitting around the sides and over the top of the head, of silver lurex covered wire shapes, filled in with silver lurex and cellophane strip braiding. Fitting over the forehead, the stalk in the air, is a downward facing geometric leaf-frond set with two iridescent faceted plastic domed ellipses, on top of which is a smaller triple upward leaf form with a central iridescent faceted plastic domed ellipse. Behind this, rising in a curve, is a similar frond set with two ellipses, and a second which continues to fit over the top of the head, finishing at the back in a large arrowhead. Fitted to the sides of the head, are curved baroque arabesques with further leaf formations fitting to the back.

Rising above the side arabesques are small wings topped with individually cut iridescent acetate feathers. The head-dress is French enamel varnished and paint-sprayed in blue tones. The ends of each inner sections are backed with stiffened muslin.

The original 1946 head-dress was much less detailed, and the wings more prominent. The sides, in leaf formation, fitted close to the head, and over the head it fitted tight, as a skull cap, with only a central 'stalk' protruding.

Lent by the Archives, Royal Opera House, Covent Garden.

y **Head-dress** for a Court Lady in The Prologue.
Wire framed triangular 'bonnet' to fit on pointed wig (see **m** above), covered with roughly pleated grey nylon net; the wired edges continue down the side, finishing in decorative bows of grey nylon net edged with gold lurex braid centred with white ric-rac braid and smaller bows of gold lurex braid with pearl ends to the ties. Fixed at the back are two pale yellow ostrich plumes held by three bows of grey nylon net randomly threaded with silver strip, edged with off-white ric-rac braid. At the apex is a pink and white five-petalled 'carnation' with a central pearl surrounded by a gold lurex tuft; from the flower emerge thin wires supporting single pearls. Around the front edge is a stylized vine of gold lurex covered wire, with 'stems' threaded with pearls and sequins set between amber beads, simulating seeds; above the 'carnation' the vine culminates in a number of these stems and small iridescent star flower sequins.

Theatre Museum. Given by the Royal Academy of Dancing.

z **Head-dress** for a Court Lady in The Prologue.
Wire framed oval to fit high on a pointed wig (see **m** above), covered with grey cotton net, the back decorated with a metal fan and two rosettes of crin threaded with fine gold strip; low on the centre back is a flat grey silk ribbon bow with long tails. The upper edge and sides are decorated with a central flower of off-white crin edged with mauve and off-white chenille with a central pearlised stud circled with gold fringe; above this is a triple leaf of white fancy plastic braid threaded with gold. To the sides are 'flowers' of white painted acetate, with a pointed centre formed of two pearls, papier mâché flower buds, long thin leaves of grey crin edged with iridescent celophane, and a triple leaf of a fancy iridescent cellophane braid with, at the base, two small flowers of white woven plastic braid threaded with gold strip, with centres of iridescent and pearlised beads.

Theatre Museum. Given by the Royal Academy of Dancing.

aa Black and white photograph, *Prologue: The Christening* with Beryl Grey (centre) as the Lilac Fairy.
By Frank Sharman, FRPS.

bb Black and white photograph, Act 1: *The Spell*. The King with the Knitting Women.
By Frank Sharman, FRPS.

cc Colour transparency of Act 2: *The Vision*. Robert Helpmann as Prince Florimund, Beryl Grey as the Lilac Fairy and Margot Fonteyn as the Vision of Princess Aurora.
By Frank Sharman, FRPS.

dd Colour transparency of Act 3, Scene 2: *The Wedding*. Leslie Edwards as Cattalabutte, Julia Farron as the Queen, David Davenport as King Florestan XXIV with Pages. (See **o** above.)
By Frank Sharman, FRPS.

The Sleeping Beauty was to be Messel's biggest and most enduring production (it was always known as the Messel Production, even though he was concerned only with the designs, and not the actual mounting of the ballet). For the initial Sadler's Wells Ballet staging in 1946 he was said to have designed two hundred and eight costumes, as well as four sets, gauzes and drop curtains. Allowing for remakes in 1952, 1959 and 1960 and the endless making of costumes for different casts, there must have been well over one thousand costumes made between the first performance in 1946 and the last by the Touring Company in 1970. The production was performed nearly one thousand one hundred and fifty times, from London to Los Angeles, from Leeds to Leningrad, becoming the Company's 'signature ballet'. And its reputation has bedevilled every attempt by the Royal Ballet (as Sadler's Wells Ballet became in 1959) to redesign it ever since.

Not that the production was without critics, and almost imperceptible, but significant, changes began at once. The first casualties were the 'lethal hats' (in P. W. Manchester's phrase) worn by several leading characters, and Aurora's sleeves in Act 1 became narrower and narrower over the years, the dancers feeling that the original full sleeves destroyed the line of their arms. Head-dresses seem to have always been subject to variation, certainly for the ballerinas (see **p** and **q** above), and it was generally felt that the original ones were too top heavy and spoiled the line of the head; over the years they gradually shrank to miniature versions of what they had once been (see **g** and **t** above). The actual shape and decoration of the tutus was subject to change over the years. The original costumes were certainly over-fussy in decoration, and this was reduced in time. After the 1952 remake Lionel Bradley recorded in his Diary that 'the fairies in the Prologue now have the fashionable horizontal tutu and the decorations ... seemed simpler and "harder".' The line of the tutus and their decoration were to continue to harden over the years.

Fabrics too changed. The first production was hampered by post-war austerity and the restricted range of fabrics available; the first remake was more sumptuous, though, as fabrics improved, the colours became, surprisingly, less subtle.

Thus, the production, like all repertory productions, underwent changes in its lifetime, some by design, some because of the availability of new fabrics or new types of decoration, or simply because of different costume-makers interpreting the designs slightly differently for different dancers; some went unnoticed by the public, others enraged or delighted them in equal measure; the Bluebird (as usual) resisted all attempts at improvement.

The production always had a particular hold on the American public and, in 1976, six years after the last performance by the Royal Ballet, American Ballet Theatre asked Messel to reproduce his designs for their first production of the full-length ballet. It would appear that the costume-makers worked from a mixed set of designs, some from the original 1946 production (the fabric pieces attached to the design for a Nymph in Act 2, see **k** above, must date from the American remake, as many of these materials would not have been available in the 1950s), and some later redrawings. But the final result was surprisingly unlike the Royal Ballet production – the spirit seemed to have departed. Once again the line of the costumes had become even harder, the now scanty decoration no longer seemed an integral part of the costume. Although Messel declared himself satisfied with the result, those who remembered the earlier staging were to be deeply disappointed.

43 The Magic Flute
Opera (1791), in two acts by Mozart; libretto by Schikaneder from Wieland's story *Lulu*. Presented by the Covent Garden Opera Trust on 20th March, 1947; directed by Malcolm Baker-Smith. English version by E. J. Dent. Settings, costumes and visual effects by Oliver Messel. With Kenneth Neate as Tamino, Victoria Sladen as Pamina, Oscar Natzka as Sarastro, Audrey Bowman as the Queen of the Night, Graham Clifford as Papageno, etc. Conductor, Rankl.

Fig. 56, **43b**

a **Model** No. 44; for Pamina's boudoir, Act 1, scene 2; with Papageno on stage.

b **Set design** for a gauze for use before Acts 1 and 2; ink, ch, w, g, gold paint. ($18\frac{3}{4} \times 30$) (Fig. 56).

c **Set design** for Act 2, scenes: 2, 4, 6 and 7; ink, ch, g. (22×30)

d **Design** for the Serpent which attacks Tamino in Act 1; p, g, w, gold and silver paints. (15×20)

e **Three black and white photographs** showing
(i) Kenneth Neate (Tamino) playing the magic flute,
(ii) Joyce Edmanson and Grahame Clifford as Papagena and Papageno, and
(iii) the Finale. Each ($8\frac{1}{4} \times 6$)
Photographs by Baron.

S.C. 1 model, 39 set details, 2 costume designs.

This was the first opera Messel had been commissioned to design, and one of the most difficult in the canon, because of the continual change of scene, and the emotional polarity between high seriousness and bucolic humour. There surely cannot be doubt that the work's core is a philosophic one, and recent productions (like Jonathan Miller's, 1983, for Scottish Opera) have stressed this to advantage. It is an older tradition to play the work for spectacle, which is the approach Covent Garden adopted in 1947. For example, Sarastro's arrival in a chariot, pulled by winged lions, was applauded by *The Times* critic, but it shows that times have changed for the better that such a thing would be impossible today. On the level of spectacle this production was praised, but musically it suffered from the largeness of the house and from the awkward placing of the singers too far back on the huge stage. For this the producer was blamed.

Also shown in this space are costume designs from the 1956 Glyndebourne production for which Messel designed costumes and settings. This was presented on 19th July, directed by Carl Ebert. Ernst Häefliger played Tamino, Pilar Lorengar was Pamina, Drago Bernardic was Sarastro, Mattiwilda Dobbs played The Queen of the Night, and Geraint Evans was Papageno, etc. Conductor, Gui.

f **Costume design** for Papageno: p, w, ch, g (15 × 10). Signed.

g **Costume design** for Papagena: p, ch, w, g (15 × 10). Signed.

h **Costume design** for Pamina: p, ch, w, g (15 × 10). Signed.

i **Costume design** for the Queen of the Night: p, ch, w, silver paint. (15 × 10). Signed.
S.C. 1 model, 53 pieces of a model, 38 plans.

This was a completely new production by Messel although it had (according to the *Daily Telegraph* critic), some feint reminiscences of the Covent Garden production nine years before. However, the general appearance of this new production seems to have been more integrated, and more charming. No designer could have had a harder problem, for not only is the Flute difficult to recount smoothly, but the Glyndebourne stage is the merest fraction of that at Covent Garden. Thus, vital scenery is at a spatial premium there and, according to Peter Heyworth in *The Observer*, Messel had not successfully solved the problem of placing monumental settings in its small area. Heyworth also pin-points what is sometimes observed now in a Messel set – fussiness of detail; however, he had good words for the costumes which were well contrasted in colour.

Room 72
MODEL SETS ON THE PLATFORM

These range from 1947 to 1959. They are made of wood, cardboard, paper, pipe-cleaners and miscellaneous materials. It is advantageous for spatial and visual reasons to show these models separately from the designs for the productions which are in other parts of this Gallery and the next. There are full details of the productions in the catalogue. In the two cases where nothing else accompanies the model, amplification is given beneath. Measurements are, $H \times L \times D$ in inches as given below.

44 The Magic Flute (1947)
Model for Pamina's boudoir, Act 1, scene 2 with Papageno on stage. ($27 \times 31\frac{1}{4} \times 22$). See related No. 43.

45 The Lady's Not For Burning (1949)
Permanent set ($22 \times 23\frac{1}{2} \times 17$). See related design No. 56.

46 Tough At The Top (1949)
Model for Act 1, scene 3, an Edwardian Derby Day. ($18 \times 25\frac{3}{4} \times 22$). This musical play by A. P. Herbert with music by Vivian Ellis was presented by C. B. Cochran at the Adelphi Theatre on 15th July, 1949; directed by Wendy Toye. Settings and costumes were by Oliver Messel. This story is of a Ruritanian princess who falls in love with an American boxer. With Maria D'Attili as Princess Philomel, Peter Lupino as Charles Lupin, Brian Reece as Count Victor, George Tozzi as Bartholomew Brain, etc. This was Cochran's 127th production and though not as successful as *Bless The Bride* (1947), which had had the same librettist and composer, it had a moderately successful run, and rather mixed notices. Model shown in Messel Exh. 1951 (p. 40). Cat. No. 11.
S.C. 1 model, 18 set designs, 86 c. designs, 2 misc.

47 Ariadne Auf Naxos (1950)
Model of the Great Hall used for the adaptation of Molière's play and for the one-act opera to follow. ($19\frac{3}{4} \times 22\frac{1}{2} \times 17$). See related No. 59.

48 Ring Round the Moon (1950)
Model for the permanent set, a winter garden in Spring. Messel says that he had the idea for this in an aeroplane, and Carl Toms has said (p. 27) that it was derived from a Portuguese railway station. ($20 \times 23 \times 17$). See related No. 57.
Made by Carl Toms; painted by Oliver Messel. Theatre Museum no. IS. 475–1980.

More material on this production is to be found on the SLIDE TAPE, Room 73 No. 99.

49 The Little Hut (1950)
A light comedy by André Roussin, adapted by Nancy Mitford, presented by H. M. Tennent Ltd, at the Lyric Theatre (Shaftesbury Avenue), on 2nd August, 1950; directed by Peter Brook; set by Oliver Messel. With Joan Tetzel as Susan, David Tomlison as Henry, and Robert Morley as Philip, etc.
S.C. 1 model.
Model: of the desert island used throughout the play. ($18\frac{3}{4} \times 24\frac{1}{4} \times 19$)

This year, 1950, was a very good one for Messel, as two of his décors for the productions (*Ring Round the Moon*, *The Little Hut*) undoubtedly helped towards their long runs of three years.
   The set of *The Little Hut*, exotically fruited, and ideally over-run with vegetation, made an ideal and highly praised setting for the slender story of husband, wife and lover wrecked on a desert island. William Chappell, dressed as a monkey, descended a palm-tree at the final curtain.

50 Under The Sycamore Tree (1952)
Model, for the throne room of the Queen Ant. One of Messel's most original sets, and where the Surrealist side of his imagination is most at work. ($19 \times 24\frac{1}{2} \times 19$). See related No. 62.

51 The Dark is Light Enough (1954)
Model, for Act 2, set in the stables. ($18\frac{1}{2} \times 23\frac{3}{4} \times 17$). See related No. 66.

52 Le Comte Ory (1954) (*Count Ory*).
Model, for Act 1; outside the castle in Touraine. ($19\frac{3}{4} \times 22 \times 17$). See related No. 68 (Fig. 9).

53 Il Barbiere di Siviglia (1954) (*The Barber of Seville*)
Model, for Act 1, outside Dr Bartolo's house at dawn. Count Almaviva has come to serenade Rosina. ($19\frac{3}{4} \times 22\frac{1}{4} \times 18$). Also q.v. No. 67.

54 Die Entführung Aus Dem Serail (1956) (*The Elopement From The Harem*)
Model, for Act 1, scene 1, the garden of Bassa Selim's country palace. This *singspiel*, in two acts, was written by Mozart to a libretto by Bretzner in 1782. This production was first performed by Glyndebourne Festival Opera at Glyndebourne on 10th June, 1956; directed by Peter Ebert with costumes and settings by Oliver Messel. The part of Belmonte was sung by Ernst Häefliger, Osmin by Arnold Van Mill, Constanze by Mattiwilda Dobbs, and Blonde by Lisa Otto; etc. Conductor, Sacher. ($19 \times 22\frac{3}{4} \times 16\frac{1}{2}$) (Fig. 57).
S.C. 2 models, 19 plans, 33 pieces of a model.

This production was well received and was the second of the three new productions Messel designed

Fig. 57, 54

for Mozart's bi-centenary year (1956) at Glyndebourne. In all of these he was assisted by Carl Toms. As might be expected Messel stressed the exotic in his settings and based his design of the harem on engravings of Turkish buildings. The predominant yellow of the set was not only a period detail but added an enlivening bustling mood to the proceedings. It is now the fashion to understate the exotic in the setting and to capitalise on the dramatic conflict.

More material on this production is to be found on the SLIDE TAPE, Room 73. No.99.

55 **Der Rosenkavalier** (1959) (*The Knight of the Rose*). **Model,** for the Inn, Act III. ($17\frac{1}{2} \times 23 \times 17$). For related designs, see No.75.

1949

56 **The Lady's Not For Burning**
A play in verse in three acts by Christopher Fry, presented by Tennent Productions Ltd, at the Globe Theatre[18] on 11th May, 1949; directed by John Gielgud and Esmé Percy. Settings and costumes by Oliver Messel. With John Gielgud as Thomas Mendip, Pamela Brown as Jennet Jourdemayne, Claire Bloom as Alizon Eliot, and Richard Burton as Richard, etc.

a **Model** No.45 (in Room 72) of the permanent set, a room in the house of Hebble Tyson, Mayor of the small market town of Cool Clary.

b **List of props** probably prepared for the stage manager. Typescript and manuscript. (10×8)

c **Costume design** for a necklace for Alizon; and a cross and a stomacher for Margaret (played by Nora Nicholson); ch, p, ink (15×10)

d **Costume design** for Thomas Mendip; ch, ink, w. Signed. (15×10)

e **Costume design** for Jennet; chalk, w, gold paint. Signed. (20×15)

f **Costume design** for Alizon; p, chalk, w, gold paint. Signed. (20×15) (Fig.7)

g **Costume design** for Nicholas (played by David Evans), p, chalk, w. (15×10)

h **Costume design** for make-up for Tyson (played by Harcourt Williams), ink, p, ch, w, g. Signed. (15×10)

i **Black and white photograph** showing John Gielgud as Thomas Mendip demanding the death penalty for an alleged crime; with left to right, Peter Bull, Richard Leech, Harcourt Williams, Richard Burton and in the foreground Eliot Makeham. ($7 \times 5\frac{1}{4}$) Angus McBean.

S.C. 1 model, 3 des. for props, 86 c. designs.

Christopher Fry's comments on the set (p.23) put very well the virtues of Messel's invention for this play. What is differently interesting is the situation as it appertained, in 1949, to poetic drama, for then it looked, to judge from the notices, that that was about to sweep the West End and re-establish itself as a commercial proposition. This did not happen but the fact that a commercial management (as opposed to a little theatre like the Arts) was willing to take such risks was not based solely on chance. There were good reasons for thinking that poetic drama was viable. Eliot was established as a dramatist by 1949, the activities of the Group Theatre in the Thirties, although not reaching a popular audience, had helped to keep alive in Auden and Isherwood's plays a tradition of verse-speaking which Gielgud had also fostered in Shakespeare. Radio drama had also taken a new turn, in the post-war period, to poetic drama in the work of Louis MacNiece, and Dylan Thomas, pre-eminently. *The Lady's Not For Burning* ran for nearly nine months until 1950 and then transferred to New York where it had another 151 performances. Likewise it dazzled its audiences.

1950

57 **Ring Round The Moon**
A charade with music in three acts, translated from Jean Anouilh's *L'Invitation au Château* (1947) by Christopher Fry, and presented by Tennent Productions Limited, at the Globe Theatre on 26th January, 1950; directed by Peter Brook. Settings and costumes by Oliver Messel, music by Richard Addinsell, dances arranged by William Chappell. With Paul Scofield playing the brothers Hugo and Frederic, Claire Bloom, Isabelle, Marjorie Stewart, Lady India and Audrey Fildes as Diana Messerschmann, etc.

a **Model,** No.48.

b **Black and white photograph** of Oliver Messel on the set. ($9 \times 7\frac{3}{4}$). Alec Murray. (Fig.58).

▲ Fig. 58, 57b   Fig. 59, 57g ▶

c **Black and white photograph** of the set by day with (from left to right), Cecil Trouncer, William Mervyn, Paul Scofield, Marie Löhr, and Daphne Newton. Miss Löhr replaced Margaret Rutherford later in the run. ($9\frac{1}{2} \times 7$). Houston Rogers, London.

d **Black and white photograph** of the set by night, probably in the ball scene (Act 2), showing Claire Bloom and Paul Scofield to right, Marie Löhr (in wheel-chair), and William Mervyn, centre. ($9\frac{1}{2} \times 7$) Houston Rogers, London.

e **Black and white photograph** showing Birgitte Federspiel as Lady India, in the Copenhagen production . ($9\frac{1}{2} \times 7$) Mydtsbou, Copenhagen.

f **Black and white photograph** showing the state of things towards the end of the evening (Act 3). Copenhagen production also. ($9\frac{1}{2} \times 7$) Mydtsbou, Copenhagen.

g **Black and white photograph** of Claire Bloom as Isabelle (10×8) Houston Rogers, London (Fig. 59). S.C. 25 set details, 80 c. designs, 2 misc.

An enjoyable evening, with perhaps not a great deal profoundly memorable about it, was the general verdict. The play brought Christopher Fry into the West End again this time as translator of Anouilh's fantasy in which Paul Scofield played twins, (Horace and Frederic, one heartless, the other shy and amorous). The set (with that for *Helen*), is probably the one most remembered of Messel's, probably because its gaunt lines, and lack of decoration are untypical of him. Despite being made of metal and glass it had, nonetheless, a quality monumental by day, and a lighter, even frivolous look when lit-up at night (q.v. Glenville, p. 26).

Ring Round the Moon ran for a year and eight months (682 performances) in London before moving to New York, and Copenhagen (with differing casts). Its success in London helped to introduce a vogue for the work of Jean Anouilh, in translation. When it reached the Folkes Theatre, Copenhagen in 1951 it had been translated and directed by Edwin Tiemroth. Angelo Bruun played the twins, Lis Løwert, Isabelle, Valdermar Skjerning Messerschmann the rich financier and Knud Heglund was Josué, the decrepit butler. According to Lisbet Grandjean, of the Danish Theatre Museum, the play was well received, the critics describing it as 'a display of fireworks and a masterpiece of design.'

1950

58 The Queen of Spades

Opera (1890), in three acts by Tchaikovsky; libretto by Modest Tchaikovsky with additions, from Pushkin's story (1834), by the composer. English version by Rosa Newmarch. Presented at Covent Garden by the Covent Garden Opera on 21st December, 1950, directed by Michael Benthall. Settings and costumes by Oliver Messel. With Edgar Evans as Herman, Jess Walters as Yeletsky, Hilde Zadek as Lisa and Edith Coates as the Countess, etc. Conductor, Erich Kleiber.

Production photograph
The Old Countess and Lisa in the Summer Garden St Petersburg; Act I, Scene I ($20 \times 15\frac{1}{2}$). Angus McBean, London.

This photograph is not only a record of a dramatic moment in the opera and the edgy relationship between the Countess and her grand-daughter, but also accentuates the detail in the costumes, wigs and head-dresses. The costume fabrics for this opera were dyed and painted by Barbara Ternouth and Beatric Bendelow while the costumes were made by Olivia Cranmer. The wigs were made by Stanley Hall and the head-dresses by Hugh Skillen whose name is often associated in this capacity with Messel's productions.

S.C. 109 c. designs.

This was the first time that *The Queen of Spades* had been presented at Covent Garden, and the first time since 1915, it had been performed in London. Although it has some fine music it is not as good overall as *Eugene Onegin* but the plot is a compelling one. Messel had already designed the film (Nos. 98, 107) to good effect and his décor, at the Royal Opera House, was generally praised, particularly by *The Observer* critic for the eeriness in the old Countess's bedroom after her return from the ball, and for a similar effect in the barrack's scene.

1950

59 Ariadne Auf Naxos

An opera by Richard Strauss, libretto by Hugo von Hofsmannsthal originally written (1912) in one act to follow Molière's *Le Bourgeois Gentilhomme*; second version (1916) with a prologue before the one act and dispensing with Molière. The first version was presented by the Glyndebourne Opera at the Edinburgh Festival on 20th August, 1950, directed by Carl Ebert. Settings and costumes by Oliver Messel. With Miles Malleson as Monsieur Jourdain in *Le Bourgeois Gentilhomme*; in *Ariadne* Hilde Zadek in the title role, Peter Anders as Bacchus and Ilse Hollweg as Zerbinetta, etc. Conductor, Beecham. *Le Bourgeois Gentilhomme* and *Ariadne* were given in English, translated by Miles Malleson.

a **Model**, No. 47.

b **Design** for a sweet dish 'in spun sugar'. Ink, w, g, gold paint. Signed. ($14\frac{3}{4} \times 10$) (Fig. 60)

c **Costume designs** for M. Jourdain, in his dressing-gown (back and front views); p, ch, w, gold and silver paints. Both signed. Each ($14\frac{3}{4} \times 10$)

d **Costume design** for Zerbinetta; p, ch, w, g, and swatches. Signed. ($14\frac{3}{4} \times 10$) (Fig. 61)

e **Costume design** for Bacchus, ch, w, g, gold paint and swatches. Signed. ($14\frac{3}{4} \times 10$)

f **Costume design** for Harlequin, p, w, g. Signed. ($14\frac{3}{4} \times 10$) (Fig. 62)

S.C. 1 model, 5 set details, 8 details of furniture, 56 costume details.

Fig. 60, 59b

◀ Fig. 6
59d

Fig. 62,
59f ▶

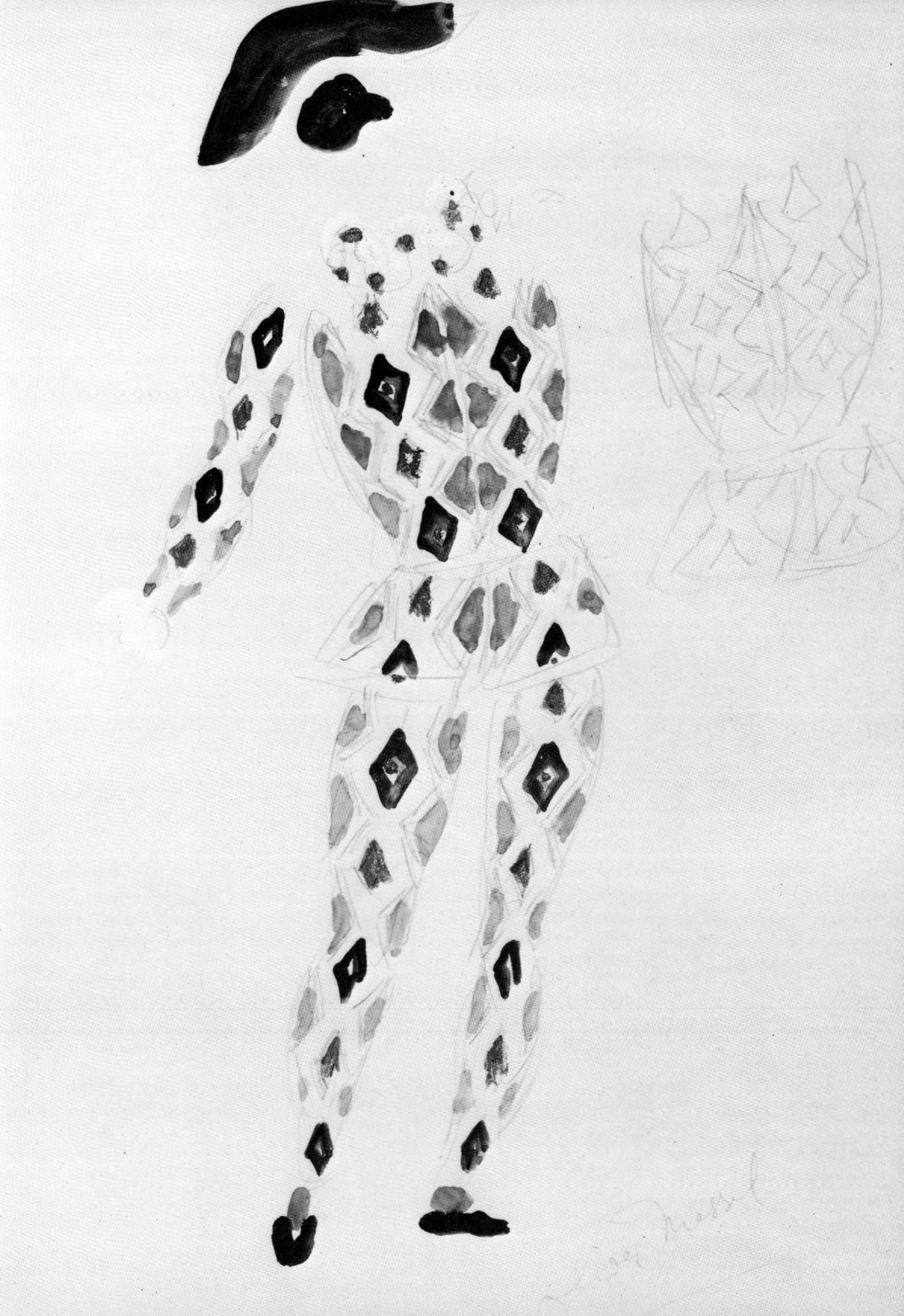

There is much to be said for both versions of the opera but it has proved to be an economic miscalculation on Strauss's part that his first version needed two casts, one of actors and one of singers. Nowadays, it is the second version which is most often done, although Glyndebourne returned to the first version in 1962. This is probably the only occasion when Messel's designs and settings for a Glyndebourne production were in the baroque style, although there are accents of this in other décors of his. However, it is seldom that the occasion arose to design so lavishly (as for M. Jourdain here). The second version of *Ariadne* does not make a full evening, so in 1954 Glyndebourne introduced the practice of a one act opera before it, and in that year Busoni's *Arlecchino* (with designs by Peter Rice) was performed. *Ariadne* with its story of the composer who had been irritated by *Le Bourgeois gentilhomme's* command that his opera and a *commedia dell' arte* troupe should perform simultaneously, became an established favourite at Glyndebourne and was revived frequently until 1962.

The performances ended with a fireworks display in proof of M. Jourdain's promise that there should be one after the opera which is about Ariadne's release from Naxos aided by Bacchus. One feature of performances of *Ariadne* by 1954 were the number of American singers who became associated with it, including Mattiwilda Dobbs as Zerbinetta, and Lucine Amara as *Ariadne*; she sang this role also in 1957 and 1958. Glyndebourne has always stated the nationalities of its singers in the programmes and American names become progressively more frequent from the early Fifties.

1951

60 **Romeo and Juliet**
A tragedy (1595–6), in five acts by William Shakespeare. Presented by Dwight Deere Wiman at the Broadhurst Theatre, New York, on 10th March, 1951, directed by Peter Glenville; settings and costumes by Oliver Messel. With Olivia de Havilland as Juliet, Douglas Watson as Romeo, Jack Hawkins as Mercuito, James Hayter as Friar Laurence, Evelyn Varden as the Nurse and William Smithers as Tybalt, etc.

a **Colour photograph** of the model for Act V (8×10). Unknown photographer.

b **Colour photograph** of the model for the Balcony Scene, Act 2, scene 2 (8×10). Unknown photographer. (Fig. 63).

c **Black and white photograph** of the duel between Tybalt and Mercutio, Act 3, scene 1 ($11 \times 13\frac{1}{2}$). John Seymour Erwin, New York.

d **Black and white photograph** of the Balcony Scene, Act 2, scene 2 (14×11). John Seymour Erwin, New York.

e **Black and white photograph** showing Juliet on the bier, and Romeo, Act 5 ($13\frac{1}{2} \times 10\frac{1}{2}$). John Seymour Erwin, New York.

f **Black and white photograph** showing Lady Capulet (Isobel Elsom) grieving over Tybalt, Act 3, scene 1 ($10\frac{3}{4} \times 13\frac{1}{2}$) (Fig. 64). John Seymour Erwin, New York.

S.C. 8 set details, 148 costume designs, 5 photographs of old Master paintings, 226 photographs of costume details, and some action photographs of the production.

The critics' reaction to this was that it was good in parts. In the action scenes the direction was considered effective; but the passion was ghostly. Olivia de Havilland (b. 1916) made her New York début in the role of Juliet, but her verse-speaking was not considered sensitive enough, although she was charming to look at. She was not completely a novice to Shakespeare. Reinhardt had cast her as Hermia in his film (1935), of *A Midsummer Night's Dream*. Of the male roles the honours went to Jack Hawkins' lively, trouping Mercutio; Romeo was considered fiery and gallant and William Smithers' Tybalt was found effective, meaning properly obnoxious in the role. While the direction was received unequally Messel's sets and costumes were thought by most reviewers to be wonderfully colourful and Renaissance in atmosphere. There was only one exception to this general view, in the voice of Brooks Atkinson in the *New York Post* who, though he praised the costumes as fine, said strongly that the scenery was out of date, because Shakespeare productions had lagged behind the main developments in the theatre. This is an interesting and arguable point but unfortunately Atkinson did not develop the theme. But what he was probably alluding to was the necessarily heavy look of the scenery in contrast to the much sparser sets in New York. In this connexion it is worth comparing No. 57 with No. 60.

This production had forty-nine performances – not long – but it is difficult to judge success or otherwise from this as the run may have been limited.

ABOVE Fig. 64, 60f   OVERLEAF Fig. 63, 60b

1951

61 Idomeneo *(Idomeneus, King of Crete) Opera seria* (1781), in three acts, music by Mozart, libretto by Varesco from that for Campra's opera *Idomeneo*. Presented by the Glyndebourne Opera at Glyndebourne on 15th June, 1951, directed by Carl Ebert; edited by Hans Gal. Settings and costumes by Oliver Messel; choreography by Sigurd Leeder. With Richard Lewis as Idomeneo, Sena Jurinac as Ilia, Simoneau as Idamante, and Birgit Nilsson as Electra, etc. Conductor, Busch.

S.C. 1 model, 14 set details, 63 costume designs, 6 production photographs.

a **Design** for the set; ch, w, g, on Whatman paper. Signed. 1951 ($16\frac{3}{4} \times 10\frac{3}{4}$)

b **Black and white photograph** showing the High Priest imploring heaven for mercy on learning that Idamante (Idomeneo's son), is to be the sacrificial victim. From left to right; Alexander Young, the High Priest, and Richard Lewis as Idomeneo. ($7\frac{1}{4} \times 9\frac{1}{2}$). Angus McBean.

c **Black and white photograph** showing the moment when the voice of Neptune prevents the sacrifice of Idamante. From left to right, Alexander Young, Sena Jurinac as Ilia, Richard Lewis, Alfred Poell as Arbace, Simoneau as Idamante, and Birgit Nilsson as Electra. ($7\frac{1}{4} \times 9\frac{1}{2}$). Angus McBean.

More material on this production is to be found on the SLIDE TAPE, in Room 73, No. 99.

Now that it is possible to have become familiar with *Idomeneo* in almost every opera house in the world, it comes as a surprise to know that the Glyndebourne production of 1951 was the first professional one to be staged in Engand. Rosenthal and Warrack record (q.v. Bib. 9b) a Scottish performance in Glasgow in 1934, but otherwise apart from amateur performances it was an unknown work, unrecorded and unbroadcast. Carl Ebert's production was generally well received. It had been mounted in memory of the late W. J. Turner, music critic of the *New Statesman*, who had tried to get the work adopted into the Glyndebourne repertoire. The performance was conducted by Fritz Busch, his last 'new' work before his death that year. According to Spike Hughes (q.v. Bib. 9b), whose long memory of Glyndebourne performances over many years is an indispensable guide, it was Sena Jurinac singing the role of Ilia, whose put-upon character has shades of resemblance to that of Pamina, who registered most of the singers. Her Fiordiligi had already been acclaimed the year before, and with Ilia and other Mozart roles, not necessarily at Glyndebourne, she was to develop into one of the great Mozart singers of this period; with an outstanding technique, always at the service of the characterisation rather than otherwise, she was also acknowledged as a superb Strauss singer, particularly as the Composer in *Ariadne*. As for Idomeneo, Richard Lewis made himself indispensable in the role, singing it in every revival until 1964.

Regarding the décor, it was not until the 1956 revival that both *The Times* and the *Observer* critics found points to irritate them. The latter felt that the effect of 'the hangings, drapes, and tassels' was deleterious to the production and reminded him too much of a Victorian drawing-room. Certainly that is borne out by the photographs. *Idomeneo* is a work already neo-classic and calls for stark décor, none at all, or the kind of formalised treatment Diamiani gave it at the Berlin Opera in December 1981.

1952

62 Under the Sycamore Tree
A 'farcical fable' in three acts by Sam Spewack, presented by Tennent Productions Limited, at the Aldwych Theatre on 23rd April, 1952, having begun at the Streatham Hill Theatre on 14th April. Directed by Peter Glenville; settings and costumes by Oliver Messel, music by Ronald Emanuel. With Alec Guinness as The Scientist, Diana Churchill as The Queen, Ernest Thesiger as The Chief Statistician and Eric Porter as The Boy, etc.

a **Model**, No. 50.

b **Designs** for a centipede settee, and a spider chair; both ink and watercolour. Signed ($14\frac{3}{4} \times 10$)

c **Designs** for a satchel, and a 'box of sweets for the Queen Ant'. Ch, ink, g ($14\frac{3}{4} \times 10$) (Fig. 65)

d **Costume design** for The Queen 'before the cocoon', p, ink, g. Signed ($14\frac{3}{4} \times 10$)

e **Costume design** for The Boy 'waiting for the baby', ink, w, g ($14\frac{3}{4} \times 10$)

f **Costume design** for The General 'as ambassador' ink, chalk, w. Signed ($14\frac{3}{4} \times 10$)

g **Costume design** for 'worker ants'. Ink, w ($14\frac{3}{4} \times 10$)

Fig. 65, 62c

satchel.

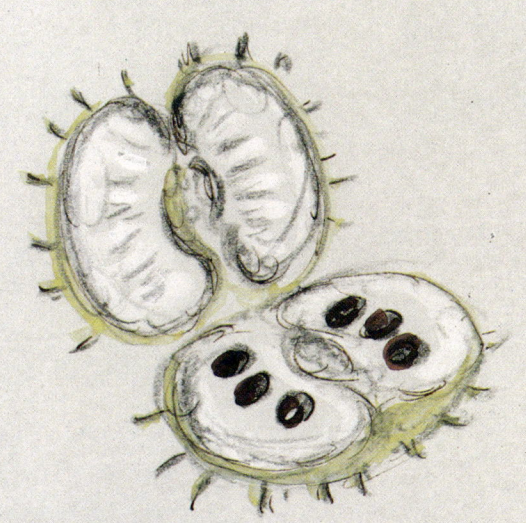

box of sweets for the queen ant.

h **Black and white photograph** showing the Queen Ant (Diana Churchill) the Statistician (Ernest Thesiger), and Worker (Madi Hedd), in Act 1, scene 1 ($9\frac{3}{4} \times 7\frac{3}{4}$). Angus McBean.

S.C. 57 set details, 30 costume designs.

If *Idomeneo* had not shown the best of Messel's décor he returned very much to form with *Under the Sycamore Tree*. Sam Spewack's satirical play about comparisons between humans and ants was cleverly directed by Peter Glenville who has written about this production in this catalogue (p.26). If Spewack's work had not the bite of Karel Čapek's *Insect Play*, to which it owed something, it did offer Messel an opportunity to let his imagination flower, so everything on his set took on a surreal look, including the furniture and accessories. The play provided Alec Guinness with a number of quick change parts and his acting of these was what impressed the critics. Guinness had become something of a specialist at this which had been seen by a wider audience in the film *Kind Hearts and Coronets* (1949).

1952

63 **La Cenerentola** *(Cinderella)*
Opera (1817) in two acts by Rossini, libretto by Ferretti, from Steibelt's opera of this name. Presented by the Glyndebourne Festival Society at Glyndebourne on 18th June, 1952, directed by Carl Ebert, the costumes and settings by Oliver Messel. With Oncina as Don Ramiro, the Prince of Salerno, Bruscantini as Dandini, Marina de Gabarain as Angelina *(La Cenerentola)*, and Wallace as Baron Monte Fiaschone, etc. Conductor, Gui.

a **Set design** for the grand salon in Don Ramiro's palace. Ink, ch, w, g, gold paint. Signed (15×10) (Fig. 66)

b **Costume design** for Cinderella, ink, ch, g, gold and silver paints. Signed. ($14\frac{3}{4} \times 10$) (Fig. 67)

c **Costume design** for Baron Monte Fiaschone, ink, chalk, w, g, gold paint. ($14\frac{3}{4} \times 10$)

d **Costume design** for Tisbe, dressing for the Ball, p, ch, g. ($14\frac{3}{4} \times 10$) (Fig. 68).

e **Costume design** for the Prince at the Ball, ink, w, g, gold paint. Signed ($14\frac{3}{4} \times 10$)

f **Costume design** for the Prince in the final scene, ink, ch, w ($14\frac{3}{4} \times 10$)

S.C. 74 set details, 81 c. designs, 2 misc.

As can be seen this was one of Messel's most delightfully light-hearted décors, and in it he caught admirably the fun of Rossini's work based on Perrault's story. It proved a popular stayer at Glyndebourne and was revived five times until 1960. The Glyndebourne public had anticipated that the opera might be a success and performances were sold out before the opening. Part of the success was no accident but based on the knowledge by the Glyndebourne public that Vittorio Gui, who was the mainstay conductor during the Fifties, had had much to do with the revival of Rossini's reputation. Rossini was to most minds in England the composer of only one opera, *The Barber of Seville*. The role of Dandini was sung by Sesto Bruscantini, a stalwart at Glyndebourne during the Fifties, and who was still singing as recently as last year (1982), at the Rossini Festival at Pesaro. Another singer (still active), in this production was Ian Wallace who sang the bass role of Don Magnifico, Cinderella's boorish father.

La Cenerentola had a great success in Berlin when the company went there in October 1954, and the opera was the subject of the BBC's first TV relay from Glyndebourne in 1959. Cinderella was sung by Marina de Gabarain the Spanish soprano who had a great success in the part and was to play the role every time the work was revived until 1956. Opposite her as the Prince was Juan Oncina, also Spanish, who was one of the leading tenors during this decade and appeared at Glyndebourne almost annually.

Fig. 66, 63a

Fig. 67, 63b

Fig. 68, 63d

1952

64 Letter From Paris
Play in three acts by Dodie Smith (from Henry James' novel *The Reverberator*). Presented by Tennent Productions Limited at the Aldwych Theatre on 10th October, 1952, directed by Peter Glenville; setting and costumes by Oliver Messel; music by Ronald Emanuel. With Brenda Bruce as Francie Dosson, Nicholas Phipps as Charles Waterlow, Jessie Evans as Delia Dosson, Peter Barkworth as Gaston Probert, Maxine Audley as Suzanne de Brecourt, Michael Nightingale as Alphonse de Brecourt, Lawrence Davidson as Maxime de Cliche, Marjorie Stewart as Marguerite de Cliche and Nicholas Hannen as Mr Probert.

a **Costume design** for Gaston; ink, ch, w, g ($14\frac{3}{4} \times 10$)

b **Costume design** for Francie, in Act 2, scene 1: ink, chalk, g, and swatches ($14\frac{3}{4} \times 10$)

c **Costume design** for Delia; pencil, chalk, w, g. Signed ($14\frac{3}{4} \times 10$) (Fig. 69).

d **Design** for a hat for Delia; p, chalk, w, g. (Fig. 70).

e **Black and white photograph** of the set in Act 2, scene 3, showing from left to right: Maxine Audley, Michael Nightingale, Brenda Bruce, Lawrence Davidson, Marjorie Stewart and Nicholas Hannen ($7\frac{3}{4} \times 9\frac{1}{2}$). Angus McBean.

S.C. 38 c. designs.

Dodie Smith's play from James' novel about the snobbery attached to acceptable and unacceptable Americans who can and cannot marry into the best French families, only ran for three weeks, and the reaction of the critics was of only mild interest. Kenneth Tynan, then beginning to establish himself (the *Evening Standard*), found it the least irritating amongst the mediocre plays of the week. Messel's costumes (*c*.1880 in period) owe something to a study of Manet and early Renoir.

◀ Fig. 69, 64c   Fig. 70, 64d ▲

1953

65 Homage to the Queen
The Coronation Ballet; one-act; choreography by Frederick Ashton. Music by Malcolm Arnold. Assistant to Oliver Messel, Carl Toms. Presented on 2nd June 1953, Royal Opera House, London, by the Sadler's Wells (now Royal) Ballet. With Margot Fonteyn as The Queen of the Air, Michael Somes as her Consort, Violetta Elvin as The Queen of the Waters and John Hart as her Consort, Nadia Nerina as The Queen of the Earth, and Alexis Rassine as her Consort, etc.
Synopsis: Entrée – Procession of the Four Elements, Earth, Water, Fire and Air. Each Queen and her Court dance a divertissement.
Apotheosis: Homage to the Queen.

a **Costume design** for The Queen of the Air, p, g, gold paint. Inscribed: 'For Margot Fonteyn'. Signed. ($14\frac{3}{4} \times 10$) (Fig. 72)

b **Projected costume** design for the Queen of the Air's Consort; p, w, gold paint.
Inscribed: 'Michael Somes'. Signed ($14\frac{3}{4} \times 10$)

The final costume was assymetric, to match that of the Queen of the Air. The wings were retained, but only worn in the formal processions, being removed for the extremely acrobatic *pas de deux* that formed the main part of the 'Air' sequence.

c **Costume design** for the male dancer in the Water *pas de trois* (Brian Shaw). w, g, gold paint.
Inscribed: (illegible) 'on shoulders [like a William & Mary] bed.' Signed ($14\frac{3}{4} \times 10$)

Fig. 71 The Queen of the Waters and her Consort, in *Homage to the Queen* (1953). **65**. Houston Rogers

d **Costume design** for an Attendant on the Queen of the Waters. Ch, p, w, g. Signed ($14\frac{3}{4} \times 10$)

e **Costume** for an Attendant on the Queen of the Waters.
Low cut sleeveless bodice; cotton foundation overlaid with flesh pink cotton and top layer of blue cotton, except at centre front where pink cotton overlaid with a toning net is visible; the sides and back bodice are overlaid with over-lapping sections of crin, painted blue, brown, green and gold to create a fin-like effect. Narrow elastic shoulder straps support a fine net and are surmounted by narrow curved petals of moulded plastic, which carry wires supporting crystal bead drops *tremblant*; the join of straps to the low back are concealed by two concertina-pleated upright points of crin, edged with sellotape. Below a line of blue cotton at the hip line, the skirt is surmounted by a peplum of milliner's buckram with scalloped lower edge, completely overlaid with crin painted blue, brown, green and gold with occasional strips of narrow velvet ribbon, creating a fin-like effect. Beneath the peplum stiffened supports create a small farthingale. At the centre front of the peplum an S-shaped motif of raised crin edged with gold lurex and knotted crin cord simulating coral. Mid-calf length skirt of a single layer of gathered jade nylon organza. Originally the dress was worn with a fitted head-dress and ruff (not shown).
Made by Olivia Cranmer.
Theatre Museum; given by the Royal Opera House, Covent Garden.

f **Costume** detail sketches for Water divertissement. Pencil. Inscribed: 'Water' ($14\frac{3}{4} \times 10$)

g **Costume design** for Queen Elizabeth I in the Apotheosis. P, g, gold and silver paint.
Inscribed: '(illegible) [gold (illegible)] trimming.' Signed ($22 \times 25\frac{1}{2}$)

h **Costume** for Queen Elizabeth I, in the Apotheosis. Costume in the style of an Elizabethan Court dress of fine gold lurex figured brocade, with square-cut neckline, exaggerated pointed front panel simulating a stomacher, very full long sleeves and boldly pleated hooped skirt.
The stiffened front panel of the bodice is of fine silver lurex brocade over-laid with two layers of blue-grey scene gauze, decorated with a 'ladder' pattern bisected by a central line, of gold tinsel edged with slightly ruched blue-grey crin braid threaded with gold lurex strip; behind the centre line is another band of crin; at each junction of the 'ladder' and centre line is a stylized flower formed of a large rhinestone surrounded by bronze leather fringe. At the lower point of the panel are six rhinestones surrounded by gold lurex fringed braid in cruciform formation. At the neck is a 'poppy' of orange-red leather with a bronze leather centre. The back of the bodice is of cream artificial taffeta.
The very full sleeves taper to the wrist; down the front of each sleeve is a panel of fine silver lurex brocade overlaid with two layers of grey-blue scene gauze; fixed to the panel are four angled strips of gold tinsel ribbon; laid diagonally across these are very broad bands of slightly ruched grey crin woven with gold lurex strip and a gold tinsel ribbon centre, fixed to the gold tinsel ribbon at each crossing by large flat stylized flowers of orange-red leather overlaid with a bronze film, studded at the centre with a large rhinestone surrounded by gold lurex lace braid.
The front panel of the skirt is of silver tissue overlaid with two layers of grey-blue scene gauze; at the hem, set between bands of bold gold lurex lace braid, is a row of stylized flowers of orange-red leather overlaid with a bronze film, studded at the centre with a large rhinestone surrounded with gold lurex lace braid. Standing very proud of the panel are alternating rows of large sunbursts and 'Tudor' architectural motifs; the sunbursts are large leather shapes painted bronze-gold, over which are fixed lengths of wavy gold tinsel ribbon covered pipe-cleaners, alternating with pairs of gold tinsel ribbon covered wires, around a central rhinestone set around with four rhinestones, each stone surrounded by gold lurex fringe braid; the architectural motifs are formed of four large loops of bronzed leather painted with white spots around a central rhinestone set around with four rhinestones, each stone surrounded by gold lurex fringe braid.
The bodice is lined with cotton and fastens at the back with hooks and eyes. The skirt is lined with bolton sheeting. Head-dress, wig and winged ruff are modern replacements.

Lent by the Archives, Royal Opera House, Covent Garden.

i **Sketches** for projected processions (Fire, Air). Pencil, pen and ink ($12\frac{3}{10} \times 18\frac{7}{10}$)

j **Sketches** for projected processions (Earth, Water). Pencil, pen and ink ($13\frac{3}{5} \times 21\frac{1}{5}$)

k **Head-dress** for the Queen of the Air.
Four rows of covered wire shaped across the head, the front forming a shallow V at the centre front, the back formed into points. Fixed on the wire, graduating from being short at the sides to higher at the centre, are wire supported crin mounts threaded with fine gold strip, the centre base of each

supporting a large oval or round faceted rhinestone; around each stone are 'flames' of gilded leather and pearl iridescent plastic 'flutes'; the largest motifs at the centre front and on top of the head are surmounted by twisted wire supporting iridescent beads.
Made by Hugh Skillen.
Lent by the Archives, Royal Opera House, Covent Garden.

l **Head-dress** for the Queen of the Waters.
Covered wires to fit across the front and crown of the head. At the centre front is a semi-circle of 'petals' in gold wired cord, the centre petal enclosing a large oval pearl and trimmed with three small hanging pearls. To either side of the head is a wing-like mount of green painted net on a wire frame with 'feathers' delineated by narrow gold braid and filled with iridescent pearlised studs. Across the head are graduated loops of heavy wire covered in gold metal braid, the centre loop being double and enclosing a large iridescent pearl; similar pearls are mounted at the lower edge and another side loop encloses a round blue jewel. Across the back of the head hang three loose loops (one missing) of solf cord covered with a random assemblage of shells and coral, pearl and red iridescent beads.
Made by Hugh Skillen.
Lent by the Archives, Royal Opera House, Covent Garden.

Messel was the obvious choice as designer for Frederick Ashton's ballet to celebrate the Coronation of Queen Elizabeth II; the formal, courtly nature of the theme obviously suggested a Jacobean masque or court ballet. Inspired by the subject, he produced several sheets of sketches for processions – which were certainly never given such elaborate choreographic form by Ashton. More elaborate processions might, in fact, have given grandeur to the Apotheosis, where the figure of Elizabeth I hands the newly-crowned Elizabeth II the orb and sceptre, which was something of an anti-climax to the work.

Some of the costumes came in for harsh citicism, though the exhibited costume for an Attendant on the Queen of the Waters was an exquisite realisation of the original design. On the whole, however, Messel's designs were not sympathetically interpreted by the costume-makers, who, one feels, had little understanding of the Masque traditions and the effects he was trying to recreate. Richard Buckle in the *Observer* (7th June, 1953), well aware of what Messel was trying to achieve, called him 'an artist in the great tradition of Inigo Jones, adept at producing effects of splendour, fantasy and romance'.

1954

66 **The Dark is Light Enough**
Verse play in three acts by Christopher Fry, presented by H. M. Tennent Productions Limited on 30th April, 1954 at the Aldwych Theatre, directed by Peter Brook; costumes and sets by Oliver Messel. Music by Leslie Bridgewater. With Edith Evans as the Countess, James Donald as Gettner, Margaret Johnston as Gelda and Peter Barkworth as Stephan; etc.

a **Model,** No. 51.

b **Costume design** for the Countes in Act 2 with swatch: ch, p, w, g. Signed (15 × 10)

c **Costume design** for the Countess in Act 3; ch, w, g. Signed (15 × 10)

d **Costume design** for Gelda (perhaps for the New York production); ch, w, ink, swatches. Signed ($14\frac{3}{4}$ × 10)

e **Costume design** for Stephan in Act 2, with swatches; ch, w ($14\frac{3}{4}$ × 10)
This design is for Paul Roebling who played in the American production.

f **Costume design** for Bella; ch and w (15 × 10) (Fig. 73).

g **Wig design** for Gelda (perhaps for Marian Winters in the New York production), to show the style of wig required; ink, ch, g (15 × 10) (Fig. 74).

h **Design** for the ceramic stove, Acts 1 and 3; p, ink, on tracing paper (13 × 9)

i **Head-dress** for the Countess (Edith Evans).
Bonnet worn across the head, of an elliptical wire frame covered with black cotton net latticed with black velvet baby ribbon, around which is a gathered band of crin ribbon overlaid down the centre with narrow black velvet ribbon, which extends at the sides into loops; this band is bordered with a goffered frill of a novelty crin braid with a narrow gathered frill of black lace. Added to the front edge is a novelty crin braid frill.

j **Head-dress** for the Countess (Edith Evans).
Head-band of stiff wire to which is attached a longer band of double wire bound together with off white net ending below the ears. Over the head is a serpentine frill of crin ribbon between each loop of

Fig. 72, 65a

Fig. 73, 66f

Fig. 74, 66g

which is set a gilt filigree bead mount on which is a smocked pearl topped with a tiny gold bead. To the back of the pearls rises a gathered frill of crin with gold metal strip edging. Below the band at either side of the head is a large oval rosette of a deep crin frill-edged with narrow crin ribbon woven with gold metal strip and off-white thread at the edge. Within this is a bold crin frill edged with narrow black lace. Down the centre are two flower rosettes of crin interlaced with gold metal strip centred with rhinestone quatrefoils and at the bottom of each rosette are three loops of narrow black velvet ribbon.

k **Hair-ornament** for the Countess worn by Edith Evans.
Curved spray of artificial flowers worn as a hair ornament on an eighteeenth century wig. The flowers are set on covered wire simulating stalks. At the base is a cluster of mauve, pink and cream old fashioned roses and rosebuds in shaded cotton and velvet, set amid leaves of dark green cotton. From the cluster curve sprays of stephanotis-like flowers of creamy pink waxed cotton with pale blue painted centres; below is a spray of forget-me-nots of white and pale blue velvet with yellow centres. Scattered amid the naturalistic flowers are seven long and short stemmed stylized open seed pods, formed on a centre pearl around which are seven small gold and bronze oval beads each surmounted with a seed pearl; at the centre of the curve are stylized leaf fronds of looped gold tinsel ribbon on green threads, the centre stems of which are set with alternating small square cut rhinestones and faceted 'quartz'; below are two small stems simulating lily-of-the-valley of gold covered wire from which hang graduated drop pearls *tremblant*.

l **Muff ornament** for the Countess, worn by Edith Evans.
Miniature version of the large hair spray, with the addition of a top curved frond from which hang wired oval milky glass beads each topped with a seed pearl.

m **Black and white photograph** of Acts 1 and 3 (10 × 8). Angus McBean.
Although a detailed design exists for **k** and both head-dresses were clearly labelled *The Dark is Light Enough*, neither appear in photographs of the production, though Edith Evans did wear a head-dress similar in style to **l** but much fuller and worn further back on the head. It is likely that both proved unsuitable when seen on stage, either because they did not 'read' effectively, or even, perhaps, in the case of **l** worn forward and over the head, impaired hearing. Both are, however, charming examples of Messel's period design.

S.C. 3 models, 9 set details, 31 c. design. 2 hats, 2 head-dresses.

This was the third time Messel had designed for a Fry play, and this one the author subtitled 'a winter story'. For the sake of completeness it is worth noting that the plays for the other seasons are: Spring (*The Lady's Not For Burning*, 1949) pp. 117, 119, Autumn (*Venus Observed*, 1950, written for Laurence Olivier), and Summer (*A Yard of Sun*, 1970). Fry's new play was about tolerance, set at the time of the Austro-Hungarian Revolution which began in 1848. The Austrian Countess rescues and shelters her mean son-in-law despite his being a deserter. She looks after a Hungarian rebel also. Thus she is apolitical, on the side of suffering and tolerance. This point is reinforced by the fact that she is herself dying. Her dying (Act 3) was regarded by most of the critics as one of the most accomplished moments of many in Dame Edith Evans' performance. The strength and yet weakness of the play, according to most of the reviewers, lay in the fact that the action related too directly to the Countess whose pacificism was too inactive to generate theatrical conflict. Despite this the beauty of the language, more tightly disciplined than that of *The Lady* five years before, was appreciated as well as the excellent supporting playing. Much of that was due to the good casting eye of the director but it is a sad fact of economic life that West End productions with such large casts are no longer possible. Even in the Fifties, Tennent's were almost the only management who could afford to mount productions of around a dozen performers. To some extent Tennent productions in the Fifties performed a service which now has been more exploratively and comprehensively filled by the establishment of the Royal Shakespeare Company (1960) and the National Theatre (1962). The play ran almost exactly seven months in London and then went to New York where it opened in 1955 with Miss Katharine Cornell and Tyrone Power in the leads. The New York critics gave the play a mixed reception on the grounds that its meaning was too elusive. But they had high praise for the acting. The run was of sixty-nine performances. Elsewhere in this book (p. 24) Christopher Fry speaks of Oliver Messel's designs for his plays including that under discussion.

Fig. 75 Sheet of colours chosen by Messel as a key for *Il Barbiere di Siviglia* (1954). **67b**

1954

67 Il Barbiere di Siviglia *(The Barber of Seville)*
Opera (1816) in two acts, by Rossini; libretto by Sterbini after Beaumarchais' comedy of the same name (1775). Presented by the Glyndebourne Festival Opera at Glyndebourne on 10th June, 1954, directed by Carl Ebert; costumes and settings by Oliver Messel. With Bruscantini as Figaro, Graziella Sciutti as Rosina, Oncina as Count Almaviva, and Wallace as Bartolo, etc. Conductor, Gui.

a **Model**, No. 53.

b **Sheet showing** the palette Messel chose to use for this production to achieve colour harmony which was his usual practice; w, g. Signed ($14\frac{3}{4} \times 10$) (Fig. 75)

c **Costume design** for Rosina, Act 1; w, g. Signed ($14\frac{3}{4} \times 10$)

d **Costume design** for Count Almaviva; ch, g, gold paint. Signed ($14\frac{3}{4} \times 10$)

e **Costume design** for Figaro; ch, w. Signed ($14\frac{3}{4} \times 10$)

f **Costume design** for Bartolo; ch, w. Signed ($14\frac{3}{4} \times 10$) (Fig. 76).

g **Costume designs** for the soldiers; ch, g, silver paint. Signed ($14\frac{3}{4} \times 10$)

h **Costume design** for the valet; p, w, g ($14\frac{3}{4} \times 10$)

i **Black and white photograph** of Act 2 (5×7). By Guy Gravett.
S.C. 2 models, 5 set details, 46 c. designs.

This production was one of Glyndebourne's great successes in a period when its public rediscovered Rossini and made him all the rage. The singers were already tried and tested in this composer and also in working together; thus Bruscantini's Figaro was well matched by Oncina's Almaviva and Ian Wallace's Bartolo. The Rosina was a newcomer, a highly attractive and born soubrette – Graziella Sciutti – who was to become well liked as Susanna, Despina, and in other roles. The fast action and amusing situations, particularly involving Rosina, Figaro and Bartolo, made this Carl Ebert's most popular and so, liked pieces of direction.

Messel chose a palette which echoed the contrasted and thus dramatic coloration of Goya's paintings. Perhaps one of the reasons why he did so was the oncoming production in 1955 of *Le Nozze di Figaro* to celebrate the twenty-first birthday of Glyndebourne. This opera has, of course, the same writer (Beaumarchais) as a source, but not the same play. Despite the popularity of this production of *Il Barbiere* it had only two revivals; one was at the Edinburgh Festival.

1954

68 Le Comte Ory *(Count Ory)*
Opera (1823) by Rossini in two acts, libretto by Scribe and Poirson from their one-act comedy of 1817. This production presented at the Edinburgh International Festival by the Glyndebourne Festival Society on 23rd August, 1954, directed by Carl Ebert. Settings and costumes by Oliver Messel. Choreography by Pauline Grant. With Bruscantini as Raimbaud, Oncina as Count Ory, Sari Barabas as Adèle and Monica Sinclair as Ragonde, etc. Conductor, Gui.

a **Model**, No. 52.

b **Sheet of studies** for reference of the colours used for costumes for Court members of the cast ch, w, gold paint. Signed (15×10)

c **Costume design** for Count Ory, ch, w, g. Signed (15×10)

d **Two costume designs** for the Countess Adèle in Acts 1 and 2; ch, w, g. Signed. Each (15×10) (Fig. 77).

e **Swatches of the materials** to be used for the costumes of the Haymaking Girls, attached to paper ($14\frac{3}{4} \times 10$)

f **Costume design** for a Crusader Knight, ch, w, gold paint. Signed ($14\frac{3}{4} \times 10$)

g **Costume design** for the Tutor, Act 1; p, ch, w, g, gold paint. Signed ($14\frac{3}{4} \times 10$)

S.C. 2 models, 30 set details, 54 costume designs.

To have to design two Rossini operas in one year was a challenge. The setting of *Le Comte Ory* was medieval, and it is not an *opera buffa* like *Il Barbiere* but an ironic philandering tale written by Rossini not so long after he had settled in Paris, and intended for a sophisticated audience. With his usual adherence to period, Messel concentrated on such designs as are found in the *Lady and the Unicorn* tapestries, and in Flemish and Netherlandish

Fig. 76, 67f

painting. As may be seen from the sheet of women's costume colours, shown here, the tonality chosen was a cool one, which would have looked odd in an *opera buffa* but goes very well with this story about the Countess Adèle and her companion Ragonde who have been left at the castle without men, because of the demands of the Crusades. Seeking advice from a hermit close by (they are in fact consulting the lecherous Count Ory), they find next he and his followers entering the castle disguised as nuns. The ensuing circumstances, with the 'nuns' raiding the wine cellars, are imaginable, but it is all sorted out in the nick of time (unfortunately for some), by the return of the Crusaders. The young Hungarian soprano, Sari Barabas, appearing for the second time at Glyndebourne, made a great success of the Countess Adèle, and sang the part in all the revivals, including the performance in Paris in 1958, where Glyndebourne had an enthusiastic reception. Count Ory was sung by Juan Oncina, by this date a very experienced Rossinian, and there was solid backing by Monica Sinclair as Ragonde making her first appearance in the role, which she was to sing in every subsequent revival.

1954

69 **House of Flowers**
A musical in two acts and thirteen scenes by Truman Capote;[19] music by Harold Arlen; lyrics by Capote and Arlen. Choreography by Herbert Ross; directed by Peter Brook. Settings, masks, and costumes by Oliver Messel. Presented at the Alvin Theatre, New York, on 30th December, 1954, with Diahann Carroll as Ottilie, Pearl Bailey as Madame Fleur, Ray Walston as Captain Jones and Juanita Hall as Madame Tango; etc.

a **Three colour transparencies** of scenes from *House of Flowers*. Richard Avedon Studios.

b **Costume design** for a carnival dancer; ch, w (15×10) (Fig. 78)

c **Costume design** for Royal; ch, w, g. Signed ($13\frac{3}{4} \times 11$)

d **Costume design** for Pansy at the carnival; ch, w, g ($13\frac{3}{4} \times 11$)

e **Costume design** for the Chief of Police at the carnival; ch, w ($13\frac{3}{4} \times 11$) (Fig. 79)

f **Message** scribbled on the reverse of a prop design for *The Little Hut*, reading; 'gone to bed at 6.0/sleep for 4 hours/done some nice work for the masks/love O'.

S.C. 69 pieces of a set, 21 pieces of props, costume designs, 4 CT's.

This production is something unexpected in Messel's work (q.v. the set and that for No. 57). The story of two rival madames of bordellos, in their vying complicating the love-life of a girl who has managed to stay virtuous in such surroundings, is a splendid excuse for exotic settings, and gorgeous costumes, as in the carnival scene. The set is reminiscent of *Ring Round the Moon* in its skeletal appearance and this may not be coincidence as Peter Brook was the same director. The New York critics found the show exhilarating, very good to look at, the critic of the New York Post thinking it the best thing visually he had seen for a long time; in this he was not out of line. The trouble with the show was that it began humourously then failed to deliver, and invention began to tail off before the end. Despite this the show was popular and ran for 165 performances. Pearl Bailey, Ray Walston and Juanita Hall were ideally cast and praised. The evening marked the début of Diahann Carroll as Ottilie, the ingénue, and she too was praised for the charm of her singing and freshness of personality.

Further material on this production is to be found on the SLIDE TAPE, Room 73, No. 99.

Fig. 77, 68d

Fig. 78, 69b

Fig. 79, 69e

1955

70 Zémire et Azor *(Zémir and Azor)*
Opera (1771), by Grétry, in four acts, libretto by Marmontel from La Chausée's comedy *Amour par Amour* (1742). Presented on 11th May, 1955, at the Theatre Royal, Bath during the Bath Festival. Directed by Anthony Besch. Choreography by William Chappell. Settings and costumes by Oliver Messel. With Huguette Boulangeot as *Zémire*, and Michael Sénéchal as *Azor*; etc.

The costume for *Zémire* remade for this exhibition is No. 32 in Room 71.

a **Costume design** for Zémire (Beauty); p, w, g, gold paint. Signed (15 × 10)

b **Costume design** for Azor (The Beast); ch, g, gold paint. Signed (15 × 10)

c **Costume design** for a Sprite; ink, w, g. Signed (15 × 10)

d **Black and white photograph** of the set for Act 2 ($5\frac{1}{2} \times 9\frac{1}{2}$). By Tony Armstrong Jones.

S.C. 2 models, 62 set details, 19 costume designs and details, 2 turbans, 3 accessories.

André Grétry (1741–1813), wrote about fifty operas of which *Zémire et Azor* is one of the several most performed. Grétry was not a great composer though he was influential (like many), on the young Mozart. The opera makes an attractive festival piece where there is no financial undertaking on the expectation of a long run. The story is a variant of Perrault's *Beauty and the Beast*.

If there is to be an ideal Messel décor, this one could vie for the title, for here he mixes fantasy, elegance, beauty of colour and charming architectural settings. The fantasy element in the costumes is very well matched to the other-worldliness of the story, and may bring reminders to some minds of those Jean Cocteau invented for his film *La Belle et La Bête* (1945).

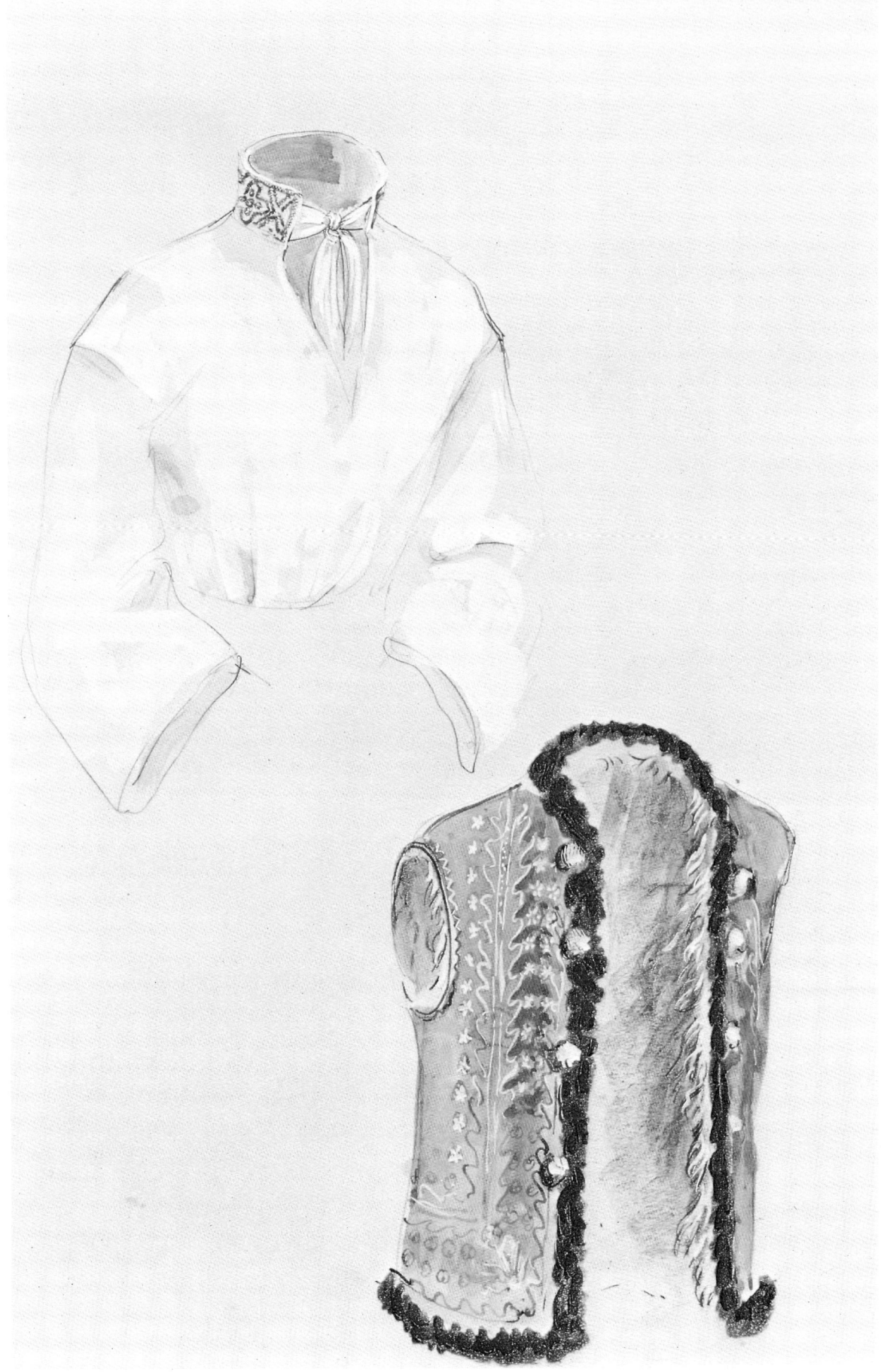

Room 73
1955

71 Arms and the Man
Film; to have been made by Alexander Korda from the play (1894) by G. B. Shaw. It would probably have been directed by Peter Glenville, and starred Claire Bloom as Raina, and Alec Guinness (probably) as Sergius.

a **Set design** for Raina's bedroom (in Act I of *the play*), ink, w, ch, g. Signed (14 × 17)

b **Costume design** for Raina's nightdress (in Act I of *the play*), ch, ink, w, g. Signed (15 × 10)

c **Costume design** for Bluntschli as an officer, p, w, g (15 × 10)

d **Costume design** for Catherine, p, ch, w, g. Signed (15 × 10)

e **Costume designs** for peasant woman in the market square.

f **Costume design details** for shoes; ink, w, g (15 × 10)

g **Costume design details** for jackets; ink, w, g (15 × 10) (Fig. 80).

h **Reference photograph** showing embroidery on the back of a newly married's dance costume. This is one of a number in the Collection for use as a source (10 × 8). Unknown photographer.

S.C. 5 set drawings, 93 costume designs, 27 photographs of costumes and details.

Arms and the Man was the first of Shaw's plays to be seen publicly. The performance was financed by Annie Horniman and presented by Florence Farr at the Avenue Theatre on 21st April, 1894. The play is about a revolution in the Balkans which Shaw (unlike any of his contemporaries), treats in a witty and irreverent way, for its false heroics. If this film had been made it would have become the second with this subject. Shaw himself provided the screenplay for the first version made in 1932, by BIP (Wardour); director Cecil Lewis.

1955

72 Le Nozze di Figaro (*The Marriage of Figaro*)
Opera (1786) by Mozart, in four acts; libretto by da Ponte, from Beaumarchais' *La Folle Journée, ou Le Mariage de Figaro*, 1778. Presented by the Glyndebourne Festival at Glyndebourne on 8th June, 1955; directed by Carl Ebert; sets and costumes by Oliver Messel; conductor Gui. With Bruscantini as Figaro, Elena Rizzieri as Susanna, Calabrese as Count Almaviva, Sena Jurinac as the Countess, and Frances Bible and Risë Stevens alternating the role of Cherubino; etc.

a **Sheet of pencil studies** principally for Acts 3 and 4 (15 × 10)

b **Design** for a lamp probably for the garden in Act 4; ch, g (25 × 19)

c **Scaled-up drawing** for the garden set in Act 4; ink on tracing-paper. (Fig. 81).

d **Costume design** for Susanna, p, ch, w, g. Signed (15 × 10)

e **Costume design** for the Count in Act 1, p, ch, g, gold paint. Signed (15 × 10)

f **Costume design** for the Countess disguised as Susanna, Act 4; p, ch, w, g. Signed (15 × 10)

g **Costume plot** for the principals, prepared probably by the director for Messel's guidance. Only one page shown. Foolscap.

S.C. 1 model unmade up, 54 set details, 57 costume designs, 18 swatches, 5 wig designs.

Le Nozze di Figaro, at Glyndebourne, has always been a rather hallowed work. It was the very first production at the Opera House and has been revived fourteen times since with widely differing casts, conductors and designers. It has only been surpassed in this by one other opera of Mozart's, *Così fan Tutte*, which has been revived one more time, and was the only other production in the foundation year, 1934. The conductor in 1934 was Fritz Busch whose conducting, revered by many, can still be heard on the set of records issued by HMV that year. In a retrospective review[20] of the first production Dyneley Hussey, the Mozart scholar, recalling it stresses, (what is often ignored today), how Busch brought out the ill-feeling, which lies in the music, between Figaro and the Count, not merely because of the latter's attempt to exercise seigneurial rights over Figaro's bride-to-be, Susanna, but because of the class conflict. The production of 1955 which celebrated Glyndebourne's twenty-first year of existence was much looked forward to but never

Fig. 80, 71g

over-shadowed the first production. In the first place, Busch's sensitive conducting, that yielded to every nuance in the music, was replaced by the driving ebullient rhythms of Vittorio Gui whose competence as a Rossinian has never been in question, but whose Mozart playing was superficial. Perhaps reacting to this the singers were dispirited, even Sena Jurinac, appearing as the Countess for the first time, disappointed. Perhaps expectations had been placed unfairly high. Revivals (and there were five subsequently until 1965) generally went better. Joan Sutherland made her first appearance at Glyndebourne in 1956 singing the Countess and was well received. Not so much later she was to leave this kind of world and concentrate on the *bel canto* of Bellini, Donizetti and others. Two years later Geraint Evans sang Figaro for the first time, the first of many occasions when his unique qualities as a great actor-singer were brought to the role.

Messel's décor and costumes were well received, though perhaps they veer on the side of prettiness, which was perhaps at its richest in the Garden Scene, Act 4. Probably the one who has put it best regarding Messel's treatment of Mozart is Andrew Porter quoted (source unspecified), by Spike Hughes (q.v. Bib. 9b): 'The great merit of his themes is that they impose nothing on the music, but seem to spring from it. Although intensely personal they reflect and decorate Mozart whereas less sensitive designers try to interpret him.'

▼ Fig. 81, 72c

Fig. 82 Portrait of Oliver Messel *c.*1956. Tony Armstrong Jones ▶

Snake.

1958

73 The School for Scandal

A comedy (1777) in five acts by Richard Brinsley Sheridan. Presented at the Det Ny Theatre, Copenhagen, on 19th September, 1958; translated by Frank Jaeger, directed by Sam Besekow. Sets and costumes by Oliver Messel. With Ebbe Rose as Sir Peter Teazle, Bodil Kjer as Lady Teazle, Olaf Ussing as Sir Oliver Surface, Olaf Nordgreen as Joseph Surface, Inge Hvid Moller as Lady Sneerwell; etc.

a **Costume design** for Lady Teazle, in the screen scene (Act 4, Scene 3), p, ch, w, gold paint. Signed (15×10) (Fig. 10)

b **Costume design** for Joseph Surface, p, w, g, gold paint. Signed ($22 \times 15\frac{1}{2}$)

c **Costume design** for Sir Oliver, ch, w, g, gold paint. Signed (15×10)

d **Costume design** for Snake, ch, w, g, gold paint. Signed ($14\frac{3}{4} \times 10$) (Fig. 83).

e **Costume design** for Lady Sneerwell in Act 5, ch, w, g, gold paint. Signed (14×10)

S.C. 37 set details, 36 costume designs.

It is probably indicative of the similarity of human nature elsewhere that Sheridan's play has proved so popular in translation. According to Lisbet Grandjean of the Danish Theatre Museum (who kindly provided details of the two Danish productions with Messel décors in this Exhibition), the performance, scenery and costumes were highly praised by the critics. A curious footnote[21] to theatre history is the fact that this play ran for nearly four years in Moscow during the Russo-German war, 1941–5.

1958

74 Samson

Oratorio (1743), in three acts, by Handel; libretto by Newburgh Hamilton from Milton's *Samson Agonistes*. Presented at Covent Garden by the Covent Garden Opera on 15th November, 1958, after some performances at the Leeds Festival in the previous October. Directed by Hubert Graf; settings and costumes by Oliver Messel, assisted by Carl Toms and Rosemary Wilkins; choreography by Meriel Evans. With Jon Vickers as Samson, Elisabeth Lindermeier as Dalila, Joseph Rouleau as Manoah, David Kelly as Harapha and Joan Sutherland, as an Israelite woman. Conductor, Leppard.

a **Scene design** the Temple falling 'all done in shadow, silhouette, lighting, etc.' for Act 3. Ink and charcoal (10×15)

b **Costume design** for Samson, chained, p, ch, w. Signed (15×10). The pose is based on one of Michelangelo's sculptures of *The Dying Slave*.

c **Costume design** for the High Priest of Dagon, ch, w, gold paint. Signed (15×10)

d **Costume design** for a Masked Official of Dagon's, ch, w. Signed ($14\frac{3}{4} \times 10$)

e **Costume design** for a Reveller at Dagon's Feast, ch, g, gold paint. Signed (15×10) (Fig. 84).

f **Costume design** for a Negro Slave, ch, g, silver and gold paints. Signed (15×10) (Fig. 85).

g **Costume design** for Dagon the God, ink, silver and gold paints. Signed (15×10) (Figs. 86).

h **Costume design** for Herapha, p, g, gold and silver paints (15×10)

i **Black and white photograph** of Act 3 (10×8). By Houston Rogers.

S.C. 33 pieces of a model, 39 costume designs, 11 designs for props.

This oratorio of Handel's which was very often performed in his life-time was presented at the Royal Opera House to commemorate the bicentenary of the composer's death; it was also the first occasion the work had been performed at Covent Garden. The effectiveness of treating this oratorio in such a way that the power of the chorus and its limited characterisation contributed to a monumental effect was commented on by the reviewers. This method of presenting an oratorio as if it were an opera was introduced in the late Twenties probably because the success of Stravinsky's *Oedipus Rex* (1928). Jon Vickers and Joan Sutherland had excellent notices. *The Times* and the *Sunday Times* critics felt that the décor, although effective, was not suitable, something sterner, bleaker, more in keeping with the urgency of the music, should have been adopted.

Fig. 83, 73d

Fig. 84, 74e

Fig. 85, 74f

Fig. 86, 748

1959

75 Der Rosenkavalier (*The Knight of the Rose*)
Opera (1911), in three acts by Richard Strauss; libretto by Hugo von Hofsmannsthal. Presented by the Glyndebourne Festival Opera at Glyndebourne on 28th May, 1959; directed by Carl Ebert. Settings and costumes by Oliver Messel assisted by Carl Toms. With Elisabeth Söderström as Octavian, Anneliese Rothenberger as Sophie, Régine Crespin as the Feldmarschallin, and Oscar Czerwenka as Baron Ochs; etc. Conductor, Ludwig.

a **Model**, No. 55.

b **Design** for the rug in the Feldmarschallin's bedroom, Act 1. Scaled up. P, ch, and w ($9\frac{3}{4} \times 14\frac{3}{4}$)
'Charles Bravery' is a reference to the scene painter who often worked with Oliver Messel, at Glyndebourne.

c **Design** for the border across the proscenium for Act 2; scaled. Ink on tracing paper ($14\frac{1}{2} \times 22$)

d **Costume design** for the Feldmarschallin; ch, ink, w, g, gold paint. Signed (15×10)

e **Costume design** for Sophie in Act 3; ch, w, g. Signed (15×10) (Fig. 87).

f **Costume design** for Octavian in Act 2, presenting the Rose; ch, w, silver and gold paint. Signed (15×10) (Fig. 88).

g **Costume design** for Baron Ochs; ch, w, g, silver and gold paint. Signed (15×10)

h **Costume design** for ruffians in Act 3; ch, w, g. Signed (15×10) (Fig. 89).

i **Costume design** for waiters at the Inn, in Act 3; ch, w. Signed (15×10)

j **The Rose** of gilded and silvered wire, gilded leather and glass used in this production ($11 \times 6\frac{3}{4}$). Lent by his sister Anne, Countess of Rosse.

S.C. 3 models, 51 costume designs, 4 set details, 4 tracings of set details.

This production was mounted as a special tribute to its retiring director, Carl Ebert, who celebrated, in 1959, twenty-five years of artistic work at Glyndebourne, exactly as long as had the house itself. Unfortunately a work written for the Dresden Hofoper was ill-suited to the small Glyndebourne stage and orchestra pit and the general impression in reading the reports, is of too much sound, and of too much jostling of characters and scenery on stage. Nevertheless, Anneliese Rothenburger and Elisabeth Söderström were highly praised and Régine Crespin slightly less so. For Philip Hope-Wallace (*The Guardian*) Messel's sets were among the best he had ever done; whilst for Edmund Tracey (*The Observer*), Messel's sets were pallid and lacking personality. But the weight of opinion was in favour of Messel whose last production for Glyndebourne this was. To have been represented by design work for eleven years in any opera house is something of a record for a British designer; thus, the danger of overkill was probably always a likelihood. Messel's work at Glyndebourne set a new level for the design standards of the house, and his followers have been of the quality expected at the big London theatres.

This is not saying that the pre-Messel period was without luminaries, but since the War, with state-subsidised theatre throughout the country, the number of experienced designers has grown enormously. Messel's best achievements, where his particular gifts were well-matched to the works, were probably these four productions, not put in order of merit: *Il Barbiere di Siviglia, La Cenerentola, Die Entführung aus dem Serail, Le Comte Ory*. But anyone knowing Glyndebourne in those years may suggest others.

Fig. 87, 75e

Fig. 88, 75f

166 * DER ROSENKAVALIER

Fig. 89,
75h

1964

76 Traveller Without Luggage
A 'pièce noire' *Le Voyageur sans Bagages*, 1937, by Jean Anouilh. Translated by Lucienne Hill. Presented by Masterson and Twain at the ANTA Theatre, New York, on 18th September, 1964, directed by Robert Lewis. With Ben Gazzara as Gaston, Mildred Dunnock as Madame Renaud, Margaret Braidwood as the Duchess, Stephen Elliott as Georges Renaud, William Cottrell as the butler, Nancy Wickwire as Valentine, etc.

a **Study** of a hare, ch, w (15×10) (Fig. 90)

b **Study** of a Great Indian Hornbill, ch, ink, w, g ($14\frac{3}{4} \times 10$) (Fig. 91).

c **Study** of a toucan, ch, w ($14\frac{3}{4} \times 10$)

d **Black and white photograph** of the set of Act 2 (8×10), unidentified photographer.

S.C. 8 parts of a model, 22 pieces of stage furniture, 6 designs for animals, some photographs of model sets.

The subject of this early play of Anouilh's is explorative rather than truly dramatic. An amnesiac who has fought in the First World War and, subsequently spent eighteen years in a mental hospital, is being claimed by two families as their son. Obviously he must choose. How he does so and why is the material of the play. Each family tries to jerk him into remembrance of them, and this is the reason why the stuffed animals are, in Act 3, brought into his bedroom since he is supposed to have been a hunter in his youth. When first produced, this play had probably more emotive effect than in 1964, as there were said to have been nearly half a million missing French combatants. The New York critics found the play flat, and more of an exercise in drama, than truly one with deeper roots. Generally they praised the acting of Gazzara as Gaston the amnesiac, Mildred Dunnock as one of the claimant mothers, and Nancy Wickwire as Valentine, the girl with whom Gaston is told he has had an affair. Messel's sets of the interior of one of those semi-delapidated French provincial houses, where fashion scarcely changed until after the Second War, were felt to be evocative, and one of its major distinctions. *Traveller Without Luggage* did not do very well and was withdrawn after forty-four performances.

More material on this production is to be found on the SLIDE TAPE, Room 73, No. 99.

a hare.

Fig. 90,
76a

a Great Indian Hornbill.

Fig. 91,
76b

1973

77 Gigi
Musical; book and lyrics by Alan Jay Lerner, music by Frederick Loewe from the story by Colette. Presented by Arnold Saint-Subber and Edwin Lester at the Uris Theatre, New York, on 13th November, 1973; directed by Joseph Hardy, settings by Oliver Smith; costumes by Oliver Messel. With Daniel Massey as Gaston Lachailles, Karin Wolfe as Gigi, Agnes Moorehead as Aunt Alicia, Alfred Drake as Honoré Lachailles, Maria Karnilova as Inez Alvarez; etc.

a **Costume design** for Gigi in the classroom, ch, w. Signed ($14\frac{1}{2} \times 10$) (Fig. 92).

b **Head-dress** for Gigi, with swatch, ch, w, g. Signed ($14\frac{3}{4} \times 10$) (Fig. 93).

c **Costume design** for Gigi in her ball gown, ch, w, g. Signed ($14\frac{3}{4} \times 10$)

d **Costume design** for Gigi in the last scene, 'accepts Gaston', ch, w, g. Signed ($14\frac{1}{2} \times 10$) (Fig. 94).

S.C. 108 costume designs.

Colette published *Gigi*, her story about a young girl being trained as a courtesan, in 1944, and it was not long (1949), before it was filmed in France. On 23rd May, 1956, a stage version by Colette and Anita Loos was presented at the New Theatre, London; directed by Peter Hall with Leslie Caron as Gigi making her stage début. In 1958 *Gigi* became a musical film with lyrics and music by Alan Jay Lerner and Frederick Loewe, respectively. This film starred Leslie Caron, and Maurice Chevalier and was designed by Cecil Beaton. For the next generation Lerner and Loewe made an adaptation from their film and presented a stage musical in San Francisco on 15th May, 1973. Thereafter the show toured St Louis, Detroit and Toronto before settling into New York. Not unexpectedly the critics and public found the show pretty familiar, but numbers like *Thank Heaven for Little Girls*, and *The Night they Invented Champagne* went down as well as usual, bringing back memories of Maurice Chevalier at his most exuberant. In comparison the new songs were rather uninteresting although Alfred Drake as the elegant *boulevardier*, with which role Chevalier stole the film, was very much liked. Also praised were Agnes Moorehead and Maria Karnilova as the scheming aunts who polish Gigi for the marriage market. Perhaps unexpectedly Gigi (Karin Wolfe), and Gaston (Daniel Massey) were found to have not enough charm to put such a trifle over successfully. This may well have had something to do with the unsettling effect of endless re-writing at rehearsals and, in Miss Wolfe's case, that she had been slipped into the show at the last moment to replace Terese Stevens who had left the cast.

Messel's costumes (the sets were designed by Oliver Smith), are the most charming group he ever designed, and would make a worthy exhibition on their own. The costumes are very much in the idiom of the turn of the century and are endlessly inventive bringing back much of the tenderness found in Renoir and Bonnard. *Gigi* was Oliver Messel's last commission in the theatre, excepting *The Sleeping Beauty*, and in many ways the essence of his style, in richness of colour and sensitivity, is to be found in the *Gigi* designs. Unfortunately, as can be seen from the San Francisco programme, the costumes in their finished form differed markedly in detail from the designs. One can only speculate as to why that was the case. Nonetheless, opinion was that the stage picture was very good to look at. *Gigi* had a respectable run of 103 performances and was to have been brought to London in the summer of 1974 but the plan did not materialise.

Fig. 92, **77a**

Fig. 93, 77b

Fig. 94, 77d

Room 73
INTERIOR DESIGN

78 The Dorchester Hotel, London

a **Model** for a suite which became known as the 'Oliver Messel Suite' on the seventh floor; consisting of a sitting-room, a single and a double-bedroom, as shown. The materials and carpets were made by Sekers and Luforma Ltd respectively, to Messel's designs. The furniture was mainly antique.
Opened in 1953. Model ($6\frac{1}{2} \times 30\frac{3}{4} \times 14$) made about 1952 by Carl Toms.

b **Model** for the Penthouse dining-room and roof garden, including the Leda and the Swan fountain, the original modelled in cement by W. Goor (of whom nothing further is known), to Messel's design. All the artifacts (excepting the furniture) were designed by Messel including the gazebos for the roof garden.
Opened in June 1953. Model ($4 \times 24 \times 14$) made by Carl Toms, about 1952.

The Dorchester Hotel was designed by W. Curtis Green & Lloyd and opened in 1930, the construction work being undertaken by Sir Robert McAlpine and Sons. In 1953 it was decided to demolish some adjacent structures on the site of the hotel and add a new wing *en suite* to the existing style of the building. This work was undertaken by the original builders. Messel's further work for the Hotel (1956) is mentioned on p. 49.

79 Shoe Shop for H. & M. Rayne, Old Bond Street, London

Model for the façade of the shop on Old Bond Street completed in 1959 ($16 \times 25\frac{1}{2}$)

This commission extended the shop into neighbouring premises (no. 15) and redesigned the showroom and the façade. The interior again employed fabrics made by Sekers and there is much decorative painting by Messel himself (Fig. 25).

80 The Rosehill Theatre, Whitehaven, Cumbria.

The interior of the theatre showing the silk-lined walls, the fabric made by Sekers. Designed c.1958 and opened in 1959. For a more detailed account of this see p. 48 (Fig. 17).
Colour photograph (8×10) unidentified photographer.
Lent by the Rosehill Arts Trust Ltd.

81 The Bath Assembly Rooms.

a **Design** for the reconstruction of the Octagon. Pencil, w, g ($19 \times 18\frac{1}{2}$). Signed.

b **Design** for 'detail of central panel for ceiling of Octagon, composed out of details from second panels of Ballroom ceiling with centre medallion...'
Pencil and ink on squared paper (17×20). Signed.

c **Design** for a bar for the Octagon.
Ink, w, gold paint (10×15). Signed.

d **Black and white photograph** of the model for the above (10×12)
Photo Studios, Ltd., London.

e **Proposed scheme of decoration** for the north elevation of the Ball Room prepared on an architect's drawing (probably drafted by Sir Albert Richardson and Partners).
W, ink, collage ($11 \times 31\frac{1}{2}$). Signed (Fig. 20).

f **Two designs** on one sheet for: pier-glasses (4) in the Ball Room; secondly, a mirror design for the Ball Room and Octagon.
Pencil and ink, on squared paper (16×11)

g **Design** for the wall-lights for the Tea Room.
Charcoal and ink ($14\frac{3}{4} \times 10$)

h **Design** proposed for one of the walls of the Tea Room. Drawn on an architect's prepared plan.
W, g (22×29). Signed.

John Wood the Elder's Assembly Rooms were opened in 1771 and were described as 'the most noble and elegant of any in this kingdom' in the Bath Guide for 1772. The Rooms survived in one form or another and were used for a variety of entertainments very different from their original purpose until they were burned out in 1942. The rebuilding finally got under way in 1956 and the Rooms were ready for redecoration in 1961. With only £4,000 to spend Messel took on the project and as Dudley Dodd says (q.v. Bib.9b), '...he evolved colour schemes which brought a festive air to the Rooms harking back neither to the frenzied stencilling of the Victorians nor the monochrome of Mowbray Green's work...'. Messel's work was generally welcomed at the reopening in 1963, but in recent years with the inclination for strict historical restoration gaining ground, his rooms were felt increasingly to be untypical of the original colour schemes which were not showy but rather the opposite; the original intention had been that apparel was to provide the colour. Of the original Messel work only the ceiling moulding, in the Ball Room, now remains.

The sketches described above must all date around 1961–62. Messel's intentions were to be as

Fig. 95, **82b**

faithful as possible to surface detail in the original; thus he followed, where he was able to, what patterns survive for plasterwork in the meagre visual documentation for the building. **c** above: this was not executed due to lack of funds and what took its place (a contemporary wooden structure more suited to the local Odeon) was for many years a point of criticism; much the same misfortune befell his furniture designs for the Tea Room these were not executed. When Messel's scheme was replaced by that of David Mlinaric (finished in 1979), only some of the fittings seem to have survived. Amongst them are the mirrors (see **f** above), originally designed for the Ball Room walls and for the Octagon. Six of these survive, in the care of the Bath Museums Service; three are shown in the Tent Room of this Exhibition (No. 1).

82 **Flaxley Abbey, Gloucestershire.**
Three black and white photographs of interiors at Flaxley Abbey. Each (10 × 8). *Country Life.*

a **View** of the Stuart bedroom in the west front.

b **View** of the Morning Room (Fig. 95).

c **View** of the screen in the bow drawing room (Fig. 19).

Mr and Mrs F. B. Watkins bought Flaxley Abbey in 1960 and with the help of Oliver Messel set about restoring the house. A full account of this has been given by Lees-Milne (q.v. Bib. 8) who has covered its complicated history, (and described Messel's alterations), and to which I am indebted for the only contemporary description of the house. Messel's work is difficult to follow otherwise. The three photographs show in **a** how the room looks after almost total reconstruction. The walls are peach coloured, as is the marble fireplace, and the bed hangings are of blue and white,[22] a pattern Messel designed to accompany the blue and white tin-glaze arranged on the furniture tops.

b this room dates from the late 1770s; here Messel has lined the walls with and provided curtains of gold damask. He set alcoves into the walls and designed the carpet which has a colour scheme of green, mauve and cream; the carpet was made in Madrid.

c originally eighteenth-century; it was composed of several rooms which Messel took down to devise a drawing room. He set up this screen to break up the impression of an unending straight room when entered.

83 **Scale plan** for the north and east elevations of 'The Gingerbread House', Mustique, built for Sig. Machado; about 1974.
Fascimile of the original pen drawing (23 × 14).
Signed (Fig. 96). Thomas Messel.

84 **Scale plan** for the west elevation of the house designed for Sen. Egas Fuente, Mustique, in the early '70s.
Fascimile of the original pen drawing (23 × 18).
Signed. Thomas Messel.

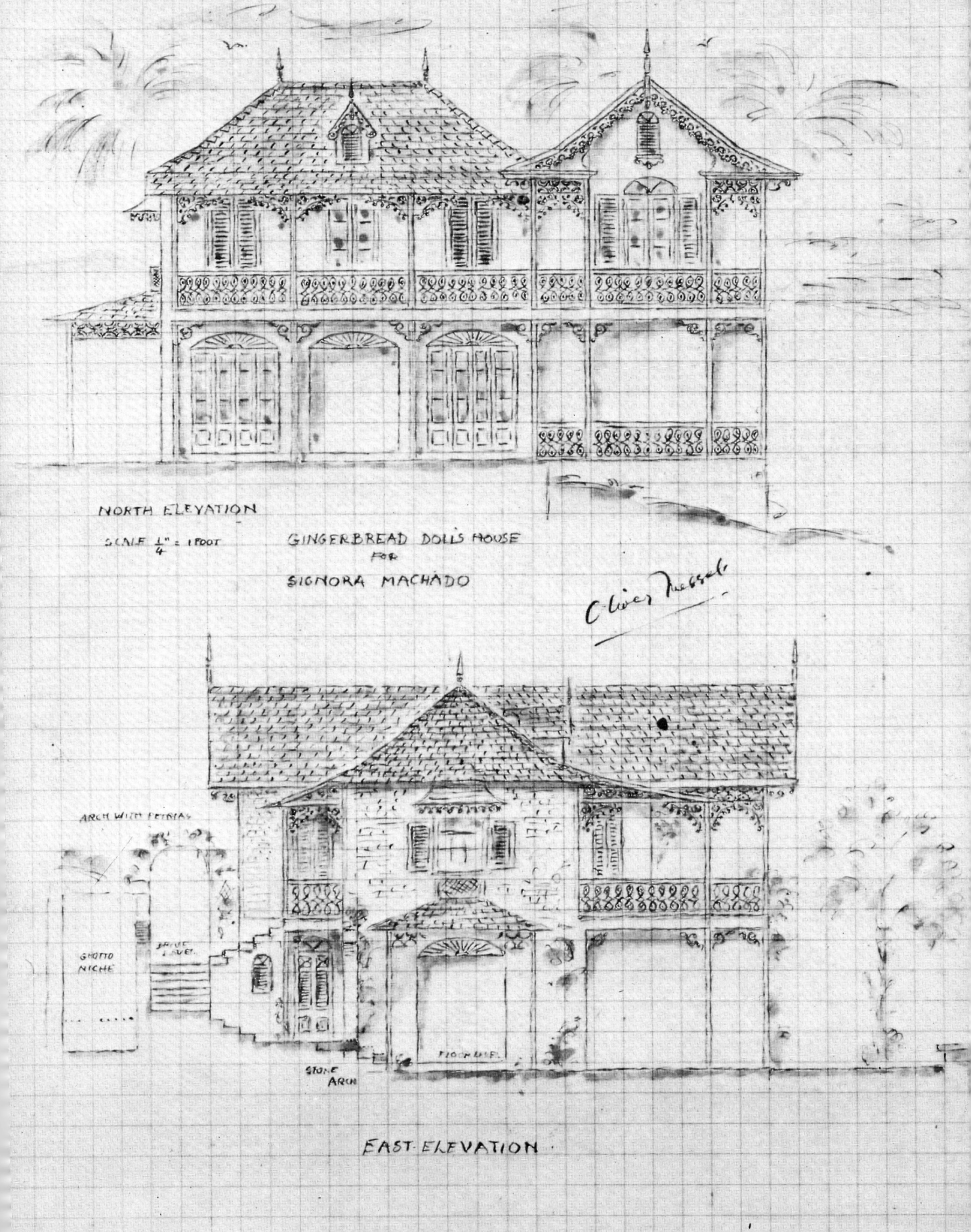

DECORATIVE ARTS DESIGNS

85 **Seven sketches** on one sheet for rattan furniture. Probably designed for Mrs Charles Gordon's house 'Nadiaville', Mustique; about 1974.
Fascimile of the original design, in ink (30 × 10) (Fig. 97). Thomas Messel.

It is not known how much furniture Messel designed in the West Indies. What is, is that he had no trouble getting such pieces made there where there was still a tradition of furniture handicraft.

86 **Design** for a motif, or perhaps the central pattern of a carpet. Charcoal, w, g (24 × 24). Perhaps for one of the carpets at Flaxley Abbey; in which case dating from the early 1960s.

87 **Glyndebourne Festival Programme** for 1954; edited by Robert Ponsonby. Printed on the outside of the front and back covers with designs by Messel based on his décor for *Il Barbiere di Siviglia* produced at Glyndebourne that year. (12¼ × 9½)
Enthoven Collection.

88 **Designs** for a knife and fork.
Pencil on squared tracing paper; according to Thomas Messel these were done before Messel's move to the West Indies in 1964. (10 × 8)
So far there is no evidence that these designs were manufactured. Thomas Messel. (Fig. 98).

89 **Mannequin** wearing a Hardy Amies dinner-gown of 'Jungle' taffeta; des. 1959; exh. Sekers Exh. (q.v. p. 58). Cat. no. 17.
Black and white photograph (9¾ × 7¾). Roy Round, London (Fig. 99).

90 **Design** 'Cape Gooseberry', for a taffeta to be made by Sekers.
Charcoal, w g (13½ × 9¼). Signed. Probably 1959.

91 **Design** 'Fibres', for a taffeta to be made by Sekers, with the instructions to the operative attached.
Ink, g (10 × 9). Signed. Probably 1959.

92 **Sample** of a taffeta with an acorn and oak-leaf design. Described on the retail label as an 'Oliver Messel design selling at £6 11s 3d per yd'. Probably designed in 1959.

93 **Sheet of pulls** for the colour lithographs for *Delightful Food* (q.v. Bib. 1), designed by Oliver Messel; publ. 1958. (21 × 26). Thomas Messel.

◀ Fig. 97, 85   Fig. 98, 88 ▼

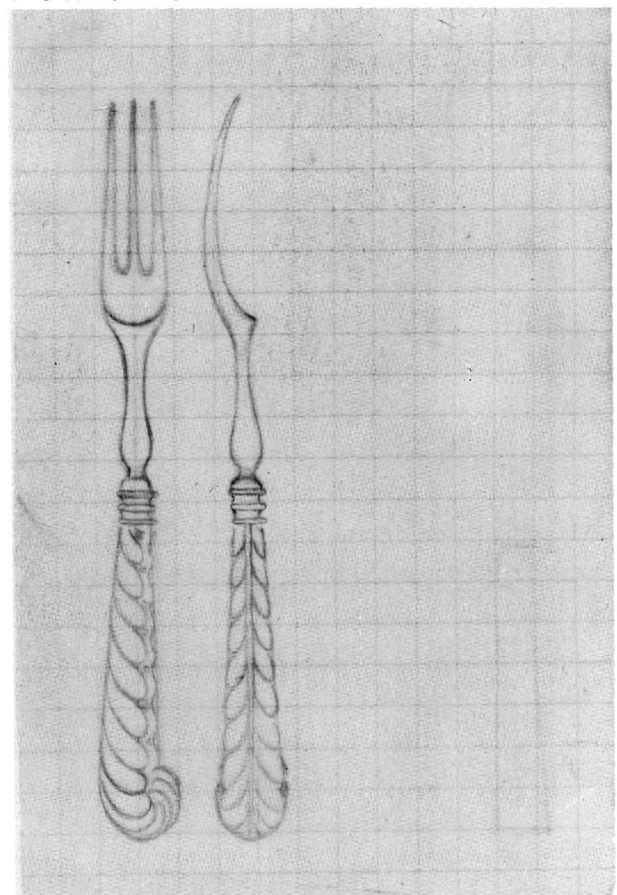
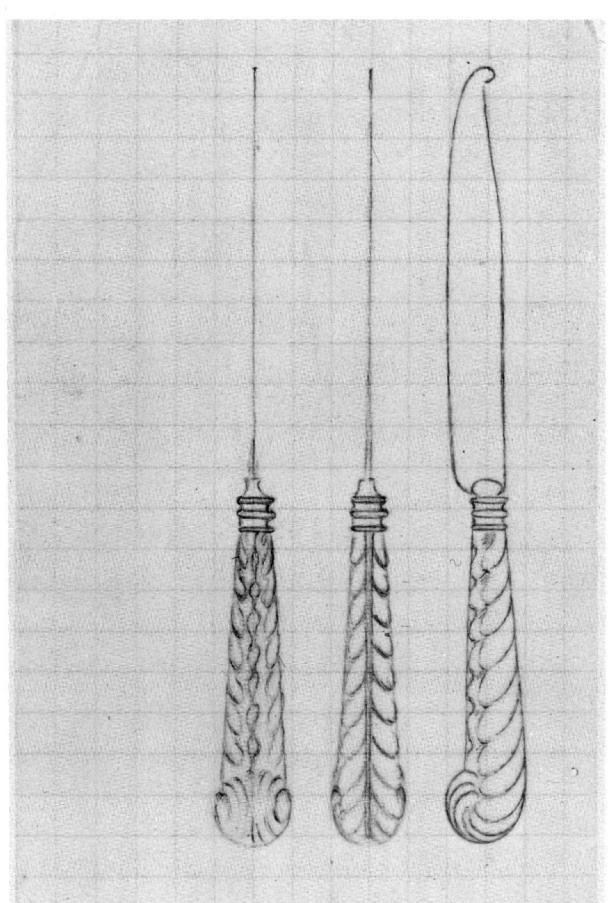

DESIGNS FOR FESTIVE OCCASIONS

94 **Black and white photograph** of the Royal Box at Covent Garden occupied by members of the Royal Family on the night of 8th June, 1953, for a performance of Benjamin Britten's opera *Gloriana* which was commissioned to celebrate The Coronation.
($8 \times 9\frac{1}{2}$) (Fig. 100). The *Daily Herald* (Syndication International).
Lent by the Royal Opera House Archives.

95 **Black and white photograph** of view of the Crush Bar at the Royal Opera House on the same evening. ($8\frac{1}{2} \times 6\frac{1}{2}$) (Fig. 24).
Louis Klemantaski Ltd.
Lent by the Royal Opera House Archives.

These two views give a good idea of the kind of decoration which Messel would create for such occasions (see p.62); for details of other events.

96 **Black and white photograph** of a view of the patio outside the Penthouse dining-room, at the Dorchester Hotel, covered over and decorated with roses and festoons, for a wedding reception in 1954, (6×8) by Millar and Harris, London (Fig. 101).
The Dorchester Hotel.

97 **Ecko television set and table,** furbished for the 'Oliver Messel Suite' at the Dorchester Hotel, 1953. Decorated with a painted crested case, plush curtains, and silk brocade.
Dimensions combined ($52 \times 18 \times 18$)
Lent by his sister, Anne, Countess of Rosse.

◀ Fig. 99, 89   Fig. 101, 96 ▼

Fig. 100, 94

VIDEO/SLIDE SHOW

98 Video Clips from:

a **Caesar and Cleopatra** (1946) Two extracts.
Points to note in the first episode are Cleopatra's golden robe and regalia; in the second the bedroom décor and the variegated costumes in the scene.

b **The Queen of Spades** (1949).
The extract shows Herman trying to wrest the secret of the cards, late at night, from the old Countess in an eery setting which is almost fifty years behind the fashion.

c **Suddenly Last Summer** (1960).
The extract shows the menacing garden – a mixture of natural and hand-made vegetation. About this Messel has spoken on p. 55.

These film extracts are interspersed by slides of design work from these productions chronologically arranged in presentation:

99 **Mother of Pearl** (1933)
Idomeneo (1951) *(Idomeneus, King of Crete)*
House of Flowers (1954)
Die Entführung aus dem Serail *(The Elopement from the Harem)* (1956)
Breath of Spring (1958)
Traveller Without Luggage (1964)
Twang!! (1965)

FILM STILLS, COSTUME, ACCESSORIES – VIDEO CHAMBER

100 **The Private Life of Don Juan** (1934).
London Films. Dir. A. Korda. Costumes by Oliver Messel. Black and white.
Still colour photograph showing Douglas Fairbanks, Snr., as Don Juan and Merle Oberon as Antonia in this film. Set in Spain, in 1650, it dealt with Don Juan, ageing, making a come-back after staging his death. Harold Saunders (16 × 20). Both costumes were designed by Messel; that for Don Juan is in the Snowdon Collection (No. 101). Lent by the National Film Archives (Stills Library).

101 **Costume** for Don Juan worn by Douglas Fairbanks, in *The Private Life of Don Juan*. Spanish style costume; shown in the still No. 100.

Short cutaway bolero jacket with long sleeves and stand up collar. The body is of a novelty plush on a gold metal threaded foundation, densely covered with lines of grey loop-embroidered misshapen squares set between vertical lines of black loop-embroidered 'flames'. From the cutaway edge hang small silver sequin covered bobbles. The tight sleeves are of grey silk velvet, fastened with seven gold shank buttons surrounded by four rows of large silver sequin covered bobbles. The collar is of grey silk velvet. The fixed revers of cream silk velvet are cut in concave curves, bordered with gold thread embroidery and braid, and decorated with ellipses of bright silver sequins and scattered silver sequins. From each shoulder is a bold epaulette of black satin embroidered with red chenille squares centred with a silver sequin covered bobble, each enclosed within lattice of mottled grey and off white chenille; the epaulettes are fringed with gold metal thread covered beads hanging in pairs. The jacket is lined with quilted white silk; the revers are faced in cream silk velvet.

Fitted high-waisted trews of light grey gaberdine decorated down the outer leg with black loop-embroidered stripes, stylized foliage and spots. On the side calf are six large silver sequin covered bobbles below which the open leg is laced to the ankle with grey silk cord. The trews fasten at the side with hooks and eyes.

String necktie of very deep purple velvet with, at each end, a large cluster of small silver sequin covered bobbles.

Cummerbund of wine coloured satin; at both ends a long tied fringe of black chenille with, at each intersection a hobble scattered with tiny gold sequins.

Long full caped coat of black facecloth with stand up collar and side vents. The cape edges are cut in concave curves, accented by borders of pale grey facecloth. The fronts of the cape, lower side sleeves and vents are trimmed with horizontal bands of grey chenille and black silk tassel fringe. Around the collar is a black silk cord tie. The coat has bold front facings of grey velveteen covered with rows of black silk bobbles.

Costume made by Simmons.

A memo from Mr Cunynghame of London Film Productions Ltd to Messel, dated 16th February, 1934, shows that the original estimate for the 232 costumes needed for the film was £3,301 14s – more than Korda had spent on either *The Private Life of Henry VIII* or *Catherine the Great*. Drastic cuts were therefore ordered in the number of costumes to be made (the remainder to be hired) and in the materials used. However, obviously no expense was spared in making the star costumes; this suit is of the finest quality fabrics and the jacket and trews are entirely hand embroidered – testimony to Fairbank's star status.

102 **The Scarlet Pimpernel** (1935).
London Films. Dir. Harold Young. Costumes, Oliver Messel. Black and white.
Leslie Howard as the Scarlet Pimpernel (Sir Percy Blakeney).
Still photograph by Harold Saunders (14 × 11)

Inscribed by Leslie Howard. The costumes for this film were designed by Oliver Messel. Lent by the National Film Archives (Stills Library).

103 **The Scarlet Pimpernel** (1935).
Six costume studies; still photographs, from this film, in many ways Messel's most stylish contribution. From left to right from the top:

a **Black and white photograph** of Merle Oberon and Leslie Howard as Lady Marguerite and Sir Percy Blakeney, who devotes his ingenuity to saving aristocrats from the guillotine, in the French Revolution the subject of Baroness Orczy's famous novel.

b **Black and white photograph** of Leslie Howard in disguise as a supporter of the Revolution.

c **Black and white photograph** of Merle Oberon waiting for news.

d **Black and white photograph** of Leslie Howard and Merle Oberon at a testing moment.

FILM STILLS, COSTUME, ACCESSORIES – VIDEO CHAMBER ∗ 187

e **Black and white photograph** of Raymond Massey as Chauvelin haunting Blakeney.

f **Black and white photograph** of Merle Oberon in outdoor dress.

All photographs of these Messel costumes were made by Harold Saunders. Each (10 × 8). National Film Archives (Stills Library).

104 **Caesar and Cleopatra** (1946).
I. P. Pascal. Dir. Gabriel Pascal. Costumes and interiors by Oliver Messel. Colour.

a **Black and white photograph** of Cleopatra (Vivien Leigh) waiting expectantly the arrival of Caesar. (Fig. 102) (top)

b **Black and white photograph** of Caesar (Claude Rains) interrupted in his study of the plan of Alexandria by Cleopatra. This film made from Bernard Shaw's play, tells how the conquering Caesar falls for the young Queen, (mid left)

c **Black and white photograph** of Caesar meeting Cleopatra. On her right, Ftatateeta played by Flora Robson, (centre)

d **Black and white photograph** of Cleopatra, (centre right)

e **Black and white photograph** of Ftatateeta restraining Cleopatra from being impulsive, (bottom)

Stills photography by Wilfred Newton. Each (10 × 8) National Film Archives (Stills Library).

105 **Black and white photograph** of Gabriel Pascal (centre) and Oliver Messel, in uniform, discuss some point in the company of Vivien Leigh, and two others, unidentified, probably during the filming of *Caesar and Cleopatra*, c.1944 (10 × 8). Unknown photographer.

106 **Head-dress** for Cleopatra, worn by Vivien Leigh. Long Egyptian-style hennaed wig with the ends caught into three net tubes. The hair is entirely covered with horizontal lines of linked chalky blue composition eucalyptus 'seed pods' which separate at the bottom to allow the head-dress and hair to fall over the shoulders.

Over the front of the wig and down the sides of the head fits a small separate head-dress in the form of a fantastic bird with outstretched wings. The miniature head and body sit proud of the forehead; the plumage is simulated by tiny ovals of gilded composition inset with ovals of green stone; the eyes are of green stone. Above the body, simulating the tail of a bird of paradise, are long narrow strips of frosted acetate painted white to simulate feathers, with 'spines' of gold paper, and three curlicues of pale gold acetate from which are suspended small coral beads *tremblant*. Below the body is a semicircle of gilded paper cut into a sunburst from which hang two gold bead chains ending in miniature lotus buds of acetate and gilded leather with stamens of coral beads. The wings are of three rows of gilded composition with zig-zag cut edges simulating feathers, the second layer decorated with small square-cut emeralds, the third with square-cut simulated sapphires; from behind the wings rise three rows of narrow strips of frosted and black acetate, painted to simulate feathers, with central 'spines' of gold paper. Fitted across the 'wings' at either side of the head, are two small acetate wings, the feathers outlined in gold cut composition inset with green. Around the front edge, matching and continuing the wig and forming a fringe over the forehead, is a formal grouping of wired chalky blue composition 'seed pods'.

107 **The Queen of Spades** (1949).
World Screenplays. Dir. Thorold Dickinson. Costumes and settings by Oliver Messel. Black and white.

a **Black and white photograph** of Herman (Anton Walbrook) making advances to Lisa (Yvonne Mitchell), the aged Countess' grand-daughter and companion, in Pushkin's story.

b **Black and white photograph** of the Countess Ranevskaya prepared for the ball. Edith Evans making her first film, played the Countess, (below)

c **Black and white photograph** of the Countess attired for the ball.

d **Black and white photograph** of Herman invading the Countess' bedroom after her return from the ball to learn her supposed secret at winning at gambling, (right)

e **Black and white photograph** of the Countess, who, threatened by Herman, has died and now awaits burial. Herman comes to believe that the secret is – three, seven, ace (of Spades), (bottom, centre)

Fig. 102, 104a

f **Black and white photograph** of Herman beginning to win with the three of Spades. Fortunes seem to be within his grasp. But in the end, he learns that the Countess has tricked him, (bottom, right)
Stills photography by George Daly. Each (10 × 8)
National Film Archives (Stills Library).

g **Two figures** of plaster, with silk costumes made small scale for a sequence in *The Queen of Spades*. Each (9 inches).
Lent by his sister, Anne, Countess of Rosse.

108 **Suddenly Last Summer** (1960).
Horizon (Col). Dir. Joseph L. Mankiewicz.
Costumes and settings, Oliver Messel.

a **Black and white photograph** of Dr Cukrowicz (Montgomery Clift) and Violet Venable (Katharine Hepburn) regard a distressed Catherine Holly (Elizabeth Taylor) in this film of Tennessee Williams' play.

b **Black and white photograph** of Katharine Hepburn ascending in an ornate New Orleans lift.

c **Black and white photograph** of Oliver Messel on the set. See his remarks on p.58 regarding the exterior garden which had the right creepy atmosphere for this story of the mysterious end of Catherine's homosexual cousin.
Stills photography by Ken Danvers. Each (10 × 8)
National Film Archives (Stills Library).

Fig. 103 Costume design for the old Countess' ball-gown for the film *The Queen of Spades* (1949)

Fig. 104 Herman studies the face of the dead Countess; still from *The Queen of Spades* (1949). George Daly. National Film Archives (Stills Library)

NOTES: CATALOGUE

Masks and Photographs of Masks (p.70)

1 Stage Society, The Incorporated; introduced in 1899 to present good though uncommercial plays when the theatres were usually unoccupied, as on Sundays. The first production was Shaw's *You Never Can Tell*, and in subsequent years works by Gorky, Wedekind, Pirandello, O'Neill, D. H. Lawrence, Odets and others, were presented. By the 1930's when more than one little theatre had appeared to undertake similar productions the Stage Society was no longer in an unique situation, and it expired in 1939.

C. B. Cochran and His Revues (pp.74)

2 In his early days as an impresario he presented Ibsen and brought Reinhardt to London (q.v. cat. *Helen, The Miracle*). He had a keen eye, and ear for fashion thus he fell to presenting annual *Revues* from the early Twenties to early Thirties, when jazz and talkies were in vogue. Despite the vulgarity this suggests Cochran had a wish for quality. Three of his *Revues* were written by Noël Coward and his designers for these shows were all beginners at this date, and he took risks with them. After the second War Cochran was more and more attracted to operetta, often to be written by A. P. Herbert, and scored by Vivian Ellis. *Bless the Bride* was highly successful and ran for three years, and there were others. Cochran was knighted in 1948 for services to the theatre.

3 Amongst those he encouraged were; Cecil Beaton, Christian Bérard, André Derain, Oliver Messel, William Nicholson, Rex Whistler, Norman Wilkinson and Doris Zinkeisen.

4 Cochran employed Messel to do masks, costumes, settings or permutations of these for: *1926 Revue, 1928 This Year of Grace, 1929 Wake Up and Dream, 1930 Revue, 1931 Revue, 1932 Helen, The Miracle, 1933 Mother of Pearl, 1942 The Big Top, 1949 Tough at the Top*.

5 Actor, director, composer, dramatist, film maker (1899–1973). Early associated with Cochran and had already made his name for *The Vortex* (1924) before writing material for *On With the Dance* (1925) and *This Year of Grace*, 1928. Coward's *Bitter Sweet* (1929) and *Cavalcade* (1931) were presented by Cochran. Coward was also knighted for services to the theatre, (1970).

The Miracle (p.80)

6 As well as the leading dailies, illustrated magazines like *The Sketch, The Illustrated London News*, and *Vogue* devoted space to the openings, in their April issues.

7 In MCKENDRY, 1976: '...She adored Reinhardt and the whole idea of the production and she would stand for an hour at a time while I'd drape plaster around her on monk's cloth to make the robes which were like a carved wooden madonna...'

8 Interview in the *Daily Telegraph*, April 1932, shortly before the first night.

The Country Wife (p.93)

9 Oct. 15, 17, 19, 1936.

10 Letter by Carroll, 'A Tax Anomaly' the *Daily Telegraph*, Oct. 15, 1936.

11 Letter by Lord Lytton, the *Daily Telegraph*, Oct. 17, 1936.

12 Article by Agate, the *Sunday Times*, Oct. 25, 1936

13 Sir Tyrone Guthrie (1900–1971); actor, director. Published three books on theatre: knighted for his services to it.

A Midsummer Night's Dream (p.97)

14 His début in London was in, *I Hate Men* (Gate Theatre) Feb. 28, 1933.

The Tempest (p.100)

15 His first was of Daphne Du Maurier's *Rebecca* (Queen's Theatre), April 5, 1940 (q.v. Wardle, op. cit.).

16 At the Royal Court actor's school Devine held classes in masks; q.v. Wardle (op. cit.).

The Rivals (p.106)

17 CEMA: (Council for the Encouragement of Music and the Arts), 1940. Reformed as The Arts Council, in 1946.

The Lady's Not For Burning (p.119)

18 It had been first presented at the Arts Theatre, 10th March, 1948, for a short run, with Alec Clunes as Thomas Mendip.

House of Flowers (p.149)

19 Truman Capote, *Building a House of Flowers; Theatre Arts*, Jan. 1955, pp.30–1, 91.

Le Nozze di Figaro (p.155)

20 Dyneley Hussey, *Figaro at Glyndebourne, a retrospective Survey* in Glyndebourne Festival programme for 1955, pp.21–24.

The School for Scandal (p.159)

21 Information from Harold Elvin.

Flaxley Abbey, Glos. (p.175)

22 Messel called this pomegranate pattern *Cluny* (Lees-Milne, Bib.8, 2nd art. p.909).

CONCISE LIST OF WORKS IN COLLECTIONS, NECESSARILY INCOMPLETE

Barbados

St Ann's Garrison; The Barbados Mus. and Hist. Soc., oil painting *Carnival Demon*; also, plans for the rebuilding (not carried out).

England

Aylesbury; Bucks. Cty. Mus., *View of Hartwell House*; oil; sgd. d.1945.

Bath; Bath Museums Service (for the National Trust) 6 mirrors in fibre-glass frames made for the Assembly Rooms (q.v. Nos. 1, 81).

Chichester; Edward James Foundation; 9 oils.

Gloucestershire; Flaxley Abbey; oil of Titania and Bottom in *A Midsummer Night's Dream* c.1937.

London: *Dorchester Hotel* (wall paintings in the Suites referred to in text), *Theatre Museum* (at the Victoria and Albert Museum); on indefinite loan Lord Snowdon's collection of costumes, model sets, designs, head-dresses, photographs, letters, etc. (inventoried). In the Theatre Museum collection there are costumes, and head-dresses for *The Sleeping Beauty*, a model for *Helen*, a costume for *Homage to The Queen*, a costume for *Samson*, a model for *Ring Round the Moon*, a head-dress for *Francesca da Rimini*, designs for *Helen*, *The Sleeping Beauty*; also many production photographs, reviews, programmes, etc.
Victoria and Albert Museum Print Room; design (not used) for *Nymph Errant* by James Laver.
Museum of London; masks for *Zéphyre et Flore*.
British Piano Museum; portrait (oil), of Peter Glenville.
Royal Opera House Archives; head-dresses for *The Sleeping Beauty*, costume for *Homage to the Queen*, photographs and programmes.

Whitehaven; *The Sir Nicholas Sekers Theatre*; drawings for the interior and photographs.

And these private collections;

Mr Roy Astley, designs, etc.

Mr and Mrs T. Fawcett; head-dresses and costumes for *Comus*.

Ms Marianne Ford; designs for *The Miracle* and *Helen*.

Mrs L. Gethic; a watercolour.

Mrs J. Lewis; flower study (oil).

Thomas Messel; designs, house plans, photographs, masks, personalia, (uncatalogued). (This is the second largest holding after that of Lord Snowdon.)

Michael Northen; working notes, photographs, etc., relating to the *Queen of Spades* (O), and *Twang!!*

Anne, Countess of Rosse (Oliver Messel's sister); a paper altar, dolls, figures, a TV set.

Mr Justin Sillman; decorated clavicord.

Lord Snowdon (see above, *Theatre Museum*).

U.S.A.

Binghamton; *University of New York Theatre Archives*; set design for the film of *The Queen of Spades*.

LIST OF LENDERS

Cooper, Lady Diana

Enthoven Coll. (Theatre Museum)

Ford, Ms Marianne

Messel, Thomas

Museum of London, The

National Film Archive, London

National Trust, The

Rosehill Arts Trust, The

Rosse, Anne, Countess of

Royal Opera House Archives

Snowdon, Lord

Theatre Museum

Watkins, F. Baden

BIBLIOGRAPHY

1. Oliver Messel – Illustrations for books: London publishers

1933 *Stage Designs and Costumes* (by Oliver Messel); introduced by James Laver; foreword by C. B. Cochran. Ills. John Lane.

1936 *Romeo and Juliet* (Shakespeare's play with Oliver Messel's costume designs for the MGM film). Batsford.

1957 *A Midsummer Night's Dream* (Shakespeare's play, ills. by Oliver Messel). Folio Society.

1958 *Delightful Food*, by Marjorie Salter and Adrienne Allen (ills. by Oliver Messel). Sidgwick & Jackson.

2. Biographical Sources

Burke's Landed Gentry, 18th ed. Vol. 1, pp. 498–499.

Maxime de la Falaise McKendry; *Oliver Messel Talks to Maxime de la Falaise McKendry* in *Interview*, May 1976 (referred to *passim* as McKENDRY, 1976).

Oliver Messel (probably taped) in HERS Magazine, Vol. 1, No. 5, 1976 (Barbados) pp. 40–41 (referred to *passim* as IHM, 1976).

Notable Names in the American Theatre: J. T. White and Coy., New Jersey, 1976.

The Times (obit.), publ. 15th July, 1978.

Who's Who: post-War, eds.

Who's Who in The Theatre, 16th ed. 1977 pp. 931–932.

3. Sources Where Messel's Stage Work is Discussed and Illustrated

Ballet Today, March–April, 1946.

John Barber, *Oliver Messel in the Theatre*: V & A Museum Album No. 1, pp. 87–90, 1983.

Cecil Beaton, *Self-Portrait with Friends*, ed. R. Buckle, Weidenfeld & Nicolson, 1978.

Cecil Beaton, *Time Exposure*, Batsford, 1941.

Arthur Boyes, *Oliver Messel*, *Harper's Bazaar*, 1st March, 1950 (Amer. edn.).

Cyril Butcher, *Oliver Messel*, *The Sketch*, 14th February, 1951, pp. 126–127.

C. B. Cochran, *Oliver Messel*, *Everybody's*, 16th February, 1946, pp. 8–9, cover.

C. B. Cochran, *Showman Looks On*, J. M. Dent & Sons Ltd., 1945.

C. B. Cochran, *Cock-a-Doodle-do*, J. M. Dent & Sons Ltd., 1941.

E. H. C. Corathiel, *Creative Artists in the Theatre; 4, Oliver Messel*, *Theatre World*, May 1950, pp. 19–20, 30.

Dancing Times, The, designs reviewed, Sept. 1937, Feb. 1942, Mar. 1946, July 1953.

Fifty Years in Stage Lighting, a History of Strand Electric, Tabs, Vol. 22, No. 1, 1964 (q.v. pp. 44–45 for comments on the lighting of *Helen* and *The Miracle*).

William Gaunt, *Masks by Oliver Messel*, *The Studio*, Vol. 96, pp. 249–255, 1928.

Derek Granger, *Oliver Messel in Glyndebourne*, Glyndebourne Festival Programme for 1955, pp. 44–48.

Oliver Messel (his view on Mozart), Glyndebourne Festival Programme, 1956, p. 76. (Mozart bicentennial year.)

Oliver Messel *A Master of Décor Speaks of His Art, Tatler and Bystander*, 29th August, 1956.

Oliver Messel *What is Good Design Worth?*, American Fabrics, No. 48, pp. 69–71, 1960.

Oliver Messel in Pelham Place, House and Garden, November 1961, p. 64.

Oliver Messel's Full New Life in Barbados, House and Garden, June 1971, pp. 60–63.

R. Myerscough-Walker, *Film and Stage Décor*, Pitman, 1940.

Roy Strong, *Oliver Messel – the master of style*, the *Sunday Telegraph*, 16th July, 1978.

Frances Tracey, *The Decorative Work of Oliver Messel*, Decoration, No. 21, January 1937, pp. 11–15.

4. Sources Where Messel's Stage Work is Illustrated '*en passant*'

Balthasar (portrait), Apollo 29, January 1939, p. 41: (Exhibition Leicester Gall. 1938. (q.v. p. 58).)

Helen (decor for); ill. *The Studio* 125, p. 149, April 1943.

(Masks) in *The Robes of Thespis*, ed. R. Mason, Benn, 1928 pls. LXXVII–LXXX.

A Midsummer Night's Dream; a design for *The Studio* 117, 67F (col), 1939. Mural in the House of Mr Wright Luddington, Santa Barbara, *The Studio* 118, p. 148, October 1939.

(Pelham Place dining-room), *Vogue*, 15th October, p. 100 (col.), 1963.

(Portrait of Joshua Logan), *Apollo*, n.s. 76, lxiv, October 1962.

Samson, costume design for (Dagon), *Vogue*, December 1958, p. 59.

Sleeping Beauty, The, (col. ills. for pp. 300–301), *American Ballet Theatre* by Charles Payne, Adam and Charles Black, 1978.

(Three Temples for *The Magic Flute*) designs for: *Burl. Mag.* 118, XXI, June 1976.

Watching the Carnival (picture), *Apollo*, n.s. 76: 715; November 1962, also the frequently illustrated spreads in these periodicals, *Dancing Times, Play Pictorial, The Sketch, Theatre Magazine*, a feature in pre-War issues when new shows were mounted.

5. Exhibition Catalogues

These are not easy to get hold of, but all the exhibitions listed had catalogues. However, the Claridge, Leicester, Chichester Antiques and the Wright Hepburn Gallery are not in business now. It has been impossible to find a Claridge Gallery cat. for the 1925 exhibition, although Laver, in the Oliver Messel book of 1933 (see Bib. 1), mentioned that the *Jehanne* mask was exhibited.

Most of the other catalogues are in the Victoria and Albert Museum Library but not that for the Sekers exhibition.

6. Reviews

(a) of painting exhibitions: q.v. p. 58 for list:
at Lefèvre Gallery, 1934; *Apollo* 19, p. 57, January 1934.
at the Carol Carstairs Gallery (NY), 1936; *Art News* 35, p. 19, December 1936.
at the Sagittarius Gallery (NY); *Art News* 58, 18th November, 1959; *Arts* 34, 70; December 1959.

(b) Reviews of stage productions in *Daily* papers after the first night:
The *Daily Telegraph* – W. A. Darlington (drama) (1920–68); Martin Cooper (music and opera).
The *Evening Standard* – Beverley Baxter (drama), d. 1964; occasionally (c. 1954) Kenneth Tynan.
The Times – (anonymous reviews); William Mann (opera in 50s, 60s on) and others.
Weekend Papers:
The *Observer* – Ivor Brown (drama) (1928–54); Kenneth Tynan (1954–58, 1960–63); Eric Blom (opera) through 30s to c. 1955; Peter Heyworth.
The *Sunday Times* – James Agate (drama) until 1946; Harold Hobson until 1976; Ernest Newman (opera) until 1958.
Well-illustrated magazines worth consulting for illustrations but with not much text are the following, though all, except 'The Illustrated London News', have now closed:
The *Bystander, Dancing Times, The Illustrated London News, Play Pictorial, The Sketch, Theatre World.*
For America, good reference materials are:
Theatre Art, which later incorporated *Theatre Arts Monthly*, New York (1932–62).
New York Theatre Critics Reviews, 1950–c. 1975 (annual compendiums), Critics Theatre Reviews Inc., New York.

7. Films

There has been little study so far of Messel's film work except *en passant* in film reviews. One exception is:

Marjorie Deans, *Meeting at the Sphinx: Gabriel Pascal's Production of Bernard Shaw's Caesar and Cleopatra* (col. ills.). MacDonald, 1946.

Denis Gifford, *The British Film Catalogue 1895–1970*, David and Charles, 1973.

8. Buildings

John Cornforth, *The Bath Assembly Rooms Redecorated, Country Life*, 9th January, 1964, pp. 56–59.

(Dorchester Hotel, London – Press Office) – *Notes on the New Suite and Banqueting Room at the Dorchester*, 1953; and *The Roof Garden Suites; Oliver Messel Suite, the Pavilion Room*, 1956.

James Lees-Milne, *Flaxley Abbey, Gloucestershire, Country Life*, I, II, III, 29th March pp. 842–845, 5th April pp. 908–911, 12th April pp. 980–984, 1973, ills.

D. Pryce-Jones, *Architectural Digest Visits Princess Margaret* ... Arch. Dig. 36, pp. 112–9, October 1979.

D. Pryce-Jones, *On Mustique; the Tropical Charm of The Gingerbread House*, Arch. Dig. 37, pp. 58–65, July/August 1980.

D. Pryce-Jones, *Mango Bay; a House of Tropical Allure in Barbados*, Arch. Dig. 38, pp. 98–103, May 1981.

D. Pryce-Jones, *An Instructed Sophistication on the Island of Mustique*, Arch. Dig. 38, pp. 116–119, November 1981.

9. General

(a) Ballet

George Balanchine (*et al.*) Balanchine's Festival of Ballet, W. H. Allen, 1978.

C. W. Beaumont, *The Sleeping Beauty as presented by The Sadlers Wells Ballet*; photographs by Edward Mandinian. C. W. Beaumont, London 1946.

C. W. Beaumont, *Impressions of The Sleeping Beauty, Ballet*, Feb. 1946.

Horst Koegler, *The Concise Oxford Dictionary of Ballet*, Oxford, 2nd ed. 1982.

(b) Bath

Dudley Dodd, *Bath Assembly Rooms*, The National Trust, 1979.

Walter Ison, *The Georgian Buildings of Bath*, 2nd ed., 1969 (Bath).

(c) Opera

Spike Hughes, *Glyndebourne, A History of the Festival Opera*, David and Charles; new ed., 1981.

Kobbé's Complete Opera Book, ed. and rev. by the Earl of Harewood, Putnam, 1976.

Norman Del Mar, *Richard Strauss, A Critical Commentary on his Life and Works*, Barrie and Jenkins (Vol. 1, 1962, Vol. 2, 1969, Vol. 3, 1972).

William Mann, *The Operas of Mozart*, Cassell, 1977.

Harold Rosenthal and John Warrack, *The Concise Oxford Dictionary of Opera*, 3rd ed. 1980.

(d) Plays

The Collected Plays of Jean Anouilh; 1 vol. Methuen London, 1966. And separately in print; *Antigone, Becket, The Lark, Ring Round the Moon*, The Plays of Christopher Fry (5 collections, in print). Oxford U.P.

(e) Revue

q.v. the autobiographies of C. B. Cochran listed in 3 above.

(f) Scene Design

British Theatre Design, 1979–83; exh. cat. Soc. of British Theatre Designers, 1983.

Sybil Rosenfeld, *A Short History of Scene Design in Great Britain*, Basil Blackwell, 1973.

(g) Theatre History

Irving Wardle, The Theatres of George Devine, Cape, 1978.

(h) The West Indies

Patrick Leigh Fermor, *The Traveller's Tree; a journey through the Caribbean*, John Murray, 1950, Arrow Books, 1961.

INDEX

Figures in **bold type** refer to catalogue entries which will be on the page following the oblique stroke; those in *italics* to illustrations. Illustrations accompanying text on the same page are not specifically listed.

Abbey, Eleanor 32
Addinsell, Richard 23, 119
Agate, James 21, 81, 88, 91, 94
Amara, Lucine 126
American Ballet Theatre 111
Amies, Hardy 179
Amphitryon 38 33
Anders, Peter 122
Anouilh, Jean 15, 23, 119, 122, 167
'Anthony' and Gordon Anthony, photographer 94, 99, 105
Appia, Adolphe 21
Ariadne aux Naxos (both versions) 40, **47**/117, *59*/122, *123*, *124*, *125*
Arlen, Harold 149
Arms and the Man 14, 47, 56, 154, **71**/155
Armstrong-Jones, Anne (later Countess of Snowdon, see below) 12, 39, 77
Armstrong Jones, Tony (later Lord Snowdon; see also below) 33, 70, 152
Arnold, Malcolm 138
Ashcroft, Peggy 48
Ashton, Sir Frederick 109, 138, 141
Atkinson, Brooks 126
Auden, W. H. and Isherwood, C. 119
Audley, Maxine 137
Avedon, Richard; studios 149

Bailey, Pearl 149
Bakst, Léon 37, 41, 71
Balanchine, Georges 77, 79, 197
Ballet Rambert 89
Barabas, Sari 147, 149
Barbiere di Siviglia, Il 9, 13, 40, **53**/117, *145*, *146*, **67**/147, 163, 179
Barkworth, Peter 137, 141
Bardon, Henry 36
Baron 115
de Basil Ballets Russes 94, 111
Bath Assembly Rooms 12, 52, 53, 70, **81**/174, 197
Baxter, Sir Beverley 106
Baylis, Lilian 93
BBC Hulton Picture Library 98, 101
Beaton, Sir Cecil 12, 21, 33, 70, 72, 84, 171, 191
Beaumarchais, Pierre A. C. de 147, 155
Beaumont, Cyril 41, 85
Beecham, Sir Thomas 122
Belle Hélène, La 84, 88
Bendelow, Beatrice 122
Benois, Alexandre 37, 41, 71
Benthall, Michael 122
Bérard, Christian 191
Berman, Monty; *costumier* 10, **32**/80

Bernardic, Drago 116
Berne Silks Ltd 48
Besch, Anthony 152
Besekow, Sam 159
Bibiena family 22, 36, 44
Bible, Frances 155
Big Top, The 38
Black & Edgington 10
Bloom, Claire 13, 24, 119, *121*
Bonnard, Pierre 171
Boulangeot, Huguette 152
Bourgeois gentilhomme, Le 122, 126
Bradley, Lionel 114
Braidwood, Margaret 167
Braque, Georges 18, 71
Bravery, Charles 163
Breath of Spring 40, **99**/184
Bretzner, Christoph 117
Britten, Benjamin, Lord 49
Gloriana 181
Brook, Peter 15, 24, 117, 119, 141, 149
Brown, Ivor 84, 106
Brown, Pamela 119
Bruce, Brenda 137
Bruscantini, Sesto 132, 147, 155
Buckle, Richard 10, 41, 141
Bull, Peter 119
Burra, Edward 22
Burton, Richard 47, 119
Busch, Fritz 130, 155, 156

Caesar and Cleopatra 15, 46, 57, **98**/184, *186*, **104** & **106**/187
Calabrese, Franco 155
Calthrop, G. C. 75, 79
Čapek, Karel and Josef 132
Capote, Truman 149
Carfax, Bruce 84
Carnival 56
Caron, Leslie 171
Carrick, Edward (T. Craig) 34
Carroll, Diahann 149
Carroll, Sydney 94
Cenerentola, La 13, 40, **63**/132, 106, *133*, *134*, *135*, 163
Chappell, William 32, 89, 117, 119, 152
Chevalier, Maurice 171
China **28**/77
Churchill, Diana 130
Claridge Gallery 15, 18, 70, 77
Claridge, John 11, 27
Clegg, Peter 111
Clement, Thérèse 99
Cleopatra 47, 56
Clift, Montgomery 189
Coates, Edith 122
Cochran, Sir C. B. 15, 18, 21, 74, 76, 79, 80, 81, 84, 117, 196
Cochran *Revues*:
1926 **24**/74
1928 **26**/75
1929 **28**/76

1930, **29**/77
1931, **30**/79
Cocteau, Jean 80, 152
Colette 171
Comte Ory, Le 12, 13, 28–29, 40, **52**/117, **68**/147, *148*, 163
Comus 13, 21, 38, 104, **40**/105
Console, A 91
Cooper, A. C. 88
Cooper, Lady Diana (née Manners) 10, 80, 81, *195*
Cornell, Katherine, Miss 144
Coster, Howard and Joan 77
Country Wife, The 13, 36, 38, 92, **36**/93
Coward, Noël 23, 72, 75, 76, 79, 106
Craig, Edward Gordon 22, 33, 34, 35
Cranmer, Olivia 122, 139
Crespin, Régine 163
Cresta Silks Ltd 48, 60
Cruickshank, Andrew 100
Cubism, and masks 18
Curtis Green, W. & Lloyd 174
Czerwenka, Oscar 163

Daly, George 187
Dance Little Lady 38, 72, **26**/75
Dante 94
Danvers, Ken 189
da Ponte, Lorenzo 155
Dark is Light Enough, The 7, 13, 24, 40, 106, **51**/117, **66**/141, *142*, *143*
Darlington, W. A. 86, 94
D'Attili, Maria 117
Deans, Marjorie 46
Debenham, J. W. 93, 99
de Gabarain, Marina 132
de Havilland, Olivia 126
Dent, E. J. 114
Derain, André 74
Devine, George 100, 102
Devine, Lauri 12, 74, 75, 76, 77
Diaghilev, Serge 18, 41, 94
Diaghilev Ballet 7, 18, 71, 111
Dickinson, Thorold 10, 46, 187
Dobbs, Mattiwilda 116, 117, 126
Dodd, Dudley 10, 174
Donald, James 141
Dorchester Hotel, The 10, 12, 27, 49, *50*, *51*, **78**/174, **96**/181, 192
Drake, Alfred 171
Dulac, Edmund 44
Du Maurier, Daphne *Rebecca* 191

Ebert, Carl 116, 122, 130, 132, 147, 155, 163
Ebert, Peter 117
Eliot, T. S. 119
Ellis, Mary 91
Ellis, Vivian 11, 77, 117
Elvin, Harold 191
Elvin, Violetta 138

Emblen, Ronald 113
Entführung aus dem Serail, Die 13, 40, **54**/117, *118*, 163, **99**/184
Erwin, John Seymour 126
Evans, Edgar 122
Evans, Dame Edith 7, 13, 46, 93, 106, 141, 144, 184, 187
Evans, Sir Geraint 116, 156
Evans, Jessie 137
Evans, Meriel 159

Fairbanks, Douglas, Snr. 185
Farjeon, Herbert 88
Farron, Julia 114
Ferretti, Jacopo 132
Fildes, Audrey 106, 119
Flaxley Abbey 12, *51*, **82**/175, 192
Fonteyn, Dame Margot 13, 44, 45, 104, 105, 108, 111, 114, 138
Ford, Marianne 10, 81, 85, 192, 195
Francesca da Rimini 13, 38, **37**/94, *95*, *96*, *97*
Fry, Christopher 7, 10, 15, 23, 36, 119, 122, 141, 144, and poetic drama, 119

Gainsborough, Thomas 44
Gaunt, William 18, 76
Gazzara, Ben 167
Georgiades, Nicholas 36
Gevergeva, Tamar 12, *71*
Gielgud, Sir John 49, 72, 100, *101*, 102, 119
Gigi 14, 40, 52, *170*, **77**/171, *172*, *173*
Gingerbread House, The 14, **83**/176, *177*
Girl in a Shawl see *China*
Glamorous Night 38, **35**/91
Glenville, Peter 10, 15, 24, 84, 126, 130, 137, 155
Glyndebourne (Festival Opera) 23, 32, 48, 116, 117, 122, 126, 130, 132, 147, 155, 156, 163, 179
Gontcharova, Nathalia 71
Goor, W. 174
Gordon, Ruth 93
Gore, Walter 89
Gorelik, Mordecai 33
Goring, Marius 100, 102
Gould, Diana 12, 82
Goya, Francisco 23
Graf, Herbert 159
Gravett, Guy 147
Great God Brown, The 12, 38, **19**/72, *73*
Grétry, André 152
Grey, Beryl 111, 114
Grigoriev, Serge 94
Group Theatre (London) 119
Group Theatre (New York) 37
Gui, Vittorio 116, 132, 147, 155, 156
Guinness, Sir Alec 26, 100, 130
Guthrie, Sir Tyrone 15, 93, 94, 97, 100, 106

Häefleger, Ernst 116, 117
Hall, Juanita 149
Hall, Sir Peter 171
Hall, Stanley 10, 30
Handel, George Frederick 159
Hart, John 138
Haskell, Arnold 94
Hassall, Christopher 49, 91
Hasselquist, Arnë 52
Hawkins, Jack 100, 102, 126
Hayter, James 126
Heaven 12, 38, *29/77*, 78, 79
Hedd, Madi 132
Helen 12, 13, 15, 21, 34, 35, 38, 41, 46, 69, 79, *34/84*, 85, 86, 87, 88, 89, 122
Helpmann, Sir Robert 13, 97, 98, 100, *104*, *105*, *108*, *109*, 114
Hepburn, Katharine 189
Herbert, A. P. 72, 88, 117
Heyworth, Peter 116
Hill, Lucienne 167
'H.H.' 100
Hofsmannsthal, Hugo von 122, 163
Hollweg, Ilse 122
Homage to the Queen 13, 40, 106, *65/138*, 140
Hope-Wallace, Philip 163
House of Flowers 13, 40, 69/149, 150, 151, *99/184*
Houston Rogers 106, 120, 159
Howard, Leslie 185
Humperdinck, Engelbert 80
Hussey, Dyneley 155

Idomeneo 40, *61/130*, *99/184*
Infernal Machine, The 38, 103

James, Henry 137
Jevons, Janet 80
Johnston, Margaret 141
Jones, Inigo 141
Jurinac, Sena 130, 155

Kanova, Germaine 105
Karinska, Barbara 94, 97
Kelly, David 159
Keystone Press Agency 79
Kleiber, Erich 122
Klementaski, Louis 63, 181
Kochno, Boris 18, 71, 77
Komisarjevsky, Theodore 35
Korda, Sir Alexander 185
Kreisler, Fritz 34

Lady's not for Burning, The 9, 12, 22, 23, 24, 25, 36, 40, *45/117*, *56/119*, 144
Lancaster, Osbert 34
Larionov, Mikhail 71
Laver, James 70, 71, 72, 74, 76, 79, 85
Laye, Evelyn 13, 34, 84, 86, 88
Lee, Marjorie 10
Lee-Elliott, Theyre 24
Lees-Milne, James 175
Leigh, Vivien 14, 99, *104/187*
Lenare 74
Leppard, Raymond 159
Lerner, Alan Jay and Loewe, Frederick 171
Letter From Paris 13, 40, *136*, *64/137*
Levinson-Brunoff 41
Lewis, Richard 130
Lewis, Robert 167

Lichine, David 94
Lifar, Serge 12, 77, 78
Linden, Anya 112
Lindermeier, Elisabeth 159
Little Hut, The 7, 9, 17, 32, 40, 106, *49/117*, 149
London Films (Korda Bros) see Korda, A.
Löhr, Marie 120
Lorelei 38, *26/75*
Lorengar, Pilar 116
Losch, Tilly 12, 20, 75, 76, 77, 80, 81
Ludwig, Walther 163
Luforma Ltd 174
Lupino, Peter 117
Lytton, Lord 94

McAlpine, Sir Robert & Sons 174
McBean, Angus 119, 122, 130, 132, 137, 144
MacNeice, Louis 119
Magic Flute, The 40, 51, 69, 114, *43/115*, *44/117*
Malleson, Miles 122
Manet, Edouard 23, 137
Mankiewicz, Joseph L. 189
Margaret, HRH Princess 7, 9, 10
Markova, Dame Alicia 72
Marmontel, Jean François 152
Masks, The 38, *24/74*
Marriage of Figaro, The 40
Massey, Daniel 171
Massey, Raymond 187
Massine, Léonide 74, 80, 84, 86, 88
Matthews, Jessie 75, 76
May, Pamela 111
Mayor, A. Hyatt 41
Mendelssohn, Felix Bartholdy 97
Messel, Lt.-Col. Leonard 15, 17, 18, 70
Messel, Maud Frances (née Sambourne) 17, 70
Messel, Oliver Hilary Sambourne (1904–78):
  awards to 15
  Bath Assembly Rooms 52
  Beaton, Cecil, and 33
  biog. outline 15
  books ill. by 179, 196
  Cochran sketches, work done for:
    China, Dance Little Lady Girl in A Shawl, Heaven Lorelei, The Masks, Piccadilly 1830 Scaramouche, Stealing Through Wake Up and Dream, What is this Thing Called Love
    (see Index for production and page numbers)
  colour sense 22, 30, 32
  costume designing 30, 32, 37
  decorative arts commissions 60
  decorative arts designs 48, 60
    carpets 51, *78/174*, *86/179*
    ceramics 49
    cutlery 14, 48, *88/179*
    fabrics 12, 14, 48, 49, 60, 61, *89/179*, *180*
    furniture 14, 48, 60, *178*, *85/179*
    designs for festivities 14, 48, 62, 63, 94 & *96/181*, *182-3*
    designs for houses 52, 54, 66, 83 & *84/176*
  design for Sekers Theatre 48

Dorchester Hotel (see interior decoration below)
eclecticism 36
exhibitions 58
films 46, 47, 56
Flaxley Abbey 51, 52, and interior decoration below
Glyndebourne work for 23
homosexuality, and 18
interior decoration 49, 51, 52, 54, 78–81/174–176
interior decoration commissions 64
Lovat-Fraser, Claude; OM compared to 106
masks 13, *19*, 38, 70, 71, 72, 75, 76, 100, 102, 149
  how to make 18
models for sets; ground plans 30
  making of 23, 30
  perspective of 23
model sets in Exhibition *31/79*, *34/84*, *36/93*, *40/105*, *41/106*, *44-55/117-9*
murals 12, 47, 64
paintings of 2, *12/70*
painting, on 23
pastiche, use of 22, 36
photographs of, 2, 12, 13, 14, 16, 21, 39, 47, 52, 59, 61, 10 & *12/70*, 20, 21 & *23/72*, *57/119*, 120, 157, *105/187*, *108/189*
portraiture 47
preparing a production 23, 30
productions; chronology of stage work 38
residences, studios of 15, 79
skills 18, 30, 31
social position 34
sources; architecture 22, 36
  costume 22
  painting 22, 23
studio; nature of 30
studio; concept for this Exhibition *31/79*
temporary decorations for festive occasions 48, 62
theatre, understanding of 34
visits abroad 15, 52
wigs, design of 31
work in collections 192, 193
Messel, Thomas 10, 111, 176, 179, 193, 195
Michelangelo 159
Midsummer Night's Dream, A 13, 35, 38, *38/97*, 98, 99
Mielziner, Jo 33, 34
Millar & Harris 181
Miller, Jonathan 116
Milton, John 105, 159
Miracle, The 12, 15, 21, 69, *33/80*, 81, 82, 83, 84
Mitchell, Yvonne 187
Mitford, Nancy 117
Mlinaric, David 52, 175
Molière, Jean-Baptiste 122
Moorehead, Agnes 171
Morley, Robert 117
Mother of Pearl 12, 38, 90, *99/184*
Mozart, Wolfgang Amadeus 69, 114, 117, 130, 152, 155, 156
Murray, Alec 12
Murray, Stephen 97
Museum of London, The 10, 71, 192
Mydtsbou, Copenhagen 119
Myerscough-Walker, R. 33

Nash, Paul 22
National Film Archive (BFI) 10, 11, 185, 187, 189, 195
National Theatre 144
National Trust, The 10, 11, 174
Natzka, Oscar 114
Neate, Kenneth 114
Nerina, Nadia 138
Newton, Wilfred 187
Nigger Heaven 38, *32/72*
Nichols, Beverley 77
Nicholson, William 74
Nikitina 12, 78
Nilsson, Birgit 130
Novello, Ivor 91
Nozze di Figaro, Le 14, 40, 147, *72/155*, 156

Oberon, Merle 185, 187
Odets, Clifford 33
  Golden Boy 33
Offenbach, Jacques 84
Oncina, Juan 132, 147, 149
O'Neill, Eugene 72
Otto, Lisa 117

Paltenghi, David 109
Park, Bertram 80, 85, 86, 88
Parkinson, Norman 10, 70
Pascal, Gabriel 187
Percy, Esmé 119
Perrault, Charles 44, 109, 132, 152
Petipa, Marius 7, 109
Petroff, Paul 94
Philpot, Glyn 81
Photo Studios Ltd 174
Piccadilly 1830 12, 38, *29/77*, 78
Picasso, Pablo 18, 97
Piper, John 22, 34
Porter, Cole 76
Porter, Eric 130
Power, Tyrone 144
Private Life of Don Juan, The 46, 56, 100 & *101/185*
Propert, W. A. 'Archie' 15, 18, 71
Pryce-Jones, David 52
Purcell, Henry 105
Pushkin, Alexander 122, 187

Quayle, Anthony 97, 106
Queen Elizabeth I 12, 59, *2/70*
Queen Elizabeth, HM The Queen Mother 70
Queen of Spades, The (O) 40, 106, *58/122*
Queen of Spades, The (F) 14, 17, 46, 56, 80, 106, *98/184*, *107/187*, 188, 189, 190

Rains, Claude *104/187*
Rashomon 15, 26, 40
Rassine, Alexis 138
Rayne H. & M. 12, 65, *79/174*
Redgrave, Sir Michael 93
Reece, Brian 117
Reinhardt, Max 34, 80, 81, 84, 86, 88, 126
Renoir, Pierre Auguste 23, 137, 171
Rice, Peter 126
Richards, Ceri 22
Richardson, Sir Albert & Partners 174
Richardson, Sir Ralph 97
Riis-Hansen, Vagn 15
Ring Round the Moon 7, 9, 12, 13, 23, 26, 30, 36, 106, *48/117*, *57/119*, 120, 121

Rivals, The 13, 36, 38, 41/106, 107
Rizzieri, Elena 155
Robey, George 84, 88
Robson, Dame Flora **104**/*187*
Romeo and Juliet (P) 13, 27, 40, **60**/*126*, 127, 128–9
Romeo and Juliet (F) 12, 22, 46, 56
Rosehill Arts Trust 10, 11, 171
Rosehill Theatre, Whitehaven 12, 49, **80**/*174*
Rosenfeld, Sybil 34
Rosenkavalier, Der 14, 40, **55**/*119*, **75**/*163*, 164, 165, 166
Rosenthal, Harold 130
Rosse, Anne, Countess of (formerly Armstrong-Jones) 7, 9, 10, 18, 70, 80, 163, 181, 189, 193, 195
Rossini, Gioacchino 69, 117, 132, 147
Rothenberger, Anneliese 163
Rouleau, Joseph 159
Round, Roy 179
Roussin, André 117
Royal Academy of Dancing 112, 113
Royal Ballet, The 109
Royal Opera House, Covent Garden (and Archives) 12, 48, 63, 109, 114, 122, 139, 159, 179, 181, *182/3*, 192
Royal Shakespeare Company 144
Rutherford, Dame Margaret 119
Rutland, The Duchess of 81

Sacher, Paul 117
Sadlers Wells Ballet (later Royal Ballet) 109, 138
Sambourne, Linley 17
Samson 14, 40, **74**/*159*, **160**, 161, 162
Samson Agonistes 159
Sacha 76, 79, 84, 86
Saunders, Harold 185, 187

Scaramouche 38, **30**/*79*
Scarlet Pimpernel, The 46, 56, 102 & **103**/*185*, 187
Schéhérazade 94
Schervachidze, Prince 97
School for Scandal, The 12, 14, 31, 40, **73**/*159*, *158*
Sciutti, Graziella, 147
Scofield, Paul 119
Scribe, Eugène 147
Sekers, Lady Agi 10, 48
Sekers, firm (now Sekers International) 10, 48, 49, 174, 179
Sénéchal, Michael 152
Shakespeare, William 97, 100, 126
Sharman, Frank 114
Shaw, George Bernard 24, 187
Shearer, Moira 111
Sheridan, Richard Brinsley 106, 159
Simmons; costumier 185
Simoneau, Léopold 130
Simonson, Lee 33, 34
Sinclair, Monica 147, 149
Skillen, Hugh 32, 106, 109, 122, 141
Slade School, of Art 15, 18, 47, 70
Sladen, Victoria 114
Sleeping Beauty, The 7, 9, 12, 15, 22, 36, 38, 40, 41, 42, 43, 44, 45, 51, 69, 106, **108**, **42**/*109*, 110, 171
Sleeping Princess, The 41
Smith, Dodie 137
Smith, Oliver 15, 171
Smithers, William 126
Snowdon, Lord 9, 10, 18, 193, 195; coll. 9; inventory of coll. 9
Söderström, Elisabeth 163
Sokolova, Lydia 71
Somes, Michael 138
Spencer, Sir Stanley 70
Spewack, Sam 36, 130
Spinelly 74
Stage Photo Co. 91

Stage Society, The 72
Stealing Through 38, **30**/*79*
Sterbini, Cesare 147
Stevens, Risë 155
Stevens, Terese 171
Stewart, Marjorie 119, 137
Strauss, Richard 69, 163
Stravinsky, Igor 79
Strnad, Oskar 80
Suddenly Last Summer (F) 12, 32, 47, 56, 57, 70, **98**/*184*, **108**/*189*
Sutherland, Graham 12, 61
Sutherland, Dame Joan 49, 156, 159

Tandy, Jessica 100
Taylor, Elizabeth 12, 47, 57, 189
Tchaikovsky, Peter 7, 45, 69, 94, 109, 122
Tchernicheva, Lubov 13, 94, 96, 97
Tempest, The 13, 38, **39**/*100*, *101*
Ternouth, Barbara 122
Tetzel, Joan 117
Theatre Museum, London 69, 192, 195
Thesiger, Ernest 93, 130
This Year of Grace 38, **26**/*75*
Thomas, Dylan 119
Tiepolo, Giovanni Battista 23
Titania and Bottom 3/*70*
Tomlinson, David 117
Toms, Carl 10, 15, 22, 27, 32, 36, 79, 117, 119, 138, 159, 163, 174
Tough at the Top 40, **46**/*117*
Toye, Wendy 117
Tracey, Edmund 163
Traveller Without Luggage 14, 40, **76**/*167*, 168, 169, **99**/*184*
Twang!! 12, 37, 40, 52, **99**/*184*
Tynan, Kenneth 137

Under the Sycamore Tree 7, 9, 13, 17, 36, 40, **50**/*117*, **62**/*130*, *131*

Valois, Dame Ninette de 7, 97, 109
Van Mill, A. 117
Varesco, Giovanni 130
Vercoe, Rosemary 32
Veronese, Paolo 23
Vickers, Jon 159
Vollmoeller, Karl 80

Wake Up and Dream 12, 20, 38, **28**/*76*, 77
Walbrook, Anton 46, 187, *190*
Wallace, Ian 132, 147
Walston, Ray 149
Walters, Jess 122
Watkins, F. B. 70, 175
Watson, Douglas 126
Watteau, Antoine 23, 41
Wedgwood, firm of 49
Wells, John 15, 18
What is this Thing Called Love **28**/*77*
Whistler, Laurence 10
Whistler, Rex 7, 18, 22, 33, 34, 48, 76, 79
Whitehaven Theatre (see Rosehill Theatre, above)
Wickwire, Nancy 167
Williams, Harcourt 119
Williams, Tennessee 189
Wolfe, Karin 171
Wood, John the Elder 174
Wycherley, William 93

Yeats, William Butler 36
Young, Alexander 130

Zadek, Hilde 122
Zauberflöte, Die 40, **43**/*114*
Zémire et Azor 40, 69, **32**/*80*, **70**/*152*, *153*
Zéphyre et Flore 12, 15, 18, 38, 17 & **18**/*71*
Zinkeisen, Doris 74, 75, 77, 79